THE
LUCKY
LIST

THE LUCKY LIST

Rachael Lippincott

SIMON & SCHUSTER

First published in Great Britain in 2021 by Simon & Schuster UK Ltd

First published in the USA in 2021 by Simon & Schuster BFYR,
an imprint of Simon & Schuster Children's Publishing Division,
1230 Avenue of the Americas, New York, New York 10020

Text copyright © 2021 Rachael Lippincott
Chapter header illustrations copyright © 2021 Lisa Perrin

1 3 5 7 9 10 8 6 4 2

Simon & Schuster UK Ltd
1st Floor, 222 Gray's Inn Road
London WC1X 8HB

www.simonandschuster.co.uk
www.simonandschuster.com.au
www.simonandschuster.co.in

Simon & Schuster Australia, Sydney
Simon & Schuster India, New Delhi

A CIP catalogue record for this book
is available from the British Library.

PB ISBN 978-1-3985-0260-4
eBook ISBN 978-1-3985-0261-1
eAudio ISBN 978-1-3985-0262-8

This book is a work of fiction. Names, characters, places and
incidents are either the product of the author's imagination or are
used fictitiously. Any resemblance to actual people living or
dead, events or locales is entirely coincidental.

Printed and bound by CPI Group (UK) Ltd, Croydon, CR0 4Y

MIX
Paper from
responsible sources
FSC® C020471

This one's for you, Mom. I love you.

1

I brought the lucky quarter.

I don't know why I did. I'd walked past it hundreds and hundreds of times without a second thought while a thin layer of dust formed around the edges. But there was just *something* about the way it was sitting there tonight, on the same bookshelf where it had sat untouched for three years.

Tonight I swear it looked . . .

Lucky.

I cringe as *that* word pops into my head, an image of blue eyes and long brown hair following it, never too far behind. Luck was my mom's thing. Not mine. But I still reach my hand into my pocket to feel the smooth metal, my thumbnail finding that familiar nick on the edge just above George Washington's head.

"This'll be fun," my dad whispers to me, turning around in

the card-buying line to give me a big, blindingly hopeful smile. A smile that acts like we didn't just spend the past three years before tonight avoiding absolutely every possible reminder of her.

I snort. "'Fun' is definitely not the first word that comes to mind," I whisper back to him as I scan the room, taking in the absolute zoo that is the Huckabee School District monthly bingo fundraiser. Even after all this time away, almost nothing has changed. My eyes move past two old ladies locked in a heated arm-wrestle battle over a premium spot near the speaker, over to Tyler Poland with his collection of rocks, each one laid carefully out in size order on top of his five coveted bingo cards.

"Chaotic," maybe. "Chaotic" would be a good word to use.

But not even the chaos of elderly people arm wrestling and prized rock collections can distract me from my uneasiness at being back here. And not just because of what this place meant to me and my mom.

For someone who just succeeded in blowing up her entire social life three weeks ago at junior prom, there is literally no worse place to be. Unfortunately, with said social life in shambles, that *also* means there wasn't a single thing I could claim to be doing to get out of coming.

And I can't talk to my dad about what happened, or about pretty much anything for that matter, so here I am. Stuck Scarlet Lettering my way around, while Dad shamelessly uses this fundraiser as a mini–high school reunion. Because tonight is "conveniently" the night his best friend, Johnny Carter, is moving back into town after twenty years away.

I say conveniently because if you want to jump straight back into the deep end of Huckabee society, this is certainly the splashiest way to do it. I mean, half their graduating class is probably still sitting in this room.

Once a month the elementary school cafetorium is turned into a group audition for a rural-Pennsylvania mash-up of *My Strange Addiction* and *WWE SmackDown*. Don't believe me? Back in fifth grade, Mrs. Long, the sweetest little angel of a kindergarten teacher, decked Sue Patterson square in the face because she thought Sue was intentionally not calling any *B* numbers.

What's even more unbelievable is that she was right.

"I'm going to get Johnny's and Blake's cards for them," my dad says, choosing to ignore my skepticism, as he pulls out his billfold. "You know how hard it is to find parking."

He's acting like I was just here last week, instead of three whole years ago.

I shrug as nonchalantly as I can muster, watching him buy three cards off Principal Nelson, the whiskery middle school principal, and the only one trusted enough for the past ten years to hand out the bingo cards without need for suspicion. There was a whole series of town council meetings and six months of rigorous debate before he was approved for the position.

"Emily! Glad to see you here," Principal Nelson says to me, that all-too-familiar sympathetic glint in his eyes. I grimace internally since "Glad to see you here" automatically translates to some variation of "We haven't seen you since your mom died!" He begins rifling through the massive deck of bingo cards and pulls out a small worn card, holding it out to me. "You want you and your mom's card? Number 505! I still remember!"

I wince slightly as my eyes trace the familiar crease straight down the center of the card, landing finally on the red splotch in the upper right-hand corner, where I spilled fruit punch when I was six. I hate these moments the most. The moments when you think you are healed just enough, and then something as simple as a bingo card makes every fiber feel raw.

Number 505.

When I was born on the fifth day of the fifth month, Mom's superstitious mind lit up like a Christmas tree, and she *swore* five was our lucky number. So that number became intertwined with everything in our lives, from the number of times I had to scrub behind my ears, to my sports-team jerseys when I attempted one spring's worth of T-ball and one fall's worth of soccer, to lucky quarters she pressed into my palm, whispering about how it was "extra special" since twenty-five was five squared.

Extra-special lucky quarters that would one day collect dust on a bookshelf. Until tonight.

But I shake my head at him. "No thanks."

There's a long, uncomfortable pause, and my dad glances at me before quickly pulling another wrinkled five out of his billfold and holding it out to Principal Nelson. "I'll take it. Thanks, Bill."

"You shouldn't have done that," I mumble to my dad as we walk away, Principal Nelson shooting me an even *more* sympathetic look now.

"It's just bingo, Em," he says to me as we zigzag our way to a

4

free table and sit down across from each other. "Blake can take it if you don't want it." He looks down at the cards as he says it, though, refusing to meet my gaze.

As if this all wasn't awkward enough, Johnny's daughter, Blake, is coming. Which I'm still not sure how to feel about yet. We got along pretty well back when we were kids, but I haven't seen her since Christmas a decade ago, when we almost set my house on fire trying to set a booby trap for Santa. Which is not exactly a conversation starter at this point, especially since we're about to be seniors in high school, instead of wide-eyed second graders. Still, she doesn't know anyone else here.

Which after tonight she will probably think is a good thing. Especially if things get dramatic.

Or, knowing the people in this room like I do, *when* things get dramatic.

I hear a laugh and my eyes automatically dart past Dad to the back corner table, where familiar long fingers comb through a familiar mess of brown hair.

Matt.

My stomach sinks straight through the floor as a sea of eyes returns my stare. Jake, Ryan, and Olivia, my former friend group, are shooting daggers at me from across the room, expressions angry enough to pronounce me guilty of first-degree murder.

But I guess after prom, all the evidence would suggest, that's . . . a pretty fair verdict.

Matt doesn't look over, though. His gaze stays fixed on the table in front of him, his dark eyebrows knit together in concentration as he shifts his body to face pointedly away from me. Which is somehow a million times worse than the glares.

I'm surprised to see they're here tonight. In the summer we'd usually all be hanging out at the Huckabee Pool after close or playing Ping-Pong in Olivia's enormous basement.

Then again, I guess I was the only thing stopping them from going to bingo night. I guess this is what summer nights can look like without me.

I pull my eyes away as my dad slides card number 505 in front of me. "I'm not going to play," I say. This whole thing is already starting to feel out of control. This is one thing I can decide.

"How about you play for me then?" he says as he shakes a bunch of red chips out of a white Styrofoam cup. I watch as they shower down in front of me, forming a small pile. "If that card happens to win, I keep the prize basket."

I stare at him, unamused. Why he even wants to play is beyond me.

Although, I guess this has kind of been his thing lately. Pretending things don't have meaning when they actually do.

Talk about my mom? Never in a million years.

Get rid of her stuff? Definitely.

Go to the monthly bingo fundraiser she religiously attended as if she didn't? Absolutely.

"The 'Football Fan Fiesta' basket, preferably," he adds, giving me a big wink as Olivia's mom, Donna Taylor, the head of the PTA and former prom queen (rumored to have *literally* bought the vote for both those elections) finally comes trotting onto the stage.

You know what? Fine. The sooner we start playing, the sooner I can get out of here.

"All righty! Everybody ready to get started?" she calls into the microphone before flashing a practiced pageant smile to the crowd.

"Fuck yeah!" Jim Donovan shouts from two tables over, causing a wave of laughter to travel around the room.

"A couple more of those out of old Jim over there, and Donna's gonna purse the lip filler right out of those babies," my dad whispers to me, his dark brown eyes crinkling at the corners as he gives me one of his smirking grins.

I shake my head, stifling a real laugh for the first time all night.

Huckabee has a weird disconnect, and Donna Taylor and Jim Donovan are the perfect examples of it. You've got the Donnas, in their McMansions, or "newly renovated farmhouses" as they like to call them, their husbands working nine to five in the city while they watch the kids and meet their mom gang at Pilates five days a week. And then you've got the Jim Donovans, living just a few miles south on farms that've been passed down since Betsy Ross first started messing around with designs for the American flag.

My dad is a slightly less yeehaw Jim Donovan. Born and raised in Huckabee, with the four generations before him sharing the "Joseph Clark" name. This town is so embedded in his blood, he'd probably crumble to dust if he crossed the limits. So, I guess it's good Johnny's moving back or Dad'd never see him.

"Will you man Blake's card for me?" my dad asks, sliding yet another card across the table at me.

"For real?" For someone who didn't want to play bingo, I sure was about to play a lot of it.

"They'll be here in a few minutes," he says, distracted, as he nods to his beat-up cell phone, the cracked screen opened to a text from Johnny. "They just found a spot."

I'm about to say I'd rather watch old Jim over there win the tractor pull for the fifth straight year at the county fair, but the familiar sound of the tiny yellow balls rattling around the ball cage stops me. I look up at the stage, and for a lingering moment I'm transported back by the sea of numbers just waiting to be called.

I learned how to count in this very room, sliding red chips over numbers as I sat on my mom's lap, rattling off the number of spaces we needed to win. My mom and I came every month for as long as I can remember, and we won nearly every time. We used to bask on a throne of wicker baskets and cellophane. All our winnings, Mom always said, were thanks to card number 505 and my lucky quarter.

The gossip was *endless*. Half the room was convinced we were cheating, while the other half was convinced we were just the luckiest two people in all of Huckabee township, my mom's charm making it pretty difficult for anyone to think bad of her. Even when the odds would suggest it.

I couldn't set foot in the convenience store without getting asked about a set of lottery numbers. I even apparently helped Paul Wilson win $10,000 on a Fourth of July scratch-off, which he spent on a finger-losing patriotic pyrotechnic show a week later.

Then, when I was fourteen, my mom died, and any luck I had

got blown to smithereens, just like Paul Wilson's finger.

Since then I've avoided this place like the plague. I'm not interested in trying my luck anymore, even if it's as simple as playing a game of bingo.

But watching Donna Taylor pick up a yellow ball in between her soft-pink acrylic nails, I feel the same pull I felt when Principal Nelson held up the fruit-punch-stained, crease-down-the-middle bingo card.

A feeling like that bingo cage inside me is one spin away from all the balls tumbling out.

"The first number of the night," Donna calls into the microphone, pausing as a group of elementary school kids three tables over start a drumroll. I catch a glimpse of Sue Patterson sitting in the corner just beside them, actively saying the rosary and sprinkling holy water over her set of four cards.

"*B*-twelve!" she calls, eliciting a cheer from some and groans of disappointment from others.

I reach out to grab a chip, knowing even before I look that it's on card 505. Even now I could name every number in every row, the card ingrained in my memory like a home address or a favorite song.

I hesitate over the chip pile and cast a quick glance down to see that it's on Blake's card too. As I slide the red chips over the respective twelves, I look over to see Jim Donovan eyeing me like this is the start line for the hundred-meter dash at the Olympics and I'm here to win gold. I stare back at him, amused that I'm counted as any kind of competition after three whole years, a swell of my long-forgotten competitiveness pulling my lips up into a smirk.

Donna calls a few more numbers: *I*-29, *G*-48, *B*-9, *O*-75, *I*-23, and *N*-40. Slowly the cards start to fill up, people eagerly eyeing one another's to compare, the cellophane over the stacked prize baskets in the front of the room glittering underneath the fluorescent cafetorium lights.

I catch sight of a basket filled with movie theater popcorn and a $100 gift card to the historic movie theater in the center of town, which Matt and I always used to go to on date nights, resting in the exact center. The thought of Matt makes my cheeks burn, and I have to resist the urge to look at him, just past my dad, a wave of guilt keeping my eyes glued to the table in front of me as I slide the red chips carefully into place, one after the other.

"Good thing I got those extra cards!" my dad says to me, letting out a long exhale as he shakes his head. "I'm striking out over here."

I glance over to see he has somehow managed to get only a single number past the free space. "Oh my gosh," I say, laughing. "How is that even possible?"

"Dang. Look at you, Clark," a voice says from just over my right shoulder. "Still can't count for shit."

My dad's face lights up as Johnny Carter's thin, tan arm reaches across the table to give him a firm handshake. I haven't seen him this excited since Zach Ertz caught that touchdown pass during the Super Bowl the winter before my mom died, securing the win for the Eagles.

I look up to see that Johnny looks almost exactly like he did when they visited for Christmas ten years ago, plus a few extra wrinkles. A loose white button-down hangs limply on his tall, lanky frame, while a mess of dirty-blond hair sits atop his head. He's even unironically wearing a puka-shell necklace, and actually pulling it off.

But I guess you can do that when you peaced out to Hawaii six months before high school graduation to become a surfing legend.

"Hey, Em," a voice says from next to me, as the person it's attached to slides onto the bench beside me.

My head swivels to the other side to see Blake.

I'm fully expecting to see a slightly taller version of the lanky seven-year-old who wore oversize T-shirts and had apparently never heard of a hairbrush, but that's definitely not who just sat down next to me.

It's safe to say Blake won the puberty lotto a million and one times over.

Her skin is a deep glowing tan, a color that nobody else in Huckabee has by the end of August, let alone now in early July. Her hair is long and wavy, darker than her dad's but with the same bright streaks of blond, like the sun rays that put them there.

It's her eyes, though, that startle me the most. Long eyelashes giving way to a warm, almost liquid honey brown. Ten years ago they were hidden behind a pair of glasses bigger than the state of Texas. Now they're on full display.

And I'm not the only one noticing. Literally everyone is looking at our table right now. So much for flying under the radar.

"I have your card," I blurt out, once I realize I haven't actually said anything back to her. Her eyes swing down to look at the two cards in front of me, and I slide hers over, careful not to send the chips scattering everywhere.

Could it *be* any more obvious I've been a social pariah for the past three weeks?

"Thanks," Blake says, smiling at me, the gap in her teeth the only constant between the girl sitting in front of me and the girl that convinced me setting off sparklers indoors would scare Santa *just enough* to get us both ponies.

"You're one away from a bingo in two places," I add, like that's not completely obvious.

I hear Donna call out a number, but it's nothing more than a hum in my left ear, my fingers wrapping instinctively around the quarter in my pocket.

"Hey! Lucky you." Blake's eyes widen in excitement, and she holds up a red chip, reaching over to carefully slide it onto my board. "You just beat me to it."

Bingo.

2

Everyone in Huckabee knows that you can't go to a bingo fundraiser in the summer without going to get ice cream after. It'd be like going to the movies and not getting popcorn. Or going to the pool and forgetting your swimsuit.

There would be no point in going.

Sam's Scoops is a block away from Huckabee Elementary, and the large crowd of people leaving the cafetorium and heading toward it trails the entire distance between the two.

Luckily, we're one of the first few groups out the door.

I power walk across the gravel parking lot, my dad and Johnny a few steps ahead of me, Blake crunching noisily just behind them. I have to jog every couple of seconds just to keep up with this above-average-height crew.

"You're bringing your prize basket to get ice cream?" Blake

asks me, cutting through my staring contest with a Carson Wentz bobblehead wedged between a rolled-up T-shirt and an Eagles hat. She slows down ever so slightly, until our feet fall into a steady rhythm on the gravel. "You doing a victory lap or something?"

I try not to snort at the idea of me parading proudly around with my dad's "Football Fan Fiesta" basket like I'd just won a Golden Globe. Although, to be fair, that's not out of character for some people in this town. I've heard of someone keeping the highly coveted, still shrink-wrapped "Wine 'n' Cheese" basket on their mantel for ten years, just to spite their in-laws. The cheese definitely got moldy, but it was never about that anyway.

I tighten my grip on the wicker basket, the plastic around it crinkling noisily. "If I put it in the car, we'll be waiting two hours to get ice cream."

It's the truth. The army of bingo goers converging on Sam's Scoops right now should be enough to give Sam and the three servers at the window carpal tunnel. A trip to my dad's car would have put us at the very back of the line, just as their arms are about to splinter into a million pieces. My mom and I figured out that scoops got 25 percent smaller and drippier if you got stuck near the end.

And after today I'm pretty sure I deserve a full-size scoop.

"So I guess you come here a lot," she says as the end of the line approaches. We've managed to walk fast enough to have only about ten people standing in between us and homemade iced sugary goodness.

"Not so much anymore," I say.

Thankfully, she doesn't ask me why. Instead, her eyebrows lift. "Wait. Please tell me this place is *actually* called Sam's Oops?"

The red-lettered light-up sign just above the white and blue shack has the "Sc" in "Scoops" out, and I laugh at the fact that most of the town is so used to it, we don't even notice it anymore. "Kind of? That sign hasn't been fixed in five years, so it's become the unofficial nickname for this place."

"What's your go-to?" she asks as she cranes her neck to squint over the long line of people at the menu board. It makes me wonder if she still wears those big-as-Texas glasses at night when she takes her contacts out.

"Chocolate and vanilla twist on a cone with rainbow sprinkles," I answer automatically, turning my attention to the front window. "I haven't had one in *years*, though." I can already feel my mouth watering, despite the pang of sadness that comes with the realization that the last time I was here was with my mom.

"Man. If you think *you* haven't had an ice-cream cone from Sam's in years," Johnny says, tallying it up on his fingers. "Clark, it's gotta be two decades since we last came here together. The summer before senior year. You remember?"

My dad nods, grinning. "You got mint chocolate chip in a cone, and I smashed it into your face about fifteen seconds after you paid. Had to get you back for pantsing me in front of the whole cheerleading squad."

They both start laughing, shaking their heads in unison.

I exchange a quick look with Blake, both of us rolling our eyes at the long night of nostalgia ahead of us.

15

"Your mom was so mad at him," Johnny says, turning to look at me, the bright light from the street lamp overhead shining directly on my face. He stops laughing, giving me a long, slightly uncomfortable look. I know exactly what's coming before he says it.

"Phew. I just can't get over how much you look like Jules."

It's a variation of a sentence I've heard more times than I can count.

"You look just like your mom."

"You're practically a clone of Julie!"

"You two could be twins!"

I used to love when people would say things like that. Now I can't seem to get away from it, her face haunting me every time I look in the mirror. Long, pin-straight brown hair, strong eyebrows, full lips.

But not her eyes. The eyes that I miss so much are never there looking back at me, no matter how much I wish they were.

Instead of her blueberry blue, I have my dad's dark, dark brown. If it weren't for that singular feature, you would never guess I was related to him. His height gene whizzed right on past me.

"Doesn't she?" my dad says, giving me one of his sad smiles.

And just like that he clears his throat and clams up, like he always does when Mom comes up. I watch as he pulls his eyes away from mine. "Did I tell you about that construction gig I had on Luke Wilkens's property? With the glass ceiling?" he says to Johnny, and suddenly we are back to boring construction talk, which I get more than enough of at home.

"So," I say, looking over at Blake as we shuffle forward. "How are you liking Huckabee so far?"

"Well, I've only been here two days, and I slept most of the first since we took a red-eye," she says, hesitating a little. "But, uh, to be honest with you? It feels almost like an alternate universe."

I snort at that generous assessment. "An alternate universe with a lot of cows."

She nods in agreement, her eyes getting a distant look to them. "A *lot* of cows."

My shoulders tense as my former friend group trudges past us, towering ice-cream cones in hand, a reward for sprinting over here. I see Jake and Ryan catch sight of Blake, the two of them slowing down, mouths slightly agape, ice cream slowly dripping down their hands as they gawk at her like she's a dinosaur that's been spontaneously dropped into the twenty-first century. Olivia jealously swats at Ryan's shoulder, but she's just as busy sizing Blake up.

It's not every day there's a new girl in town. And definitely not one who's as pretty as Blake. I'm just relieved that she's a distraction from the fact that they're supposed to be judging me.

The only one not looking at her is Matt.

He glances in my direction for a fraction of a second, his eyes peeking out from underneath the swoopy chocolate-brown hair that my mom always said was so adorable.

All I see now is the hurt and disappointment that's painted across his face.

I stare after him, feeling pretty awful. Which I absolutely

17

should, since I just broke the heart of the nicest guy in Huckabee.

"What'd you do to *him*?" Blake asks when they're out of earshot. I was hoping she wouldn't notice, but that look packed quite a punch.

"Oh, you know," I say as I let out a long sigh, trying to keep my voice light. "The usual. We dated. We broke up. We dated. We broke up again." It's not a lie. It's not the whole truth, either.

She whistles, raising her eyebrows in surprise. "You think you'll get back together again?"

"No. I don't think that's going to happen this time." Three years of making up and breaking up cycle through my mind, Matt always finding a way to make things right again. But now that cycle includes the night of junior prom, and it's ground everything to a halt. He won't even talk to me. "I mean, you saw the look he gave me. Pretty obvious he's going to hate me for all eternity."

"Really? Hate? I didn't get that." Blake bites her lip thoughtfully. "Seemed to me like he isn't over you. Maybe he's just waiting for you to talk to him."

Mercifully, Sam's oldest daughter, Amber, calls "Next!" from the middle window, so I don't have to acknowledge the tiny bit of hope fluttering into my stomach at Blake's words.

Hope that there might be a way I can fix all this.

The full-scoop, front-of-the-line cones come out in the blink of an eye, and I juggle the prize basket to grab ahold of mine, taking a big lick before it starts to melt.

In an instant I'm transported back to summer nights with my mom after bingo and pit stops after tough days of elementary school.

I have to remind my feet to keep moving.

The three picnic tables are already filled, so we start the trek back over to the elementary school, the line of people still waiting eyeing our ice cream longingly.

Blake looks over at me and makes a face, rubbing her temple. "Brain freeze."

"Put your tongue on the roof of your mouth," I say, hearing Mom's voice in my head, telling me the same words hundreds of times. I always used to scarf my cone down in under a minute, writhing in pain after. I take a slow, focused lick, no longer rushing straight into my rainbow-sprinkle-covered twist. Or anything, for that matter. "It works like a charm."

Within a few seconds she nods, her face impressed, the brain freeze gone as she starts right back in on her cone like nothing happened.

I look past her at the line of people, noticing all the eyes drawn to Blake as we pass. She is something new, and shiny, and beautiful in a town where very little changes. If she feels like Huckabee is from another universe, it's pretty clear that everyone here feels the same way about her.

I look over to see if she notices the stares she's getting, but she's just merrily licking her ice cream. Not a single care in the world other than brain freeze. I can't help but feel a sudden wave of jealousy at that.

My dad nudges me, and I swing my head around to look up at him. "Still good to pack tomorrow? I brought a couple of boxes home from work."

I grimace as the for-sale sign outside our house pops into my head, my childhood home soon to be ripped out from under me. Just another reason this summer completely sucks.

"Packing?" Johnny skids to a stop.

"Didn't I tell you we're moving?" my dad asks. Guess Dad didn't mention it in their monthly phone calls.

"You're kidding!" Johnny exclaims, his eyes wide, looking almost as shocked as I was when my dad told me. A glob of ice cream drips off his cone and lands smack on the pavement below him, somehow managing to steer clear of his shirt. Ah, to not have boobs. "The second I get to town you're packing up?"

"Not out of Huckabee," my dad says, pointing his spoon at Johnny as he replies. "Just into something smaller." "Smaller" was a code word for "cheaper," but Johnny probably didn't know that.

"Like he'd ever leave Huckabee," I whisper to Johnny as my dad "hi"s and "hello"s his way down the long ice-cream line. Our own unofficial mayor.

"I don't know what I was thinking," Johnny says with a laugh, turning to say hi to an old classmate.

If Huckabee were the *Titanic*, my dad would definitely be the captain, saluting proudly as the ship nosedives straight into the ocean.

"We could swing by tomorrow to help you pack for a bit," Johnny offers when we hit the gravel parking lot and there's no one left to say hello to but the cars.

"Don't you guys have some *un*packing to do?" my dad asks.

"Our boxes don't come in for another three to five business

days," Johnny says, grinning widely. "How about we do a trade? We help you tomorrow, and in exchange, you help us later this week."

"Deal," my dad says, crushing the empty cup in his fist and holding out his free hand. They do a firm manshake, like this is some kind of solemn oath and not just casual plans.

"Does three work? Or three thirty?" Johnny asks, nodding to Blake as we head slowly to the farthest corner of the parking lot, where they managed to find a space. "This one's still a little jet-lagged."

I see it now, in the faint dark circles under her eyes, the rasp encircling some of her words.

"Three is perfect," my dad says, nodding. "Em works Saturday mornings at Nina's Bakery in town."

"Nina?" Johnny asks. "As in Nina Levin?"

"Nina *Biset* is what she goes by now," my dad corrects, grinning. "But, yes, *that* Nina. Her daughter, Kiera, is best friends with Emily."

"Was that by choice or predetermined?" Johnny asks me with a wink.

"A little bit of both," I say, laughing. Kiera and I always joke that we were born best friends, like our moms.

I finish off the rest of my ice cream, the sweet taste lingering in my mouth as we walk slowly through the parking lot. We reach the last row, cars squeezed together just past the fifth-grade wing and right before the soccer field, the forest beyond the goalpost looking dark and ominous in the moonlight.

Back in middle school, after the bingo fundraiser was over, a group of us used to dare each other to run past the soccer goal and touch one of the big trees just inside the brush. It would take twenty minutes of talking smack and wide-eyed creeping through the grass for someone to be brave enough to actually do it.

Nine times out of ten, I was the one whipping through the darkness to tap the uneven bark, still flying high from my bingo-winning luck.

It's crazy how much has changed since then. How much *I've* changed since then.

"Well, this is us," Johnny says.

I'm looking at an old, rusty, forest-green Jeep, but I'm surprised when the lights on the blacked-out Porsche next to it blink twice as he unlocks the doors.

I exchange a quick look with my dad, trying to hide my shock. I can tell he's just as shook as I am.

Johnny doesn't notice our wide-eyed reaction though and gives me a one-armed hug, the cellophane around the prize basket crinkling noisily as he leans in. "See ya tomorrow, kid!" he says, then gives my dad a handshake before opening the door to the Porsche and hopping in.

This must be a family of huggers, because Blake gives me a hug next, her arm wrapping quickly around me, bringing with it a wave of fresh linen and warm sand and salty ocean water all wrapped together.

She smells like a day at the beach.

"See you," she says, tugging herself away. Apparently, I'm so busy smelling the ocean that I hold on for a second too long. What is wrong with me?

She waves to my dad. "Bye, Mr. C!"

We watch them pull out, the engine revving gently as they slide smoothly through the aisles and out of the parking lot.

"What is it Johnny does again?" I ask as the headlights slowly fade into the distance.

"Tech stuff," my dad says with a shrug.

"Tech stuff?" I say as we head to the car, doubling back across the parking lot. "What? Like . . . Google? Matt's dad doesn't even drive anything like *that*."

He looks over at me, the both of us surprised I brought up Matt. He doesn't know the specifics, and won't ask unless I tell him, but he *has* to know something big enough is amiss that Matt hasn't come by and I haven't left the house to see anyone but Kiera in weeks.

"Yeah," my dad says, grabbing the basket from me and lightly nudging me. "And to think, neither of them has a bingo prize basket!"

I smile at him, nudging him right back.

"Thanks, by the way," he says as we get to his red, slightly rusty Chevy. He holds the basket up and smiles at me over the truck bed.

"Nope!" I say, yanking open the truck door, the hinges screeching noisily. "Your card, your money, your basket."

"I don't know about that. That card doesn't win like that for anyone but you and your—" He stops short before saying it, hitting

23

me square in the chest with more than just the prize basket.

The both of us fall silent, but I can feel the missing word ringing in my ears.

He was able to *go to bingo*, to be in that room and pretend it didn't mean anything, but he can't even say her name.

"Buckle up," I say, eyeing his seat belt as he puts the car in drive. I don't know how many times I have to tell him practically half of all motor vehicle fatalities could be prevented if the person had a seat belt on.

He nods, quickly braking the car and clicking it into place. He shoots me a sincerely guilty look. "Sorry, Em."

I nod, pretending it's no big deal, but I'm already down one parent, and I'd rather not make it two.

We drive off, the elementary school fading into the distance, just like it had hundreds of times in my mom's lemon of a silver Toyota Camry. I watch the people outside Sam's Scoops, kids running around, their parents trying to wrangle them and slowly accepting defeat, a group of middle school girls gossiping in the corner. I try to picture myself in the middle of it all, if everything were different.

Would Mom and I be driving off already? Or would we be stuck in the thick of it, talking about Jim Donovan's antics or the latest gossip at school or how wild it is that awkward seven-year-olds can grow up to be Instagram-model pretty. I'm sure that in that universe, things would be okay between me and Matt and my friends, that the person whose advice I need now more than ever would know some way to fix this.

But the image fades just like the school in the rearview. There's always this empty void, a gap in space and time where my mom should be but isn't.

Shifting in my seat, I rest my head against the glass of the car window and close my eyes, reaching in my pocket to wrap my fingers around the lucky quarter.

I usually push these thoughts away because I can never picture it, but for the first time in a long time, one arm cradling the familiar shape of a bingo prize basket, the taste of our favorite ice-cream flavor still on my tongue, I can feel her.

I can actually *feel* her.

My thumbnail finds that familiar nick just above George Washington's head, and I can't help but think that maybe this bingo night wasn't so bad after all.

3

The rising sun is already ridiculously hot, and I'm relieved when my bike picks up speed and I feel the wind pulling at my hair, the for-sale sign on my front lawn fading farther and farther into the distance as I head off to work the next day.

I could do this ride with my eyes closed, the route carved deep into my memory. It's crazy to think I won't be riding along it soon. Every familiar turn and hill and landmark will be a thing of the past, since we'll probably move into an apartment in town, and Nina's will be just around the corner.

Not that Dad has said *anything* about it.

I turn out onto the main road that'll take me straight into the heart of Huckabee and scan the horizon as a single red car lumbers past me. Behind the car sits a blanket of farmland, cornstalks growing taller and taller with each pedal.

And, of course, there are the cows.

Anytime there's a stretch of farmland in between a development of McMansions, you see them, loafing around in a field of grass, not a single care in the world.

Each stretch marks a Huckabee family that's refused to be bought out and shoved a few miles south to the cheap, rickety town houses that no one really wants to live in.

I pedal past Devonshire Estates, a development of cookie-cutter houses that were built on top of my grandparents' farm back in the mid-2000s. My grandfather died just after I was born, and when the real estate developers came knocking, my grandma didn't really have a choice. The farm where she grew up, where she raised my mom, was ripped right out from under her. She lived in the town houses until she passed away.

I stare at a golden retriever sunbathing in a sprawling back-yard, wondering what part of the farm used to lie underneath him. Wondering if my grandma was just as devastated about losing the home she had grown up in as I am about losing mine.

Saint Michael's Church comes swinging into view, with its stoic brick and stained-glass windows and ancient wooden door, and the playground next to it where I used to jump off swings and play tag and hang upside down on the monkey bars with Kiera.

Admittedly, I probably won't miss this part of the ride all that much, since when I slow to a stop at a big red stop sign, I find myself trying, like I always do, to ignore the black sign looming in the distance just in front of me, HUCKABEE CEMETERY painted in thick gold letters.

I duck my head and pedal quickly past, the black sign and the wrought-iron gates whizzing by me as the center of Huckabee pulls me safely inside. Yet even when I can breathe again, there's still a crater inside me that feels like I've left her behind. Again.

The business district, or, really, the heart of Huckabee, hasn't changed a single bit in my entire life. Sure, a few of the buildings have been renovated and modernized, likely because they had lead paint from the fifties, but it still has the same feel, good and bad memories around every corner. Memories I don't want to think about.

I see Judy through the window at Hank's Diner, where my dad and I went almost every day for three months when we just didn't have it in us to make dinner. She blows me a kiss, and I can already feel the bone-crushing hug she'll give me when she finds out we're selling the house. Judy is the cornerstone of Hank's, having worked there since she was a freshman at Huckabee High. She'll be seventy-five this fall.

The Coffee Bean is a few doors down, followed by a slew of other shops, like O'Reilly's Used Books and a hardware store my dad frequents. I wave to Mr. O'Reilly as he unlocks the door to his shop, his carefully maintained mustache turning up at the corners as he gives me a smile, even though I haven't set foot in there in years. The creaking wood floors and the smell of old books are still too much three years on.

As I pedal down Main Street, I watch the giant clock in the center of town tick slowly closer to seven forty-five, the morning sun already shining brightly in the sky behind it. I slide onto the sidewalk, hop off my bike, and walk it over to the rack at the bottom of the library steps. Taking my U-lock out of my bag, I glance up at the huge old building with its wide windows and century-old red brick. And sitting in stark contrast across the street from it is . . .

Nina's Bakery. Relief washes over me at just the sight of it.

Whitewashed brick gives way to a large circular sign, spelling out the name in a loopy black cursive.

I catch a whiff of the heavenly pastry smell that forms a cloud around the building, luring passersby in for a donut or a cupcake or an apple tart made with fresh apples from Snyder's Orchard just a few miles north.

I've spent so many days and nights here since Kiera's mom quit her nursing job when my mom died, and decided to chase her lifelong dream of owning a bakery. "Live your life how you want to live it, ladies," she said to me and Kiera after she signed the lease for the building, the two of us tucked safely under her arms. "Tomorrow is never guaranteed."

I usually hate it when people say stuff like that, but not Nina. I click my lock into place, then jog across the street and push open the door. The bells jingle noisily as I slide inside.

Nina's is one of my favorite places ever. Aside from the hundreds of baked goods, every corner of this place feels special. From the white walls we all spent hours painting, to the wooden industrial-style shelves my dad hung with practiced precision, to the kitchen in the back we slowly put together one oven and fryer at a time.

But more than that, it also feels *new*. Sometimes I feel like

29

there's not a single inch of space in this town that isn't saturated with old memories. Nina's is different, though. It's a product of the after. It's a blank slate. It's safe.

The people inside the building help with that feeling too.

"Hey, Emily!"

I look up to see Kiera's older brother, Paul, sitting behind the cash register, twirling a pen effortlessly in his right hand. His curly black hair is pulled back into a small ponytail; his nose piercing, a small diamond stud, glints brightly against his dark skin.

"Hey, Paul," I say, unclicking my helmet, the door closing noisily behind me. "Any news from Kiera? Did she get the box?"

Every summer Kiera goes to Misty Oasis, a no-cell-phones-except-for-Sunday-evening, long-letter-writing, let's-relive-pioneer-America style sleepaway camp. Nina went, and, in turn, Kiera's gone religiously since she was eight and a half years old. This summer she was promoted from CIT to junior counselor, a job she is apparently taking very seriously.

"Nah. Haven't heard from her." He drops his pen onto the napkin he was doodling on. "She's too busy making fires and, like, trying to make sure her campers don't die."

"That sounds awful," I say, sliding behind the counter. Paul and I are decidedly not the camping type. We've each done a one-week stint at Misty Oasis and are still traumatized from it.

"What'd you put in it this year?" he asks.

I make Kiera a homesick box every single summer, filling it with small trinkets that make the month away a little easier. I tick the items off on my fingers as I list them all for him.

"Three packs of her favorite gum, a vanilla candle that smells *just* like your mom's Very Vanilla Cupcakes, four different shades of red nail polish, the latest copy of *Seventeen*, and twenty-five notes, one for every day she'll be gone."

To be honest, I don't think she gets homesick anymore, but it's tradition.

And this year I'm extra homesick for her. Not only do I wish she were here to help with the move, but she's the only one who stood by me when shit hit the fan with Matt.

I glance at the napkin in front of Paul and see he's drawn an intricate machine, a cake sitting underneath what looks like a fancy waterspout. He's a mechanical engineer in the making, working toward his BS at Carnegie Mellon, on the other side of the state.

"What's this one do?" I ask, leaning over his shoulder to get a better look at it.

"Streamline cake icing."

"You trying to put me out of work?" I say, nudging him playfully. Cake icing is my specialty. I always get tapped by Nina to do the birthday and graduation and wedding cakes. Yeah, it takes hours, but it's worth it. There's nothing more rewarding than seeing the designs in my head come to life.

"That's the plan!" he says, giving me a wide grin. "Free you up to have the wild summer you've always dreamed about having."

I roll my eyes at him. "Very funny."

I head toward the back office to drop off my stuff, passing Nina on my way. "Hey, baby!" she says as she looks up from the dough she's mixing. "How are you doing this morning?"

"Good! Only sixteen more days," I say as I push open the office door. Sixteen more days until Kiera comes home from Misty Oasis and I won't be all by myself, smack in the middle of the worst summer in history, rotating between packing and waiting for the junior prom aftershocks to settle. Which they aren't. At all.

I hang my helmet in the closet under my self-decorated name tag, swapping my backpack for a black apron and my pink Nina's Bakery hat. Tying my apron as I go, I head back out into the kitchen, eyeing the bowl of dough Nina is mixing.

"Are those—" I start to ask.

"You bet!" she says, pouring some more chocolate chips into the mixture. "Secret Ingredient Chocolate Chip Cookies!"

I steal a little bit of the dough, tasting the sweet, but not too sweet, chocolatey goodness. "Is it nutmeg?"

She gives me a warm wink. "Em, I told you it's—"

"Love. Yeah, yeah, so you say. Nina, I *know* there's something else in there!" I laugh, giving her a quick hug.

"Nutmeg?" I whisper to Paul as I pass him to make sure the napkin dispenser is fully stocked.

He snorts. "The woman gave birth to me, and it took me eighteen years and a blood oath to get ahold of that thing," he says loudly, shooting a quick side-eye at Nina before lowering his voice to a whisper. "Think a little sweeter."

We start to get everything set up for the morning rush while I tell him about bingo the night before, from Johnny's and Blake's arrival to the unexpected appearance of my friend group. I'm still not used to having Kiera gone, and I find myself holding out trays of donuts or a stack of bags to the open air, to the place where she should be, empty. We have to work twice as fast to get everything done without her, the entire morning flow thrown off.

The most important part of the preopening setup is making sure the donuts are on display, the pink Nina's Bakery bags sitting poised just next to them. Nina is *known* for her donuts. We always sell out of them before noon, and on Saturdays we're lucky to have any left by ten. She has to make an extra four dozen every Sunday so the churchgoers don't forget their teachings at the door and square up near the glass display case.

"Everything ready?" Nina asks, wiping her hands with a towel as she walks to the front from the kitchen, her eyes scanning the pastries to make sure everything is neatly in place.

"Ready!" Paul says, saluting confidently, but sweat lines both our brows.

She rolls her eyes at him, the corner of her mouth twitching up into a smile as she pushes open the windows. Slowly, the scent from her Secret Ingredient Chocolate Chip Cookies wafts through the bakery and out onto the street. It's like a siren's song, drawing out the donut lovers and the baked-good regulars from every corner of Huckabee.

Practically the second she turns the sign to open, the front door of the library busts open and Mrs. McDonell, the head librarian, begins trotting eagerly down the steps for her two glazed. She's surpassed being just a regular and is now a certified addict, pairing her Nina's with a cup of coffee and a book every single morning. Somehow though, she's still barely more than ninety pounds, her tiny, elderly frame all sharp angles and knobby knees.

The bells on the front door jingle as she comes in, and they don't stop jingling for the next two hours straight. The noise is almost constant, as customer after customer comes inside, eagerly eyeing the display case. I work the cash register as Paul grabs the donuts and slides them into the pink bags, handing them out to everyone with a toothy smile. Nina sticks to the kitchens, churning out the goods.

It's a blur of people from around town until the clock lands on ten, and I couldn't be happier. I'm so busy moving at light speed, I don't even have time to think about Matt or my friends or the move. Instead, I focus on the people right in front of me: Annie from Hank's, Mr. Schmidt, the principal at Huckabee High. I do my best to put a name to every face, which always earns a warm smile and the clattering of change in the tip jar.

Luckily, it's pretty easy to do when you've lived in the same small town your whole life.

When there's a lull, Paul slides a stool over and sits down next to me with a long exhale, his shoulders slumping.

"Stop playing. You missed it," I say, nudging him.

"Working with you? Absolutely not," Paul says, grinning back at me.

The three of us, Paul, Kiera, and I, would work every weekend together during the school year before he went to college. On Sundays we used to plot some new variety of pastry or some funky cookie combination to cook up. If Nina taste-tested it and gave it the stamp of approval, she would put whatever we made out and let us keep all the profits from it. It was harder to find time to do it after he left, especially when the rush at Nina's became more and more hectic with each year that passed.

The bells on the front door jingle, and we both look up, plastering artificial customer-service smiles on our faces. But I'm surprised when I see Blake standing in the doorway, a white Ron Jon T-shirt making her arms look even tanner than last night.

"*Blake?* What are you doing here?" I blurt out, my brain and my mouth working on two different wavelengths. Luckily, she cracks a smile. Her golden-streaked hair is pulled back into a ponytail, full and wavy and swinging gently as she moves.

"Nice to see you, too," she says, closing the door carefully behind her. "I Yelped the best place to get a donut in Huckabee, and this was the only place for, like, twenty-five miles."

"That's *almost* true," I say with a nod toward the window. "There's a gas station about ten minutes down the road with a whole display case of them. I think they put new ones out once a month, just to keep them fresh."

"Once a month? What am I doing here, then?" she asks, throwing her hands up with fake exasperation.

I laugh, quickly fixing my hair and smoothing out my Nina's Bakery shirt as her eyes dart down to look at the cupcakes on the other side of the glass. I glance over and catch Paul looking at me, a faint smirk on his face.

I roll my eyes. With Kiera gone, he knows Blake is my one chance at having a friend this summer. There's no need to rub it in.

"I think I'll just take a glazed donut," Blake says finally, both of our heads whipping back around to look at her. "Is that lame?"

"Nah," I say as Paul dramatically pulls a single sheet of waxed paper from the box. "They're the cornerstone of Nina's."

"You're in luck!" Paul says from behind me. "You got the last one."

He puts it carefully in a bag and holds it out to her. "I'm Paul, by the way," he says when she takes the bag from his blue-gloved hand. "Brother of Emily's best friend, the better-looking sibling, former resident gay of Huckabee."

Blake laughs, her entire face lighting up in the morning sun, trickling in through the storefront window. "Nice to meet you. I'm Blake."

She doesn't even raise an eyebrow at his gay comment. It's good to know she isn't homophobic. It can be pretty hit or miss around Huckabee, but I guess where Blake grew up things are probably a little different.

"Are you here visiting?" he asks her.

She shakes her head, the bag in her hand crinkling noisily. "No, I just moved here with my dad."

"Oh my gosh. I'm so sorry," Paul says, shaking his head mournfully.

Paul is *not* a fan of Huckabee. Which is absolutely fair, because Huckabee has been really hard on him. He was always a little smaller, a little quieter, a little darker, and a little gayer than anyone at Huckabee High, and people weren't shy about letting him know that. When he came home for Christmas break last winter with a boyfriend, it was like meeting an entirely different person.

36

Like he came into his own the second he put his suitcase in the car and drove past the town limits. It's honestly no wonder he drives back to visit his boyfriend every chance he gets.

Sometimes I wonder what that would be like. To go somewhere where no one sees someone else when they look at me.

"It doesn't seem too bad," she says, pulling her wallet out of her back pocket, her eyes flicking to me. "I mean, there *are* a lot of cows."

I laugh as she pulls out a couple of ones, crisp and free of crinkles.

"How much for the donut?" she asks.

"Don't worry about it," I say, waving my hand at her. We get a free baked good of our choice every day, and I feel like being generous.

"For real?" Blake asks, surprised.

"Yeah." I nod to Paul. "Think of it as an apology donut from all of Huckabee."

"Thanks," she says, smiling down at the bag.

"Don't mention it," I say with a shrug. She reaches out and puts the money in the tip jar. "I'll see you in a few hours," she adds as she heads for the door, flashing a big smile in Paul's direction as she pulls it open. "Bye, Paul!"

"Bye! Come back soon!" he calls, waving until the exact second the door clicks shut. He lets out a low whistle as we watch her walk down the street, her outline disappearing around the corner and out of sight. "What is *she* doing stuck in a place like Huckabee? I mean, why on earth would Johnny Carter move back here?" He pulls off his blue gloves with a snap and tosses them into the trash can.

I shrug and reach out to adjust the stray napkins spilling out of the dispenser. "I don't know. Something to do with her family." At least that's as much as my dad mentioned. He was predictably light on the details.

When I push a stray hair behind my ear, I realize he's raising his perfectly even eyebrows at me. "Well, she definitely wants to be friends with you," he says as he grabs the empty donut tray.

"What? No." I shake my head. "She probably just wanted a donut."

"Emily, come on. You know Nina's Bakery sure as hell isn't on Yelp. Nothing in this fart of a town is on Yelp," he calls over his shoulder as he heads for the kitchen sink. "She definitely just came to see you."

Huh, he's . . . right. I glance out the window, at the corner Blake disappeared around, and wonder if that's the truth. If this might not be the loneliest summer after all.

4

A few hours later I push open the door to my dad's bedroom, lugging a big, empty cardboard box behind me.

Carefully, I creep across the space, a reflex from my usual secret trips in here. I close the distance to my mom's closet door, and my hand reaches out to wrap around the silver door handle.

I've been putting this room off since the house went up on the market three weeks ago. I knew it would be the hardest one.

I'd put it off for longer if my dad hadn't just handed me a box downstairs, motioning up the steps and mumbling, "Closet today," before ducking out of the room to go rummaging through the stuff in the basement.

I take a deep breath and turn the handle. Immediately the smell of her sweet lilac perfume radiates off the dresses and shirts and skirts, warm and safe and fading from this house and this room and this closet and my life by the second.

But for now, still here.

For a moment I stand there in the darkness and it's like . . . I can *feel* her standing next to me. I let her wrap around me once more, let the horribly overwhelming sadness climb out of the box I usually keep it in. The one I only open here. It tightens its grip on my chest, reminding me why I always try to avoid this feeling, but this move is making it harder and harder to do that.

Bingo night is making it harder and harder to do that. Maybe I need to stop trying to push it away all the time.

Because pretty soon we will be in a new house, without a closet filled with her scent, and I will have nowhere to crawl into to try to feel close to her when I am sad or angry or heartbroken and only want to talk to her like I always did.

I flick on the light and gently run my fingers along the row of hangers, trying to convince myself that they are just *clothes*. Bits of fabric. Nothing more and nothing less.

It's impossible, though. To not make every single thing feel like a memory.

I start with a black cardigan. It's just a normal black sweater, nothing fashionable really. But she always used to wear it when we'd decorate cakes together in the kitchen, the pockets wide enough to hold pastry bags, and icing smoothers, and glass jars filled with sprinkles.

I pull it off the hanger and stare at it, trying to find the strength to turn around and drop it in the box.

To just let go.

I mean, I know. On some level I *know* this needs to happen. I've known for a long time.

When the medical bills started rolling in after that summer, past due turned into WAY past due in the blink of an eye. My dad did everything he could to keep it at bay. Everything but give up the house.

He never said it, but I think for a long time he felt like if he let go of the house, he had to let go of her. I think it's why he fought so hard to keep it.

Maybe longer than he should have.

A month ago, though, it all caught up to us. I found him sitting at the kitchen table a little before midnight, still in his dirty clothes from working his third overtime shift that week, eating reheated pasta from another dinner he had missed out on.

"Second mortgage was denied," he said, the ripped-open envelope still sitting in front of him, his eyes glued to the rejection letter. "I'm going to go into town tomorrow morning to talk to a real estate agent."

"Summer is almost here," I said, desperate. "I'll be able to work more! I can take on some extra shifts, and I can pay the electric bill, and—"

"Emily." He cut me off, his voice firm. "It's done. It's over." He pushed his chair back, the legs screeching against the floor underneath them. "It's time to let go."

He got up from the table and it was like a light switch. He couldn't part with anything, and now it feels like there will be nothing left. Every day there's a new pile of boxes, filled to the

41

brim with stuff to donate. It's like because he was forced to get rid of the house, he's also fine with throwing out every reminder of her.

And he wants me to be fine with it too.

But standing here, holding this tiny, pretty insignificant piece of my mom that I can't give up, it suddenly feels impossible. There's a part of me that can't let clothes just be clothes and can't let a house just be a house. This disconnect between knowing what is good and right and what has to happen and this feeling like I'm losing her all over again.

Just differently this time.

I slowly loosen my grip, my fingers letting go one by one until the cardigan falls from my hand into the box, landing at the bottom with a soft rustle.

"How's it going in there?"

I start, peering out of the closet to see Blake wearing the same white Ron Jon T-shirt from earlier, another empty cardboard box tucked under her arm.

"Uh, fine!" I call back. I pull myself together and quickly scan the clothes in front of me before grabbing a shirt with a price tag still on it and tossing it into the box at my feet so it isn't *completely* empty. "About to . . . get started on the shoes."

My eyes travel over the floor-to-ceiling shoe rack as I let out a long exhale. For some reason, shoes feel at least slightly less sentimental.

Black cardigans: definitely cry inducing, strong potential for an existential crisis.

A pair of brown loafers: instantly ready to be put into the

garbage disposal, will burn if given the chance.

Blake appears in the closet doorway, leaning against it as she drops the box behind her with a thud.

"Well, I am here to help!" she says, her voice a little too awkwardly cheery, just high enough to tell me she knows how weird this is. I see her cringe at herself out of the corner of my eye and can't help but crack a small smile.

"Sounds good," I say as I scoop up a pair of heels, tossing them on top of the cardigan and the unworn shirt.

"Anything off-limits?" She eyes the shoe rack, her hands on her hips.

"No," I say, but my voice cracks unexpectedly. I clear my throat, trying again, firmer now. *"No."* The new place won't have space for a bunch of clothes that no one will wear. And if I start picking and choosing, I'll want all of it.

We get started, pulling out the shoes by twos, the rack slowly emptying. I don't know if it's because we tried to blow up Santa together or the fact that our dads have such a strong bromance, but a comfortable silence settles over us, the hum of the air-conditioning in my parents' bedroom the only noise. Every now and then our hands brush lightly against one another, but it's just for a second and then she's pulling away, redirecting to another pair of shoes, her movements smooth and focused.

I notice a leather bracelet around her tan wrist, seagulls flying around the perimeter of it, stretching their wings alongside small teal circles. I watch it move as Blake reaches out to grab a flip-flop and attempts a backward shot into the box, but it smacks off the corner and lands on the ground in between us.

"Nice try, LeBron," I say as I bend down to grab the flip-flop. I duplicate the shot. This time it makes it safely inside.

She laughs as she rolls her eyes at me, and I notice the dark circles around them have faded slightly since yesterday.

"How's the jet lag?" I ask her.

"Better! The donut *definitely* helped."

"I didn't even know Nina's was on Yelp," I say, eyeing her as Paul's words from earlier come back to me.

I almost expect her to be embarrassed, but she laughs and shakes her head. "It's not. I just remembered your dad said you were working this morning, so I thought I'd swing by. It's not like I have anything else to do." She tosses another pair of shoes into the box. "I mean, what do *you* do for fun around here?"

"This year . . . I'm not doing much. Just working at the bakery and . . . waiting for school to start."

The past friendless weeks have been beyond boring. My usual days off would be spent lounging at the Huckabee Pool, eating cheese fries from the concession stand. But since Matt and a giant fraction of the Huckabee High population are employed there, there's no way in hell I could set foot in there without drowning in a wave of passive-aggressive judgment.

"You're telling me you don't do *anything*? Like . . . with your friends?" Blake asks, surprised.

Realizing we burned through the shoes pretty quickly, I look away and step onto a stool to get started on the top shelf of stuff. Blankets, a few hats and scarves, a couple of odds and ends. Things

I can part with. She picks up the other box, catching the items I toss in her direction.

"Well, my best friend goes to this sleepaway camp in the middle of absolute nowhere for half the summer," I say, throwing a pair of gloves before picking up an Eagles hat my dad bought for my mom during treatment. I cringe and chuck it to Blake, eager to be rid of the painful memories it brings up.

I don't add the fact that, besides Kiera, none of my friends wants to hang out with me right now. If Blake finds out the whole story, I doubt she's going to be making impromptu visits to Nina's. "So, aside from a phone call every Sunday and the occasional letter in the mail, I don't really have anything planned until she gets back."

I grab a rolled-up fleece blanket, stopping short when I come face-to-face with a cardboard box shoved into the very corner of the closet. Printed in dark Sharpie on the side of the box is HIGH SCHOOL MEMORIES, a small heart drawn next to the words.

I've never seen this box before.

I don't know how. I used to spend nearly every morning in here with her, helping her pick the perfect outfit for the day. But really, more than outfit picking, it was the time it was just the two of us, talking about the latest gossip at school, or getting advice about whatever drama was bubbling up in my friend group.

I've been in this closet hundreds of times since, my eyes looking over every inch of the space for pieces of her.

But I never found this one.

I can feel my heart pounding as I reach up, stretching as much as I possibly can, my fingertips clawing at the edges of the cardboard. No matter how hard I stretch though, I'm not even close to getting it down. Even *with* the small stool, which starts wobbling dangerously underneath me.

"Here," Blake says as she puts the donation box down. I step off the stool and she slides past me, a wave of that warm-sunshine, blue-ocean smell mixing with Mom's lilac.

I rub my arm, watching as she reaches up and smoothly pulls the box down like I didn't just dislocate my elbow trying to get it.

She doesn't tease me though, just turns and carefully holds it out to me, like she can sense the importance.

I walk out of the closet in a daze, the worn cardboard corners slowly wilting open from age as I place the box on the ground. I slide onto my knees as I begin to pull out the contents hidden inside. Blake sits down on the opposite side of the box, her hands crossed in her lap, her honey-brown eyes wide as my mom's high school years pool on the ground in front of us.

The first few things are what I expect them to be. Royal-blue varsity letters for cheerleading and soccer. Medals from her statewide competitions, earned her sophomore and junior years. A soccer T-shirt with HUCKABEE HIGH stamped across the front. A picture of her with a group of her soccer besties in their matching, brightly colored late-nineties tracksuits.

I stare at the picture for a long moment, recognizing Nina and Donna Taylor's sister, Samantha.

I put it down and move on to the rest of the box, my hands eagerly wrapping around a manila envelope.

"Can I?" Blake asks as she reaches out for the soccer-team photo I put down.

"Sure." She picks it up, her eyes widening as she looks at it. "*Wow.* You do look just like your mom."

"Yeah," I say, prickling slightly.

"Do you hate it?"

She's the first person to ever ask that. I jerk my head up to look at her, and our eyes meet as she peers at me from over the photo.

"No," I say, but then I hesitate. "It just . . . makes me feel like a walking memorial card." I unfold the metal prongs of the envelope, trying to keep my hands busy.

A small line forms in between Blake's eyebrows as she processes my comment. "It's kind of cool, though, isn't it? That people see her in you. That you keep her memory alive without even trying."

I've never thought about it like that.

"Yeah," I say, nodding, my eyes falling to the picture in her hands, my mom's face staring back at me. "I guess it is."

I pull the envelope open and find it's full of certificates, none of them surprising. Honor Roll, Perfect Attendance, Most Likely to Be President.

Crazy to think that she barely lived long enough to be *eligible* to run for president.

Blake whistles as I sift through them all. "Jeez. What *didn't* your mom do? I'm surprised someone like that was hanging out with my high school dropout of a dad."

I laugh, my wrist honestly aching from the weight of all these awards. "Well, it was our dads who put a stop to all this. Look. . . ."

I fan out the papers in my hands. "Nothing after her junior year."

"What'd she do instead?" Blake asks, reaching out to pluck a Hall Monitor certificate from the bunch.

"Started actually living the life she *wanted* to, I guess. Started doing the things she always wanted to do, instead of trying to be president of every club on campus and having panic attacks over AP English presentations," I say, thinking back to what my mom had told me. "She said after she started hanging out with our dads, she realized what she thought was living really wasn't."

"That summer changed everything, Em. Everything just . . . fell into place." She would always say that to me, a wistful look in her blueberry-blue eyes.

She never told me why though, and looking at all the stuff in this box, I feel like I understand it even less. It looks like she already had everything in place.

I always thought maybe she'd tell me more when I was the same age she had been that summer. That the summer before my senior year would be the same. Big. Life changing. Things falling into place for me the same way they did for her.

I wonder what she would say to me now. Instead of everything falling into place, my senior year has blown into a million pieces before it even starts.

I go to slide everything back into the envelope when I catch sight of a ripped-up piece of paper, tape holding it together.

It's my mom's SAT scores from the spring of her junior year. I scan the page, surprised to see she *bombed* the reading section. Like . . . a 230.

I'm pretty sure you get 200 just by signing your name.

That's weird. And, sitting in this stack of accolades, it's . . . *super* not like her.

"Henry Huckabee Lodge?" Blake asks. I look up to see she's holding a metal room plate, the number five embedded on it. "What's that?"

I put the taped-up paper on top of the stack, closing the envelope. "It's this big lodge three hours away that the family of Huckabee's founder still owns," I say, pulling a moose stuffed animal out of the box. "My school has a lake trip there every August for the incoming senior class as a 'Congrats, you *almost* survived high school' kind of thing. It's a tradition. They've done it for, like, a hundred and sixteen years. My parents actually started dating during their senior-year lake trip." I toss her the moose, grinning. "*Our* school, rather."

She grins back at me, catching the moose and holding it up, her brown eyes inspecting its face. "It kind of looks like your dad," she says as she spins it around to face me.

I pretend to be offended on his behalf, but . . . I definitely see it. The eyes, the unruly brown hair, the stocky build.

"So, are you going?" she asks as she carefully places the Joseph Clark moose down on top of the manila envelope. "On the lake trip?"

"Absolutely not." I grimace. I decided pretty much my first day of high school I wouldn't be going because of 1) the three-hour bus ride there, 2) the three-hour bus ride back, and 3) I'm definitely not a Lake-Going Person.

Oh, and, newly added: 4) I'd rather not be stuck at a lake for three days with my ex and a bunch of people who either want to gossip about me or hate me.

"Why not?" she asks, clearly surprised by my adamant decision.

Blake is *obviously* a Lake-Going Person.

"Do you have any idea how much bacteria is in a lake?" I ask. "When I was in middle school, Huckabee Lake was shut down for the whole summer because of a massive breakout of carp herpes. The shore was literally lined with dead fish."

Carp herpes is no joke.

She snorts, shaking her head as she puts the room-number plate down. "I didn't even know carp could *get* herpes."

I turn back to the box, pulling out two cassette tapes' worth of music, a worn blue baseball cap, a small jar of sand, a worse-for-wear book by Albert Camus, and wait. . . .

My eyes widen when I see what's at the very bottom.

I've just hit the jackpot.

A yearbook. "Huckabee High Class of 2000" is printed in big block letters on the front of it, a picture of the graduating class on the cover in matching royal-blue graduation attire. I pull it out, flipping through the brightly colored pages.

"Oh my gosh," I say, "look at this."

I spin the yearbook around to face Blake so she can see the picture that stopped me dead in my tracks. Two boys decked out in face paint, one perched on the other one's shoulders, swinging a T-shirt wildly around over his head. Joseph Clark and Johnny Carter, our dads, in all their high school glory.

My dad looks almost exactly the same, except for the lack of a beard and the backward blue cap he's sporting in the photo. He's even got on a leather jacket that I am 99.9 percent certain he still has to this day.

Johnny, on the other hand, looks *completely* different. Perched on my dad's shoulders, he looks nothing like the lady-killer at bingo night. He's pretty much just a clone of young Blake. Small, lanky, and wearing a pair of glasses that takes up most of his paint-covered face.

"I can't believe your dad was so tiny!" I say, shocked.

Blake laughs and takes the yearbook from me. "He grew five inches the year after he left for Hawaii." With her free hand, she reaches into her back pocket and pulls out her phone. "I actually have a picture."

She scrolls through her photos, stopping finally on what's clearly a picture of a printed photo, the color slightly faded, the image just a little blurry. As she turns her phone around, I see Johnny Carter in all his chiseled bronze glory, one arm slung around the shoulders of a stunning Japanese woman while they stand on a breathtaking Hawaiian beach. They're sun kissed and in love and wearing matching blue-and-white-striped bathing suits as they gaze into each other's eyes in that magical way we all hope someone will share with us one day.

I wonder what that must be like.

If this were Tumblr, I'd reblog the crap out of that photo. It looks like it's something out of a magazine.

"That's your mom?" I ask, seeing Blake in her eyes and the bridge of her nose and the curve of her smile.

"Yep!" Blake says happily, nodding as she cranes her neck to look at the picture, an identical smile playing on her lips. She definitely isn't a carbon copy like me, but you can still see their shared features.

I'd never seen Blake's mom before, but I knew the story. She'd died six hours after giving birth to Blake. A hemorrhage of some kind.

I meet Blake's eyes, wondering what that must be like. Never having known your mom. To only have that picture on your phone, or stories told over dinner about a person you know but never really *knew.*

When my mom died, it felt like everyone I knew had a story about her. Every story was a different flavor of grief, a memory that would just pour out of people to absolve a wound far beneath the skin. To make sense of something that couldn't make sense. As they talked, I would wonder if it was for me or for them, the stories slowly becoming empty words. Empty words passing over lips in an attempt to reconcile a loss that couldn't be reconciled.

Sometimes the things people told me didn't even *sound* like her. Like the parts of my mom they were giving me were all wrong. Like they didn't even add up to the person I knew.

What would it be like to *just* have those stories? To maybe not even know what was real. Or . . . what was fake.

"Well," I say to her, not wanting to pick at either of our wounds, my eyes moving back to the yearbook picture of her gawky teen dad. "It's good to know the whole crushing puberty thing is genetic for

52

you Carters. All I got was boobs and a tick mark over five-three."

She pockets her phone, giving me a long look.

"Fine. A tick mark over five-two."

She shakes her head and holds out the yearbook to me, but as she does a folded piece of paper falls out of the very back. I watch as it floats down to the worn wood of my parents' bedroom floor, the faded page landing gently on the ground between us, with a whisper too quiet for me to hear.

I can feel it in the air though, the hair on the back of my neck standing on end when I catch sight of my mom's handwriting, bleeding through from the other side.

I reach out to pick it up, carefully unfolding it to see JULIE MILLER'S SENIOR YEAR SUMMER in thick, bold letters. TWELVE ADVENTURES BEFORE TWELFTH GRADE is written just under it, slightly smaller.

The paper is crisp but thin underneath my fingertips, holding all the years between the last time my mom touched it and right now.

The handwriting is the same loopy cursive I remember. More legible, perhaps, with the forced neatness we all try for when something is important. Every line is written in a different color ink, still vibrant after all this time.

1. Get a tattoo.
2. Get over my fear of heights.
3. Go on a picnic.
4. Try a new food.

5. Get out of Huckabee.
6. Sleep under the stars.
7. Go on the Huckabee Lake trip.
8. Skinny-dip in Huckabee Pool after hours.
9. Buy a book in another language.
10. Steal an apple from the First Tree at Snyder's Orchard.
11. Find a four-leaf clover.
12. Kiss J. C.

"What is it?" Blake asks.

"It's like . . . a bucket list," I say, holding it up for her to read. "From the summer before their senior year."

I watch her eyes move down the paper, quietly taking it all in.

"How's it going up there?" my dad's voice calls up to us, the bottom step creaking under his weight as Blake and I jump.

"Fine!" I call back, quickly folding the paper and shoving it into my pocket. I start to load the stuff back in the box, the yearbook, the stuffed moose, the varsity letters. "Just got done packing up the shoes!"

I don't look at Blake, but about halfway through my manic packing, she starts helping me, quickly stuffing the last few things in the box and standing up.

"I'm taking a truckload of stuff over to Goodwill," my dad calls, which has been his catchphrase for the past week and a half. "You guys want to bring your boxes down?"

"Yeah, definitely!" I call as I slide the Huckabee Lake

room-number plate inside and fold the cardboard corners of the box shut, over, under. "We'll be right down!"

Blake stands and grabs the first box of shoes from the closet, heading toward the bedroom door.

But then I see the black cardigan peeking out through a small hole in the side.

"Wait!" I exclaim, jumping up. Before I can process what I'm doing, my emotions get the better of me.

She stops dead and looks back, our eyes meeting as I run over to her, pushing aside the mound of shoes to dig the black cardigan out of the box. The second my fingertips touch the soft fabric, a feeling of relief pours over me.

"All good?" she asks.

I nod. "Yeah, I just . . . couldn't let this go yet."

She nods, like she gets it.

As she heads out of the room, I shuffle off down the hall, hiding the box of high school memories and the cardigan underneath my bed before booking it back to my dad's room. I grab the second box of shoes and assorted top-shelf items, almost buckling under the weight as I stumble down the glossy wooden steps, trying my very best not to trip over my own two feet and face-plant.

I'm relieved when my foot hits solid ground, and I stop to adjust the box, my arms burning. The black front door is thrown wide open, and I can feel the afternoon heat radiating slowly into the house.

I lug the box the rest of the way to my dad's beat-up pickup truck, where Johnny swoops in to take it from me. A pained expression appears on his face as he pretends it weighs a million pounds, staggering his way over to the truck bed.

"Phew, Em. You got some muscles!" he says, and my dad lets out a booming laugh, the likes of which I haven't heard in . . . forever.

I watch as he slides the box of shoes onto the back of the truck, and it becomes just another box in a sea of boxes. I try not to look too hard at the items peeking out of corners and edges, knowing I'll probably see something else that will make me sad.

"We'll be back in a bit," my dad says as he pushes up the tailgate. He gives me a hug, his strong arms wrapping around me, his shirt smelling of dust and sweat. Normally, I'd grumble about it, chide him to take a shower in a voice I know is as similar to my mom's as my face, but this time I don't try to resist.

They hop in the truck, turning the radio up and rolling down the windows like they're back in high school. It's wild how things can change so much and still be exactly the same.

I wave as they pull off, driving down Green Street and out of view.

"This is a pretty house," Blake says from somewhere behind me. I start at the sound of her voice, realizing we're going to be completely alone now. No packing left to do today now that my dad's been appeased by a donation run and we're out of boxes. Just me . . . trying not to be awkward.

I turn to look at the house, taking in the familiar crisp-white exterior and the sash windows and the front porch with a swing. The afternoon sunlight trickles softly through the large trees around our house, and I can't help but smile at the deep green of the grass and the bright yellow sunflowers in the garden that my dad and I carefully tamed in the spring.

It hits me that that was it. The last spring sunflower bloom, already over.

We definitely don't have the same green thumb my mom did, but we've worked tirelessly the past three years to keep the garden looking as good as she left it, from testing the pH of the soil to pest-control stakeouts on the front porch. I saw my dad get into it with a squirrel just last week after it tried to get some sunflower seeds.

"It was pretty perfect." I spy the red and white for-sale sign smack in the middle of the lawn, the flaw in it all. "Someone's sure going to love it."

I head up the front path and the steps and across the porch, Blake following just behind me.

"You want some water?" I call behind me as we round the corner into the living room.

"Yeah, sure."

We head into the kitchen, and I swing open the fridge door, grabbing the water pitcher off the top shelf, the cool air feeling nice after being outside.

"So," she says, sliding onto the marble kitchen counter as I take two cups out of the cabinet and start pouring out the Brita. "Why don't you want to move?"

I'm so surprised, I nearly dump all the water onto the counter.

"Who said I don't want to move?" I ask, quickly pulling myself together and handing her one of the cups.

"Oh, I don't know. Maybe just the look of disgust you gave the for-sale sign five minutes ago," she says, pausing, the glass halfway to her mouth. "Or maybe it was the look you gave the pile of boxes in the back of the truck."

She raises her dark eyebrows at me and takes a long, slow, calculating sip.

"Jeez, Blake," I say with a laugh. "You didn't have to call me out like that."

I'm surprised to find, though, that I like the honesty. It's refreshing. It's been three years and I still find people tiptoeing around me, bullshitting.

It makes me want to be honest too. To not tiptoe around the things my dad wouldn't want to hear.

"Because," I say, taking a deep breath, "all of this just feels like I'm getting farther and farther away from my mom. The move. Cleaning out her closet. All of it."

Blake is quiet for a moment. Thoughtful. She pulls her hair slowly into a bun, and I try to focus on the cup of water I'm drinking from instead of the way her face looks when her hair is pulled back. It's not fair for anyone to be that pretty.

Finally, once her hair is tucked away, she starts talking again. "Back in Hawaii, I used to go rock climbing at my mom's favorite spot. When my dad first showed it to me, he told me she liked it the most because when you get to the very top, everything else looks small. The people down at the beach. The cars. The trees, even." She puts her cup down on the counter. "She used to say that when you're that high up, even your problems can look smaller."

I nod. I like the idea of that. Though I'd probably need to be on the moon to make all my problems look small.

"You know I never met my mom, but whenever I wanted to feel close to her, I would go rock climbing at that spot because it made me feel like she wasn't that far away," she says, pausing for a moment to tuck a stray hair behind her ear. "Anyway . . ." She shifts her position, her eyes meeting mine, like she can sense I'm wondering where she's going with this beyond commiserating about our joint membership in the Dead Moms Club. "What I'm *trying* to say here is that you should do something to feel close to her. In a new way. New memories to substitute for that house-shaped void you're feeling."

She grins and points at my pocket, the outline of the folded list pressing through the fabric. "Actually, you could even do that bucket list. I mean, what've you got to lose?"

I laugh at that, but her words stick with me. Through our conversation about our shared love of *Schitt's Creek*, through our dads coming back from Goodwill, through the Carters leaving to go walk their golden retriever named Winston, through a quiet dinner of spaghetti and meatballs with my dad.

Not just something to feel close to her. *Twelve* somethings I never even knew she did before.

Could I do them too?

5

The next morning I lumber down the steps, my phone in one hand and my mom's list in the other. I make a beeline for the living room couch, plopping down on it and swiping up to unlock the phone screen.

No new notifications.

This shouldn't surprise me. Why would Matt wake up and send me a text on this random Sunday after nothing but weeks of radio silence?

I spend *hours* every day trying to find the right words to say, staring at the keyboard on my phone, but I can never find them. I want to explain to him why I did what I did, but I just . . . can't. How can I give him an explanation when I can't even give myself one?

This is one breakup I don't know how to fix. Especially because *he* was always the one who found a way to fix things before, whether it was showing up at my doorstep with flowers or pulling me aside to talk in between classes.

I don't know how to fix this on my own. And, maybe, there's some small part of me that doesn't want to.

I burrow down into the couch as the guilt swims over me, washing that thought away, the move making this additional betrayal of my mom's wishes feel just that much worse.

"Hey!" my dad's voice thunders unexpectedly from the kitchen, nearly giving me a heart attack.

He is usually working overtime by the time I get up on Sunday. I wasn't expecting to see him until our weekly Hank's date, gorging ourselves on their Sunday Special.

And . . . I definitely wasn't expecting to see him in *this*.

It takes me a second to fully process what I'm seeing.

"Where'd you get the new outfit?" I ask, and he cranes his neck to look down at himself, a smirk playing on his lips.

My dad, the six-three, pickup-truck-driving, thick-beard, arm-full-of-tattoos guy, is standing in the kitchen wearing an ancient pink flowery apron. An ancient, pink, flowery apron I remember my grandma wearing. But never quite like . . . this.

I try to shake my head at him, but I am laughing so hard, I can barely breathe. Before he can protest, I hold up my phone and snap a picture, wiping away the laugh-tears with the back of my hand. "I can see the caption now. 'Who wore it best?'"

"I spent my morning slaving away making pancakes, and you're going to fart around on your phone instead of eating them

61

with me?" He points a butter knife at the stack already sitting on the kitchen table with a defensively dignified look.

He's got a point.

I push myself off the couch and pocket my phone, the smell of the pancakes pulling me across the room and into the kitchen. "I thought you'd already left for work!"

"Sitting there texting . . . didn't even compliment my new apron . . . ," he grumbles as I slide into one of the kitchen chairs, an empty white plate resting in front of me. When his back is turned, I pull the list out of my pocket and unfold it, putting it carefully on the table next to me, hoping either he sees it and says something, or that I'm bold enough to just *ask* about it.

I feel my heart hammering in my chest. I know it's hard for him to talk about her. I know it's hard for *us* to talk about her.

But if he can move out of this house and get rid of her stuff, and pretend going to bingo night isn't a big deal, then he should be able to at least do this.

I force a huge grin as he spins back around, syrup and butter clutched in his hands. I use my fork to get a pancake from the top of the mound as he sits, scooting his chair into the table. "You're killing it, Dad. The apron really brings out your eyes."

"I thought the exact same thing!" he says, laughing.

"You staying late tonight?" I ask as I cover my pancakes in a layer of syrup before handing the bottle over to him.

"Yeah," he confirms as he takes it from me, slowly swirling the syrup onto his plate. "You know how it is with weekends . . . fewer guys . . . double the pay."

"So, no Hank's?" I ask, even though I already know the answer.

He nods, looking sorry. "No Hank's."

"But we've got pancakes!" I say quickly. I hate making him feel guilty.

He smiles and holds up a forkful. "We *do* have pancakes."

Then . . . his eyes follow mine down to the table where the crinkled piece of paper sits. Am I going to pass out? Maybe.

He raises his thick eyebrows as he points in its direction. "What've you got there?"

I swallow my mouthful of pancakes and cautiously pick it up. "I found this yesterday. When I was cleaning out the closet."

I hold it out to him, and he reaches for it, nodding as his eyes run down the piece of paper, his expression unreadable. I stay silent, waiting for him to talk. "Yeah. I remember this."

"You do?" I ask, trying not to appear too excited. I know by now that I'm definitely walking on eggshells. He'd do anything to get out of a conversation about Mom, and I usually would too. But I can't now. Not this time. "Did you, uh . . . ?" My voice trails off, and I have to force the words out. "Did you help her with it?"

He smiles faintly. "Yeah. Me and Johnny both did. Nina for one or two, but she was away at that camp for most of the summer. I even came up with a couple of them. We went on a day trip to the beach and rode on roller coasters until she wasn't afraid of the drop. A whole bunch of stuff."

My eyes land on number twelve: "Kiss J. C.," and I give my dad a big grin. "Plus, number twelve certainly worked out well for you. Did you come up with that one?"

He snorts, rolling his eyes. "Yeah, right."

I see his face change the longer he looks at it, his eyebrows furrowing, his jaw locking. I can tell he's closing off, a door slamming shut.

I claw my way into the tiny space, wrapping my fingers around the doorframe before it can close completely. "Why did she do it? Do you know?"

He takes a bite of his pancakes, chewing slowly, swallowing deliberately. "Your mom spent most of her life doing what people expected of her. She was the president of all the clubs at school. She was always on honor roll. She was always doing what her parents wanted her to do." He reaches out, taking a sip of his coffee. "But then she bombed her SATs."

My head snaps up as I remember the taped piece of paper I found yesterday.

"Didn't get a lick of sleep the night before and ended up passed out over her reading section. She'd completely worn herself out. Me and Johnny found her crying in the parking lot afterward. But it wasn't hard to see it wasn't really the test that was weighing on her." He stares at his plate, his face thoughtful.

"Is that why you decided to help her? How did she come up with the list? Was it like—"

"I gotta get to work," my dad says, cutting me off midsentence. He shovels the rest of his breakfast into his mouth and stands up, the wooden chair screeching loudly on the kitchen floor.

I glance at our oven clock. Ten fifty-five. He'll be a whole ten minutes early if he leaves now. I should've quit while I was ahead.

"I can clean up," I say as he puts his plate on the counter.

He nods and rips off the apron. Hard to believe we were just joking about it ten minutes ago.

I watch as he takes one more swig of coffee. "Thanks, Em," he says, giving me a quick kiss on the top of my head before heading to the hall closet, where his work boots are. "I'll see you tonight, okay?"

"Okay!" I call after him, hearing the front door creak open. "I love you."

"Love you too," he calls back, the door slamming shut behind him.

I eat the rest of my pancakes slowly, the silence of the house ringing uncomfortably in my ears. I turn on music and clean the dishes, putting the syrup in the pantry and the eggs back in the fridge, all the while Blake's words from yesterday still circling around in my head, my conversation with my dad layered just over the top of it.

My mom, completely worn out, bombing her SATs, wanting to . . . what? Do the things she had always wanted to do? Face her fears? Have a fun summer?

His closed-offness makes me want to know more.

But it's pretty clear he isn't going to tell me.

If I want to find out more, if I want to *have* this connection, I have to . . .

I grab my phone and bring up Instagram, my thumb finding the tiny circle that's Blake's smiling face, an unwatched story tempting me.

I click it to see her launching a tennis ball in the middle of a spacious field, a blur of a golden retriever barreling after it.

I let out a long sigh and chuck my phone onto the table, watching as it lands on top of my mom's list, the paper crinkling underneath the weight, the thought I'd tried to push away coming back to me.

I have to do it myself.

I picture it for a second, seeing myself getting a tattoo at the parlor over on Sycamore Street, and watching the sunset on the beach, and being jostled around on the rental bus on the Huckabee Lake trip. Facing the fear of heights I apparently inherited from her, and . . .

My eyes land on the last item of the list, "Kiss J. C.," and I fold the paper directly below number eleven. Even if I change the initials to M. H., with Matt not even talking to me, this one is a definite no-go.

Although . . . isn't that the point of a bucket list? Doing things that seem impossible or scare you?

Maybe by the end of this I can find a way to make things right. A way for things to fall into place the way they did for Mom. If anyone could show me how to fix this, it's her.

My eyes travel back up to the top of the paper. *Where do I even start?* Mom at least had Dad and Johnny.

I take a deep breath, and for the first time in a long time, I decide to try my luck.

Before I can talk myself out of it, the phone is back in my hand and I'm pressing the call button under Blake's contact info, the phone ringing noisily in my ear until her voice comes through the speaker.

"All right. Where are we starting?" she says, like she already knows why I'm calling.

I'm stunned for a second, but then I smile and shake my head. "I honestly have no idea."

Blake laughs. "Perfect."

6

Lounging upside down on my bed later that day, I pull up my phone calendar, counting down the days until the end of the Huckabee Lake trip. The last day of the trip is my newly planned goal for finishing the list, according to Blake, at least.

Twenty-one.

Twenty-one days to get this list done, the trip being the very last item.

Twenty-one days from now, I will have *finished* my mom's bucket list. Provided I actually pick an item to get things started.

I switch over to Instagram and scroll through Sycamore Street Tattoos' page for the millionth time, since that's number one. Photos of newly decorated arms and legs and underboobs glide across my screen as I try to make a plan of attack. I pause on a familiar picture of a red rose, planted for all eternity on the side of my best friend, Kiera.

We went last Galentine's Day for a discount special that Sycamore Street runs for just about every major, minor, and entirely made-up holiday. You could go and pick from an overflowing binder of artwork, the price always ringing up under fifty dollars. They even ran a special on National Cheese Day, which I'm pretty sure isn't actually a real thing.

True to Huckabee form, Sycamore Street Tattoos doesn't bother with carding, which was why Kiera and about half our classmates have gotten their first tattoos long before their eighteenth birthdays. Like we were going to this past February.

"Come on, Em!" she had said. "Let's do something bad for once. Like we—"

Like we used to. She stopped herself before she said it, but I could still feel the burn.

I remember Kiera spinning the binder around to face me after flipping through only two pages and pointing to the rose. "Arm or rib cage?"

I said arm, but she went for rib cage.

I chickened out a few minutes later at the sight of the needle, wondering when they'd last been cleaned, as the statistics I'd read on infections circled around and around inside my brain. I could tell Kiera was disappointed, but she still faithfully went through with hers, squeezing my hand so tight, I had entirely lost feeling in my fingers by the end of it.

Which had *absolutely* affirmed my decision not to get one.

Until now. If I can stop chickening out.

My phone starts vibrating in my hand, and Kiera's name flashes up on the screen in white letters. Our first call since she left. She gets thirty minutes of phone time every Sunday night, and a chunk of it usually goes to Nina, so I don't want to waste a second.

If she's calling me first, it means she has some news.

I sit bolt upright and tap the green accept button for her FaceTime.

"Kiera! Hi! How are you?"

"Em, are you *trying* to give me a cavity?" Kiera's voice pours through the speaker of my phone, her box braids and smiling face slowly coming into view, as blurry as it always is when she's away at Misty Oasis. The service is so bad up at camp, most of the calls are glitches and frozen screens. She holds up the three shiny packs of Bubble Yum Cotton Candy Bubble Gum. "You know once I open a pack, I have to finish it."

Even through the screen I can tell her nails are freshly painted, one of the nail polishes I sent her being put to use. Homesick box success!

"Give some to your campers! It'll be a welcome relief from the cardboard and water they usually get."

She rolls her eyes, but the corners of her mouth turn up. From what I remember from my traumatic week there, Misty Oasis made the sketchy buffet by the Goodwill look like a gourmet meal.

"How's it going so far?" I ask.

"Pretty good! I got a weird rash on my leg a few days ago on our nature hike, but other than that I'm doing great."

I grimace as she flicks the camera down to show me a lumpy red patch just above her ankle. Of course *this* is the moment the quality shoots straight from pixelated to ultra HD.

"Ew. That's gross as hell."

I still don't fully understand how the same girl who cried over breaking a nail at our freshman formal two years ago transforms into a mountain man each summer. It's like two versions of Kiera simultaneously exist in one body.

She laughs and the camera moves back up to her face. "Could be worse. One of the campers had to be sent home a few days ago after they got poison ivy on their eyelid." Her eyes widen slightly, the horror still palpable. "Now, *that* was gross."

"I don't even want to begin to picture that," I say, glancing over at my alarm clock, the bright red numbers blaring out 7:43.

I jolt, realizing how close it is to eight. My dad will be home from work soon. And I know for a fact he hasn't eaten since pancakes this morning. I push myself up and head down the hallway, giving Kiera a wry smile as I tuck my long brown hair behind my ear.

"So. How's 'Nice Arms' Todd doing?" I ask, eager to get the latest Misty Oasis gossip. Kiera has been nursing a crush on Todd Thomas since he came back to camp two summers ago redefining the words "glow up."

"Emily. His nice arms got *even nicer*. I swear they quadrupled in size over the course of the school year. It is unreal how good he looks. And"—she glances behind her to make sure the coast is clear, her voice excited—"I found out his girlfriend broke up with him a month ago because she's going to UCLA this fall."

"No way."

"Yes!"

"That's amazing!" I say, stopping to quickly backtrack to the place where sympathy should've been instead of celebration. "I mean, like, poor Todd."

"Oh, yeah, I mean . . . total dick move. Major bummer," Kiera says, nodding in agreement as we both offer up a moment of silence.

"So . . . ?" I say, grinning since I've clearly found the reason behind the phone call.

"So . . . ," Kiera says, smiling around the word. "We maybe made out after the bonfire last night!"

We both squeal, and I do a little excited dance as I make it to the kitchen. This has been two whole summers in the making.

"I can't believe you actually kissed him!"

"Oh my gosh, I *know*," Kiera says, swooning a little bit. "And let me tell you, it was WORTH the wait."

I put the phone down on the counter just for a second, reaching up on my tippy-toes to grab a box of pasta out of the pantry.

I'm about to ask for more details when I hear her say, "So is there any—"

She cuts out, the image freezing suddenly, her voice coming out in garbled spurts.

"Kiera?" I say, watching as her face finally starts to move again, the glitching fading as the connection returns.

"Sorry," she says with an eye roll. "I asked if there was any news on the Matt front."

I groan internally. I was really hoping we'd get cut off before we got to this.

"No," I say, shaking my head as I slam the pasta box onto the counter with more force than I intended, the bow ties rattling noisily around. I meet Kiera's gaze. "I *did* see him, though. And everyone else. Two days ago at the bingo fundraiser."

"You *went*? To play bingo? Are you . . . okay?" Kiera asks, a twinge of concern in her voice.

"Yeah! I mean, I'm fine," I say quickly, grabbing a pot from inside the oven to fill with water. "And I didn't *really* play. I played for my dad. I was forced to go because THE Johnny Carter moved back into town this week."

"Oh my gosh! I totally forgot that was this week!" Kiera says, surprised. "He's got a daughter, doesn't he?"

"Yeah," I say, Blake and the list popping back into my head. "They came over to help us pack this weekend."

"Is she cool?"

"Too cool," I say, thinking of all the jaws that dropped Friday night. Growing up in Hawaii apparently instantly made you *way* cooler than growing up in Huckabee ever could. Though, I couldn't help but feel like Blake's chill demeanor was probably cool just about everywhere.

"She's nice, too. And she's in our grade. You'll definitely like her."

"Mmm," Kiera says, her voice distracted. I watch the pot fill slowly with water, knowing she's about to drag the conversation back to what I was hoping she'd forget about. "So you saw everyone? At the bingo fundraiser?"

I sigh, shutting the water off and lugging the pot over to the stove.

"Look, I know you *both* needed some space after it happened, but you gotta talk to him, Em! You said you would before I got back from camp, just like *I* said I would make a move on Todd if he was single. Which I did! You know as well as I do that you have to make things right before school starts, or it's going to be super weird for all of us," Kiera says. I know she's right. If I make things right with Matt, it makes things right for *all* of us. Jake, and Ryan, and Olivia, and Kiera. No one will have to choose—though for everyone but Kiera it doesn't seem to have been a hard choice.

"This is just like the other breakups. You're psyching yourself out. Like last year, when you broke up with him because you thought he was being too clingy. Or the time before that, when you felt like you weren't focusing on your schoolwork enough." She rolls her eyes, and the reasons sound even thinner when she says them.

"This one is worse than any of the others," I argue, turning the dial on the stove top up to boil the pasta water. "Like, *way* worse. I *kissed* someone else!"

I cringe as I think back to that night. Matt's hand finding the small of my waist as he pulls me in for a long kiss, the countdown clock in my head ticking down the seconds until it is over. His voice in my ear, asking if I want to take things to the next level.

His parents were out of town and I was spending the night at his place. Even *I* could see it made sense. Which was probably why I couldn't figure out how to tell him no. Since that would've meant explaining why my stomach had just sunk to my feet, which . . . I couldn't.

So I didn't say anything. I just stumbled over to Jake, my red dress getting tighter by the second, the Huckabee High gym feeling more and more claustrophobic. I remember sneaking a big drink from his silver flask, the burning taste in my mouth, and Kiera grabbing my hand to pull me into a big group of people. And then the room spinning, a blur of arms and legs, streamers hanging limply from the walls and around the basketball hoops, Matt weaving through the crowd to get to me.

I needed a way out.

My eyes locked with this sophomore guy I'd seen a few times in the hallway, somewhat familiar blue eyes and a buzz cut. I didn't even stop to think, didn't even know his name. I just walked right up to him and planted a kiss right on his mouth.

I thought it would be freeing. Doing something I couldn't take back. But I couldn't have been more wrong. As soon as I came up for air, I knew I'd ruined everything.

"You were drunk!" Kiera exclaims, bringing me back to the aftermath. "*Everyone* got drunk on that shit that Jake brought to prom. It was his uncle's homemade apple pie moonshine. You could probably start a car with that stuff."

"That's not an excuse, Kiera," I say, watching the small bubbles appear at the bottom of the pot. As much as I've tried to sell myself on that, it isn't. Alcohol wasn't what fueled it. And lying isn't the route I want to take to fix this.

"It sounds like you're *trying* to keep everyone mad at you.

75

And you're always talking about how perfect Matt is, so it just . . . doesn't make any sense."

"I don't know, okay? Can you just stop bugging me about it!" I blurt without thinking, the frustration I've kept pent up from hearing this question asked over and over again in different ways suddenly spilling out.

She just stares at me, her dark eyes serious. "Listen. You're my best friend, and you know I've always got your back, but I'm going to be real with you. If we have to spend senior year smack in the middle of this drama between you and Matt, it's going to suck. I mean, just *think* about it. I'll have to alternate lunch tables! And don't even get me *started* on Senior Skip Day. How will we do that without the whole crew together? If we can't have an awesome Senior Skip Day with our friends, with Jake making his crappy jokes, and Olivia staring at Ryan like the sun comes out of his ass, I'm going to hold a grudge so big, your great-grandchildren are going to feel it." She pauses, raising her eyebrows at me.

When I don't say anything, she lets out a long sigh. "Em, I am here to help you, but you are the only one who can fix this."

"I know. I'm working on it," I say, thinking of the list. But I don't want to get her hopes up yet. And I don't know how to tell her this pressure is not helping. Like . . . at all.

We're both silent for a long moment, then Kiera finally clears her throat to break the tension.

"Well, I gotta call my mom before my phone goes back in The Locker," she says, nodding behind her to a closet covered in National Park stickers. "Talk next week?"

I nod. "Yeah. For sure." Things still feel prickly between us, so I give her a small smile. "Can't wait to hear about what happens this week with Todd."

She returns it, but it's not her usual smile. "I'll keep you updated. Love you."

"Love you," I echo, the screen going dark, the call ending.

Sighing, I lean against the counter.

I *hate* this feeling.

Everything about this moment feels awful and unfamiliar. I can't believe I snapped at her. If Kiera were here in Huckabee, and not all the way at Misty Oasis with a time limit on phone usage, I'd ride my bike over to her place to shake off the weirdness.

I turn my head and watch the pasta water instead, the small bubbles growing and growing, slowly turning into a rolling boil. I add the entire pasta box to the pot. Far more than two people can eat in one sitting, but whatever. I can refrigerate it for my dad to take for lunch for the next couple of days.

My phone vibrates, and I grab it, hoping to see Kiera's name, a final text to say things are fine even though they don't feel it. But to my surprise, it's from Blake.

I tap on the notification, and a text bubble appears.

What are you doing tomorrow?

Why? I type back automatically, the response I've conditioned myself to ask before I accidentally open myself up to something I might not want to do.

I hesitate before deleting it and trying again. **I work in the afternoon, but I'm free before that.**

She replies right away. **I was going to head to the pool to see if they're still hiring lifeguards. You want to come?**

I groan, tossing my phone onto the counter. The pool. Of *course* she's going to get a job there. It's only the mecca of Huckabee High summer employment, staffed by Jake, Matt, Ryan, and everyone who knows exactly what went down between us.

I can see it now. One sunny day they'll all be lounging around the infamous lifeguard picnic table, generations of Huckabee Pool employees' names carved into the worn wood, a historic roll call sitting right alongside a couple of overexaggerated penis drawings.

My name will come up. Matt will get that stoic look on his face that I know so well, jaw locked, eyebrows jutting downward, and before you know it, no matter how much he tries to stop them, Jake or one of the gossipy junior girls will tell the tale of my very public cheating, ruining any chance of Blake not thinking I'm a total shit and my one opportunity to actually have a friend this summer. Which I apparently need more than ever, since things are weird with Kiera now too.

I'm relieved Olivia works at the mall in the next town over. She'd *for sure* tell her within the first ten minutes.

The daydream fades, and I pick up my phone, making up an excuse.

No . . . I just remembered I said I'd help my dad—

I pause, trying to think of something moving related.

I said I'd help my dad clean the windows before a showing on Tuesday.

It's lame, but I send it anyway, sighing as I put down my phone and turn the stove top off. So much for Blake helping me with the list.

I feel in my pocket, my fingertips finding the worn paper I've tucked away there, a small comfort.

Maybe it's the one thing that can help me fix all of this.

7

Scrolling through Instagram at the kitchen table on Wednesday morning, I tap on Blake's story for the millionth time. It's a boomerang from an hour ago at the less-than-sanitary Huckabee Pool, the caption reading, "FIRST DAY OF WORK!"

We haven't talked since Monday afternoon when she said she was hired, and after today I'm sure I'll never hear from her again. It'll be super awkward when my dad and Johnny inevitably try to force us to hang out.

Sighing, I take another bite of my cereal and open my photo gallery. I scroll all the way back to the first couple of photos on my phone, taken just before my mom died. I usually avoid them at all costs, but today I'm looking for something.

A picture of my mom's tattoo.

"Maybe try to figure out more of the backstory for some of

them," Blake had said on our phone call a few days ago. "Maybe that'll tell you where to start."

That led me to the only direct link between the list and something I knew about. Something I saw every day.

My mom's tattoo.

I pause on a photo that my dad took of the two of us at the garden store over by the apple orchard. She's pushing a bright orange cart around the greenhouse, pretending to struggle from the weight, while I lounge dramatically on top of the cart, two bags of potting soil sitting underneath me.

I swipe right, moving farther and farther back in time. It's strange to see my mom getting healthier and healthier with each passing picture, when all I know is the opposite. I watch as the dark circles around her eyes fade, her gaunt cheeks fill out slowly.

I pause on another photo, of my mom fast asleep on my dad's shoulder after a rough doctor's appointment, then a photo of her and Nina laughing at Kiera's birthday party, followed by a photo of the two of us after a long day of gardening, lottery tickets from the small gas station by the highway clutched in our hands, dirt stains on our jeans.

Finally, I find it.

A picture of my mom holding a sparkler on the Fourth of July, just before her brain cancer diagnosis, her blue eyes shining, her forearm tattoo faint in the fizzing glow of light. Zooming in, the words become clearer, the block letters spelling out AN INVINCIBLE SUMMER.

I remember asking her about it when I was pretty young, my chubby first-grader fingers tracing the letters over and over again.

All she had said was that it reminded her of the summer she became friends with my dad and Johnny. She never said any more than that. I'm missing the *why*.

"Morning!" my dad says as he lumbers sleepily into the kitchen.

I put my phone down quickly, instantly transported back into my *super* not-invincible summer.

"Morning," I say back, half-heartedly picking at my Cheerios while I eye his dirty work boots. Mom would've thrown a fit to see him wearing those anywhere past the front door, but this isn't going to be our house anymore, so I guess none of that really matters.

"You good?" he asks as he pours some cereal into a bowl, sloshing milk on top of it a moment later.

"Yeah." I shrug.

"That wasn't very convincing," he says, leaning against the counter and pointing his spoon at me.

"I'm great! Never better!" I say, faking a huge smile.

He chuckles at that, scratching his thick beard. "You got work today?"

I shake my head no. Nina kept me late last night, the two of us making a wedding cake for the Mckenzies. In trade, she gave me today off. I'd insisted it was fine, since working kept my mind off everything, but she told me to "go do something fun with my friends."

I didn't have the heart to tell her I don't exactly *have* any friends right now.

He nods to my phone, munching noisily on his cereal. "Whatcha looking at?"

I look down to see the picture of my mom still filling up my phone screen. Instinctually, I reach out to tap my home button before he can get a look, but something stops me before I press down. I want answers. And I'm in a bad enough mood today to risk some discomfort if it means I'll get them.

"Just trying to figure out what this means." I grab my phone, turning it to show him the picture.

"Mmm," he says, swallowing his mouthful and averting his eyes to his bowl, his Cheerios suddenly becoming incredibly fascinating.

For a solid minute it's just crunching. I push a Cheerio around and around in the leftover milk in my bowl, watching it dunk below the surface, reappearing a moment later. I *know* he remembers the list discussion we had. I know he knows what I want to know.

"An invincible summer," he says, exhaling. I look up at him, our identical dark eyes meeting. He shrugs and gives me a small smile. "It's a part of a quote. Some translated lines from this thing a French guy wrote. I think his name was Albert Camel? Camera?"

"Camus?" I ask, practically jumping out of my seat as I remember the worn book I found in my mom's box of high school memories. A worn book by *Albert Camus*.

"Yeah, him," he says, nodding to confirm my suspicions. "I don't know what the whole quote was. She found it in a book the summer we all became friends. I think in a lot of ways, it kind of set the list in motion. She said the words summed up what she wanted that summer to be for her. A moment in time, in her life, where nothing could touch her, where she could do anything."

His words give me chills.

He takes a bite of his cereal, talking through a mouthful of Cheerios. "Did you know your mom liked that book so much she actually wanted to go live in France at one point?"

My eyes widen in surprise. I had no idea. "Wait. She *what*? *France*?"

"Yeah," he says, chuckling. "She studied French in high school and was determined to get out of Huckabee one day and board a plane there for good. You know, marry some stylish Parisian and eat baguettes by the Eiffel Tower and shit."

I laugh, giving him a once-over in his torn jeans and sweat-stained T-shirt.

"Eventually, she just wanted to go to France," he says, noticing my look and smirking. "And then we got married, and had you, and she realized she had everything she needed right here in Huckabee."

He gets a distant look in his eyes, a furrow forming on his forehead. Finally, he clears his throat, taking one last solemn bite of his cereal.

"You good?" I ask him as he puts his bowl in the sink, the spoon loudly clattering against the porcelain bottom.

He nods, looking back to give me a small, thin-lipped smile.

"That wasn't very convincing," I say.

He laughs, calling out, "I'm great! Never better!" before kissing me on the top of the head and leaving for work.

I look down at the tattoo on my mom's arm, processing all this new information. An invincible summer. *Her* invincible summer.

If the quote is the key, I finally know what I have to do.

I don't even bother to clean the dishes. The second my dad crosses over the threshold, I'm tearing up the stairs to my room. I duck under the edge of my floral bedspread, my hands clawing at the box I've hidden under my bed.

I rifle through everything, the manila envelope, the stuffed moose, the soccer T-shirt, until I see the book, nestled into the corner.

I pull it out to see "L'ÉTÉ" is written across the front in a bold red, "par Albert Camus" just underneath it in black.

And . . . there's my first problem. As I flip through the yellowing pages, I realize this entire book is in French. With three years of Spanish under my belt, I couldn't find the quote she'd pulled her tattoo from even if I tried.

I stop my flipping, my brow furrowing when I see there's a page missing, a gap between 156 and 159, the jagged paper near the binding the only clue that something had been there.

She'd ripped a page out.

I could probably just Google it? Or . . .

I flip back to the title page and see a faded blue stamp reading "O'Reilly's Used Books," and suddenly the possibility of my first bucket list item is sitting right in front of me.

9. Buy a book in another language.

If they have this exact book, not only would I check my first list item off, but I could figure out what that missing page said. And, if I could figure out what the missing page said, I bet I could figure out what the whole quote was. I could find my answer.

It isn't much, but it's a place to start. Finally.

8

I peer at the sky, the downpour of rain ricocheting off the metal overhang in front of Nina's.

Just perfect.

Of course I forgot my rain jacket on the one day the sky decides to dump out an ocean of water. That, and my bike tire popped on the way here, so I'll be stuck not only walking to O'Reilly's, but also waiting in sopping-wet clothes for my dad to come pick me up at Hank's to go to the Carters' to help them unpack.

Talk about bad luck.

I would just hide out at Nina's, but . . . I've put off starting the list for almost a whole week now, and I'm not going to let some rain and a missing jacket ruin it for me. The Huckabee Lake trip deadline is getting closer with every day that passes, so even if I have to walk the half mile to O'Reilly's Used Books in the rain, I'm going to do it.

Gritting my teeth, I step out onto the sidewalk, and the rain instantly soaks straight through my shirt and pants. I clutch at the strap of my tote bag as I slosh my way straight down Main Street, I feel my shoes getting heavier and heavier with each passing second, my fingertips finding the lucky quarter I'd tucked into my jeans pocket this morning.

Something about starting the list made me feel like I should bring it along. Although it isn't proving to be much help.

I keep my head down, counting my steps as I go, to distract myself, the numbers blurring together as I pass forty.

I pull the quarter out and squint down at it, rain pelting me in the eyeballs. "Aren't you supposed to be lucky?" I mutter.

Out of the corner of my eye, I see a faded light blue truck pull over onto the shoulder, the window rolling down.

"*What* are you doing?" a voice calls out to me.

I turn my head and squint into the truck. "*Blake?*" She's wearing a red lifeguard sweatshirt, the hood pulled up over her wavy hair. Or at least I think she is. It's hard to see through the rain.

"Uh . . . walking?"

Talk about stating the obvious.

She grins and shakes her head at me. "You want a ride?"

I nod gratefully as she reaches across to unlock the door. I pull at the handle, clambering inside with a sigh of relief, my wet clothes squeaking on the worn, aged leather, my tote bag tumbling onto the floor.

"Isn't this your grandpa's old truck?" I say, once I can finally see again. When my mom died, Blake's grandma and grandpa would pop over every now and then to see how we were doing, this truck chugging noisily into our driveway, Mrs. Carter lugging a giant casserole up our front steps. But Mr. Carter died two winters ago, and I haven't seen it since.

"Good eye," Blake says, nodding as I manually roll up the window. "My grandma gave it to me a few days ago to get around."

"Johnny won't let you borrow the Porsche?" I ask. She gives me an amused eye roll as I sit back in the seat.

"I wouldn't drive it even if he let me," she says, the corner of her mouth ticking up into a smile. "Way too flashy. He's always been a fan of attention. I think it's some pro-surfer residual."

I pull my seat belt on and study her face as she shifts the truck into drive, wondering if she knows anything yet.

So far, things don't seem awkward, and *she's* the one who stopped, so that's a good sign.

She peers in the rearview mirror for traffic. True to Huckabee form, there isn't any. "So, where are we heading?"

"O'Reilly's Used Books," I say, nodding straight ahead as the seat belt I'm pulling on clicks noisily into place. "It's four blocks down on the right."

"Are you working on the list?" she asks, her eyes wide with unfiltered excitement as she eases us back out onto the road. "Wasn't there a book-related thing on there?"

"There might be." I push my wet hair behind my ear and pull the tote bag onto the seat, digging inside to find the folded list and the Albert Camus book, tucked safely in the rain-safe plastic of three Ziploc bags I'd stolen from Nina's.

Carefully, I pull out the book, holding it up to Blake as she slows to a stop at a stop sign. "I'm looking for this. Page one fifty-seven and one fifty-eight are missing. Torn out. I think the quote my mom's tattoo is from is on one of those pages, and I think it can give me a bit of context. Backstory. What set the list in motion. Like what you said on the phone."

Blake nods, taking it all in. "You think he'll have a copy?"

"I hope so," I say as I point halfway down the block at the O'Reilly's Used Books storefront, relieved to see there's a parking spot right out front. "Only problem is that if he does, it's in French." I peer at the peeling gold lettering just above the door while Blake parallel parks the grumbling truck like a champ. "I'm banking on Mr. O'Reilly maybe knowing enough to translate."

I shiver, my soaked clothes making my teeth chatter in the AC. Blake's dark eyes glance over at me as she puts the gearshift in park, the sound of the motor dying away, the rain falling onto the metal of the roof overtaking it.

"Here," she says, unclicking her seat belt and pulling off her sweatshirt. I can't help but notice the toned lines of her lower stomach. She holds it out to me, her arms tan against the white of her lifeguard tank top. "This'll help."

I slide the warm sweatshirt on gratefully, and a wave of her ocean smell and the balmy scent of sunscreen surround me. "You always smell like a day at the beach," I say as I squeeze my head through the top and shimmy my arms through the open holes, the sleeves continuing on long past the tips of my fingers.

Blake raises her eyebrows, amused, and I realize just how weird that sounded.

Why can't I be normal around her? Have I seriously lost all my social skills in just a few weeks of exile?

Luckily, Blake doesn't make it weird. "Soon I'll smell like a day in Huckabee!"

"Oh God," I say as I throw open the door, the metal hinges squeaking noisily. "Let's hope *that* never happens." I pull the hood of Blake's sweatshirt up and hop out, the two of us laughing as we run together through the rain.

The inside of O'Reilly's is exactly like I remember it.

The smell of old paper wraps around us the second we step inside, warm and comforting. There are piles and piles of books everywhere, tucked onto towering wooden bookshelves and stacked on top of tables, tiny signs tacked to the ends of aisles to guide you to what you're looking for. The lighting is dim, and some of the corners are thrown into darkness, faded red and blue and brown spines barely peeking out at you from their hiding places.

"Go find it, Emily."

Suddenly, I am back here with my mom, grabbing her hand tightly as I peer into the dimmest, spookiest aisles, afraid of something coming at me from the darkness.

Hearing her ask me, "Find a book with gold writing on the cover," or, "Find a cover with a dragon on it." She made me fall in love with the place, dark corners and all, by coming up with little games to play.

Pretty soon I didn't need the games anymore. We'd come almost every weekend, just the two of us. She'd browse the romance section, while I'd wander back to young adult, the two of us finding our way back to each other as we worked our way across the store.

It feels wrong to be here without her.

I don't turn, but I feel Blake standing just behind me, and feel some small comfort that I'm not here completely alone.

"Emily Clark!" a voice says. I turn my head to see Mr. O'Reilly is propped up on a stool just behind a tiny, worn wooden counter, a pair of glasses perched on the edge of his nose, a red cardigan tucked around his narrow shoulders. He reaches up to tug at the corner of his mustache as the door closes noisily behind us. "It's been a while. What brings you in today?"

"Hi, Mr. O'Reilly," I say, digging around in my bag for the book. "I know it's a bit of a long shot, but I'm looking for . . ." I pull the book out, still tucked in a Ziploc bag. "This."

He holds out his hand and I give it to him. Blake shifts excitedly from foot to foot next to me, her eyes wandering around the shelves like she's determined to find it first.

"Ah," he says, studying the cover. "Camus. This is an older one. Nineteen fifty-four, I believe." He stands, teetering off through the store, Blake and I following eagerly after him. "I might just have a copy. . . ."

We weave down an aisle and around the corner, the sloped wooden floor giving way to science fiction books, and World War II history, and, finally, the foreign language section. He taps two enormous bookcases as the bell rings noisily from the front desk, an eager customer waiting to check out.

"If it's anywhere, it'll be here," he says, giving my mom's copy back to me with a wink before rushing to the front of the store to make his sale.

Blake takes a step closer, putting her hands on her hips as she cranes her neck to look at all the books.

I push a small stepladder over to her, nudging her lightly in the side. "You start on the top shelf, I start on the bottom?"

She nods, her eyes narrowing at the challenge. "Deal."

We work in silence, sifting slowly through the mishmash of books, titles and covers blurring together, whites and yellows and blacks and blues. This would be *way* faster if Mr. O'Reilly organized by language, but they're all just piled together, Mandarin next to Italian next to Portuguese.

I have a couple of close calls, and I know Blake does too, tiny intakes of air followed by a mumbled, "Never mind."

We're about halfway done with the second bookcase when Blake triumphantly holds up a faded white book, nearly teetering off the ladder. She steadies herself, then holds it out to me. "Found it!"

I look down to see an identical book to the one in the Ziploc bag, completely intact except for a small tear in the cover. I flick quickly through the book to see that the missing pages are still there. I could kiss her.

I grab it, flying through the aisles to the front of the store, butterflies swarming my stomach. Mr. O'Reilly looks up in surprise when I plunk it down on the counter next to his ancient cash register. Then a twinkle of excitement sparks in his eyes.

"You wouldn't happen to speak French, would you?" I ask as he begins to ring it up.

He shakes his head. "I could do Latin and some Spanish, but I don't speak a word of French."

My stomach sinks ever so slightly as I hand over the money in exchange for the book. I think I was hoping to keep this pure, like how my mom did it, but I could still figure it out with an app.

Google Translate, maybe? It would take a while, but I guess it's better than nothing.

"Thanks, Mr. O'Reilly," I call as we head out the door. I'm relieved to see the rain has stopped.

Blake opens her mouth to say something, but I grab her hand, excited to get to work. The postrain humidity instantly clings to my arms and legs as I pull her down the steps and across the street.

"Strategy meeting at Hank's. Blake, we've got some French to translate."

9

Even though I'm semidry by the time we slide into a bright red booth,
Judy gives us our milkshakes for free, chattering away about how I
look like a limp rag.

"We missed ya last Sunday," she says as she slides two towering chocolate shakes onto the table, her arm reaching up to lean
casually against the booth.

"My dad had work," I say, pulling the new book and my mom's
list out of my bag. "But we should be in this weekend."

She pops her pink bubble gum and gives me a warm smile,
glancing back at the kitchen to make sure her husband, Hal,
isn't listening. He's got a thing about not telling people specials
before the day or else they aren't "special" anymore. "We've
got your dad's favorite on the menu. Hal's making his meat
loaf," she whispers with a wink. She nods to Blake. "Bring your

friend! I'll make sure you get an extra-big slice."

"All right, Judy," I say, even though I bet the last place Blake wants to be this Sunday is eating meat loaf at Hank's Diner with me. I'm honestly surprised she's still here now.

But I glance across the table, shocked to see she's nodding enthusiastically, totally game for the heartburn-inducing meat loaf Hal puts out once or twice a month. I smile to myself as Judy trots away to take another customer's order.

I send a quick text to my dad to let him know Blake will be driving me over to the Carters' before I begin to scroll through the translator apps available on my phone. I tap on Quick Translate, an app with 4.3 out of 5 stars, supposed to be able to take photos of words in real time and translate them. I let out a groan as the page takes a century to load. "I forgot how bad the service is here. The second you pull open those heavy glass doors, you lose about three bars."

"What was your mom's tattoo?" Blake asks, reaching out to take the book off the table. She flips through the pages with her thumbs, leaning forward to take a quick sip of her milkshake.

"It was on her arm," I say, swiping out of the app store to bring up the photo of my mom from the Fourth of July. I turn it around to face her, zooming in on the words. "It says, 'An invincible summer.'"

Blake studies the picture, nodding, before turning her attention back to the book, while I turn my attention back to the small blue and white app taking a million years to download onto my phone. I let out a long sigh. "This is going to take—"

"Au milieu de l'hiver, j'apprenais enfin qu'il y avait en moi un été invincible."

My head snaps up to see Blake reading from the book in perfect French. Her eyes move from page number 158 up to meet mine, my heart hammering noisily in my chest.

"You *speak* French? Why didn't you say something!"

"I wanted to, but *someone* was a little too eager to get over here to let me get a word in edgewise." There's a teasing glint in her eyes, and I feel my cheeks begin to burn. "Took it since middle school. I was thinking about maybe minoring in it in college."

My phone pings, the pointless, no-longer-necessary app finally starting to download. "So do you know what it means?" I ask, sliding around the table and sitting down in the booth next to her.

I peer over her tan shoulder at the book, and she taps the sentence she just read aloud. "It means something like, 'In the midst of winter, I found there was, within me, an invincible summer.'"

I nod slowly, taking it in, trying to find a connection. Trying to find *something* hidden in there. Something about her and her experience.

I squint at the words, thinking of Matt and junior prom, and the past three years without my mom, filled with ups and downs. Thinking of the taped-together SAT results I found in my mom's box of things.

But nothing about those words makes any of that come together for me.

"Well, that's just great," I say, throwing my hands up. "I mean, what does that even *mean*? Leave it to me to tear through a bookstore, expecting this quote from some old French dude to tell me some long-lost secret about my mom."

Blake laughs and pulls out her phone. I watch as she types the translation into it, sending the words to me in a text. She leans on her elbow, looking directly at me, her sun-streaked hair hanging over her arm. "Well, maybe that will change. It may not mean anything now, but maybe it will one day. Maybe you just need to finish the list or something first."

"I am *deep* in winter, Blake! Nothing about this summer is invincible," I mutter, reaching out to grab my milkshake and taking a long, slow sip.

"Not *yet*," Blake clarifies, giving me one of her big, ear-to-ear smiles, which makes me remember how she convinced me to light a sparkler in my living room ten years ago. I have a feeling I'd probably still go along with that. "I mean, maybe it didn't make sense to your mom at first either. Maybe her summer didn't exactly start out as an invincible one. But it *became* one."

I bite my straw thoughtfully.

"Besides, you've already taken the first step," she says, reaching past me to grab the pen Judy left on our table. She holds it out to me, spinning my mom's list around to face me, my eyes landing on number nine.

Buy a book in another language.

My first list item.

I feel a swell of happiness as I take the pen from her hand, carefully putting a small blue check mark next to the line.

The first step. One item checked off my mom's bucket list.

10

The drive to Blake's house sends us into the winding back roads of Huckabee, the fading sunlight carefully cutting through the trees as we drive. Remnants of the earlier rainstorm cling to the branches and the road, making them sparkle.

I shift in my seat, my jeans finally dry after our milkshakes at Hank's. We pass the development Matt lives in, and I crane my neck, my eyes searching for and finding his black Honda Civic in the driveway.

Fridays were always our day. Just for us. No Kiera, or Jake, or Ryan, or Olivia. We used to go out to the historic movie theater in the center of town, or just stay in, watching Netflix on his basement couch and making peanut butter cookies using the recipe we perfected together. Matt was always really into filmmaking, and my favorite part of the night was listening to him talk about every little behind-the-scenes detail, from how they did certain special effects to the accolades of the director. It always made the movies we watched more fun.

I wonder how he's spending his Fridays without me. If he misses hanging out with me, like I miss hanging out with him.

Or if this radio silence means he doesn't anymore.

An unsteady feeling swims through me, and I look down at the road underneath us, watching as the unbroken yellow line turns into a dotted one.

How can I possibly fix this when I don't even know *why* I can't get it right?

I feel like things were so easy for my parents. That all the romantic stuff just . . . happened naturally. They didn't break up once. Why can't things be as easy for us?

We keep driving, heading onward toward the big houses on the edge of Huckabee, just on the border of Cherryfield, the next town over. Each of the houses in this neck of the woods is surrounded by acres of trees, its nearest neighbor nowhere to be seen.

I know some people think that would be peaceful, all that space, but there are times late at night when there is nothing but darkness. A scary, overwhelming darkness, everything past the headlights disappearing into nothingness. I always hated it when Matt would drive us through here.

I see lights peeking out from between the trees as Blake slows at a mailbox and then carefully turns onto a long driveway, turn signal flashing.

"I'd hate to have to take the trash all the way down there on trash day," I say to her.

She nods in agreement, then gives me a mischievous grin. "I *conveniently* forgot yesterday and my dad had to do it. To be honest, I'm not sure how my grandma did it at all before we got here."

I open my mouth to say something, but stop short when I see the house we're pulling up to.

I stare at the modern design in awe, the entire structure sleek and carefully constructed. Floor-to-ceiling windows take up the entire first and second floors of the house, giving way to sharp metallic angles. On the second floor, a deck extends out, carefully enclosed by trees on either side of it. All browns and silvers and grays, everything uniform in a beautiful way.

"This house is insane," I say, my eyes wide. I knew the Carters' refused to sell their farm until Johnny Carter Sr. couldn't work anymore, making their plot of land the final puzzle piece in a massive development plan the real estate developers had been trying to build for years, but I had no idea their payout was enough for *this*.

"It's my grandpa's dream house," Blake says as we pull slowly up the driveway. "He designed it entirely by himself."

"He *designed* this?" I ask, completely in awe.

"Yep," Blake says, peeling her eyes away from the driveway to admire the house. "Architecture was his passion, even though he didn't get an education in it." Her gaze is almost reverent. "He didn't live to see the *Architectural Digest* article about it, but he'd have loved it."

I wonder what that must have been like. Having enough money to build something like *this*. Or, just enough money to stay in the house you grew up in, where your parents built a life together, and where your mom's garden sits out front, and where your favorite memories of cake decorating and closet conversations with her feel etched into the very foundation.

I try to shake off the move vibes. "Those are some windows," I say with a whistle.

"Yeah, the views are beautiful. Zero privacy, though!" she says with a laugh. "It's a good thing we live in the middle of nowhere. The whole neighborhood would have seen my butt by now."

We reach the top of the long driveway and see my dad's truck already parked in front of the spaceship-size two-car garage. Blake pulls up alongside it and reaches up to press a button. The right door of the garage slowly opens, but unlike our garage at home, there's no clutter to be seen. Just Johnny's car, and four surfboards hung in ascending size order on the wall.

I'm surprised when she puts her car in park instead of pulling inside.

"You're not pulling into the garage?" I ask.

She shakes her head as she turns the key in the ignition, the truck noisily cutting out. "My dad won't let me park it in there. He got upset with my grandma because it leaked oil onto the 'superior concrete floors.'" She says the last bit with air quotes and an eye roll. "Which is really rich coming from the man who would track sand around our old house like it was his job."

We laugh as we unbuckle our seat belts, then head inside.

No sooner have I crossed over the threshold than a blur of fur and slobber comes slamming into me, almost knocking my feet out from under me. A single paw finds my shoulder, and suddenly the droopy brown eyes of a golden retriever are staring lovingly into mine as my face is coated in sloppy dog kisses.

I laugh, patting the dog's sides, and realize with a start that he only has three legs. The smooth skin of his chest extends all the way around on his left side, a tiny nub the only sign anything had ever been there.

"*Winston*," Blake commands, and Winston immediately stops car washing my face, dropping down onto all threes and sitting with a loud, obedient thump.

He stares up at Blake, his tail keeping time on the chilly concrete floor. She stares back at him, her face serious for a few seconds before cracking into a big smile. Winston immediately launches himself at her in a similar greeting.

We follow the smell of pizza up a set of metal stairs. Framed house blueprints Blake's grandfather must've drawn are hung carefully along the wall. Winston hops noisily up the steps behind us, the last few giving way to an open living room and kitchen. I peer up at the high ceiling, the decor right out of Pinterest, everything simple in a neat and trendy way, from the potted plants, to the pillows on the couch, to the pictures hung on the wall.

The only thing out of place is the pile of moving boxes sitting in the corner, Sharpie-covered labels indicating their contents.

Our dads are right in the middle of the room in full lounge mode, mine on the leather couch, Johnny in an armchair that clearly prioritizes style over comfort, beers in front of the both of them.

"Hey, girls," my dad says, looking over at us. "How was—"

"Took you two long enough!" a voice says, cutting him off. A glass door across the room swings open as Blake's grandma trots in from the huge balcony, a cane clutched in her hand. She looks frailer than I remember, her cheeks gaunt.

She nods to the two pizza boxes on the glass coffee table, her white beehive of hair refusing to budge even an inch. "The pizza almost went cold!"

"I got stuck at work," Blake says, covering for our stop at Hank's as she gives her a hug hello, the tiny woman's body disappearing from view. Winston peers up at Blake, sniffing the air like he senses the lie. She shoots a glare at him.

"Besides, Grandma, the pizza probably went cold on the delivery driver's way out here!" Blake's grandmother smiles warmly at her before nodding in agreement. I stifle a laugh at Winston's lie detector of a nose, giving Mrs. Carter a quick hug before plopping down beside my dad on the couch.

I gaze around the brightly lit room, taking in the fireplace and the view of the sunset. This place is even cooler inside than it is outside, the concrete floors accenting the sleek kitchen design. "This is a really great house, Mrs. Carter."

Blake's grandma laughs, the tan skin around her eyes wrinkling at the corners. "Oh, not you too! It's all Blake ever talks about," she says. "Good thing my husband isn't here to hear this. His head would be too big to fit in this house of his."

We grab some plates and eat our pizza, and as usual the

simplest thing has Johnny diving straight into storytelling mode. Today it's tomato sauce.

"What year was it, Joe? Tenth grade? The Cafeteria Incident?"

My dad smirks, taking a swig of his beer. "Yep. Tenth grade. It was lasagna day in the cafeteria, and I sent a sauce-covered brick of it across the room at Luke Price. It exploded all over his white shirt."

"All hell broke loose," Johnny says, setting the scene. "In an instant, food was everywhere. Kids diving under tables for cover. The lunch ladies barricading themselves in the kitchen." He grins at me, touching his cheek. "Your mom hit me square in the face with a tuna sandwich before running off to a calculus class she was probably the only one to show up to. I think Joe fell in love with her right then and there."

"It got so bad in the cafeteria, the police had to be called," my dad says, all of us laughing. "A kid got carted off for a flying-milk-carton-induced concussion."

It's weird to hear my dad talking so openly about the past, especially a story that has my mom in it. Maybe even the moment he first started falling for her. How can he talk so freely with Johnny but always clams up with me?

We've never been big on talking, especially about feelings, but I can't help but be . . . I don't know. Jealous? Hurt?

"It took the whole school two days to clean up the mess we made," Johnny says, wiping away a tear from all the laughter. "I'm pretty certain there's still a chocolate-pudding stain on the ceiling."

"I almost killed you both," Mrs. Carter adds, still doubled over.

I watch in awe as Johnny and Blake down an entire pizza by themselves through several more stories, having absolutely no idea where it could possibly fit inside their lanky bodies. Soon the plates rest on the coffee table, the laughter dying down, a single slice sitting in the center of the second box.

"We'll clean up," Johnny says, reaching for it. "You girls can work on Blake's stuff. I got a bit of a head start today while you were at work."

"If you call unpacking a single box and watching TV a head start, I'd hate to see what the rest of the race looks like," Mrs. Carter says, roasting her own son. Blake snorts, a look of camaraderie passing between the two of them.

"I brought most of my boxes upstairs this morning," Blake says to me as we head over to the pile in the corner. "Didn't want my grandma to have to do it," she adds in a whisper. She rifles around in the corner, pulling three boxes out of the mix, a strong cursive on the top differentiating them from the others. "Just gotta take these up."

I hold out my arms as she hands me a single box, then balances the remaining two in her arms, letting out a long exhale as she stands under the weight of them.

I follow her up another set of metal stairs and down a long hallway. The walls are a stark, barren white, so different from the photo-lined ones at my house. Winston trails just a little bit behind us, his claws clicking noisily on the floor. At the very last door, Blake turns, pushing it carefully open with her foot.

"I don't think it'll take us that long to get everything unpacked," she says over her shoulder. "I got a little done last night."

I step inside, and the room instantly feels homier than the rest of the house. Mostly just because it feels more like . . . well . . . *like Blake*. Her warm, familiar smell washes over me, like the whole room is her cozy sweatshirt.

I add my box to a small pile on the floor, looking around at everything. The walls are the same bland white of the hallway, but Blake has added string lights around the entire ceiling, which cast a warm glow on the overflowing bookshelf in the corner and the row of plants sitting in front of a wall of glass.

I see what she meant about the no-privacy thing. If there was anyone even remotely close by, they'd get a clear view straight into here.

"I got mostly cacti for a reason," she says when she sees me staring at the row of plants. "Sometimes I forget to water them." She takes a step closer, carefully inspecting them. She reaches out to prod at the soil. "I think it's genetic. Unlike your mom, my mom apparently had the polar opposite of a green thumb. One look at a plant and it dropped dead."

I laugh at that before catching sight of the frames hanging around the room, tiny pinpoints of color against the white wall. They're all pictures of houses. A split-level perched on the edge of the sand, a cottage surrounded by a wall of trees, a white bungalow with Winston out front, tongue lolling as he chases a tennis ball.

I take a step closer, astonished when I realize that they aren't pictures.

They're paintings.

"Did you do these?" I ask, pointing in awe at one of them.

"Yeah," Blake says, like it's no big deal, sitting down on her gray-and-white-striped bedspread. She peers at the small pile of boxes. "My easel is somewhere in here."

"You're *insanely* good," I say, looking from the painting to the real-life Winston over and over again. Winston wags his tail at my excitement, trotting over for a pet. "Like . . . I have never seen anyone our age this talented before."

"Thanks," Blake says, blushing slightly at my praise.

"Is that what you want to do?" I ask her.

"Pretty much," she says, nodding. "I want to go to school in New York. Or California, maybe, so I can be close to the beach. Get a degree in architecture. Do what my grandpa never got the chance to." I can easily picture her in a class on top of some high-rise, her hair pulled back into that messy bun, ink splattered on her hands and her tan arms as she works at a drafting table.

She leans back, looking around the room, the house he designed. "We used to FaceTime a bunch and talk about it, especially when the house was being built. He'd show me pictures of cool buildings and send me floor plans in the mail, try to teach me the way he had learned. It really sucks I couldn't spend more time with him in person before he died."

She shrugs and gives me a thin-lipped smile I recognize all too well. "Anyway, what about you? What are your plans postgraduation?"

I freeze and search for words, but come up empty. To be honest,

I haven't *really* thought about it. Not since Mom died, at least. Matt was always bringing up college applications and where we should go, but I'd just clam up. We already have so much debt, there's no way I can go into more just to go to school. Especially when I don't even know what I want to do there.

In a lot of ways, Blake's future is way easier to picture than my own.

I think about working at Nina's. The smell of flour and butter and chocolate. How the rest of the world fades away when I'm decorating a cake or weighing dough or cooking up a new recipe. "I don't know. I guess I . . . like baking," I say, which is a start.

But do I really want to work at Nina's forever? I could go to culinary school, I guess, but that's not something I could do here in Huckabee.

"Secretly, I think the one thing I do want is to get out of here. To go to a big city somewhere, away from all the sympathetic, knowing smiles. Away from everybody knowing everything about everyone else. Where I'm able to figure out who I am and what I'm like, without an entire town of people thinking they already know."

It feels weird to say it out loud. Matt may have money, but he's like my dad. He loves it here. Leaving doesn't even occur to him.

"Why couldn't you?" Blake asks as she rips the tape off the top of one of the boxes.

I look away and shrug. "I don't know. There are a lot of reasons, I guess. I mean, could I leave my dad alone here in Huckabee?"

"Would he want to be the reason stopping you?"

I open my mouth to say something, but nothing comes out,

her words taking me by surprise. I don't know how to tell her that it just feels . . . impossible. Too big. Too risky. I haven't even left Huckabee for a single *day* in the past three years.

I put my hands on my hips. "I thought we were here to unpack your stuff, not my problems," I say, and Blake laughs, chucking the balled-up hunk of packing tape at me. I swat it away with a grin.

We peel off the rest of the tape and start to unpack the boxes we brought up. I sit on the floor, handing stuff to Blake for her to put away, one of her Spotify playlists playing softly in the background. She likes a lot of the same stuff I like. Indie. Folk pop. Some Billboard Hot 100 hits. She hums along to "Alaska" by Maggie Rogers, her head moving back and forth to the beat as clothes and shoes give way to art supplies and sketchbooks, sand embedded in the bindings.

From the bottom of a box I pull out a pile of pictures, and . . . I'm not sure if I should look. It feels super personal. Like each one is showing some small part of the life Blake lived before coming here.

And I know better than anyone that some parts you just don't want to show.

But she smiles, sitting down next to me, her leg close enough for me to feel the heat radiating off it. The two of us flip through the photographs of sandy beaches and surfing and happy faces.

"These are my friends Jay and Claire," she says as I take in a picture of her sitting on a curb, a girl with brown hair next to her, a guy in a gray T-shirt on the other side, all of them clutching Styrofoam cups. "We would always get shave ice at this spot down the street from my house on Fridays after school. It's pretty big in Kauai. The tourists, thankfully, don't know about this particular spot. You flavor it with a bunch of syrups, and real fruit and stuff." She flips to the next picture, a close-up of a yellow and orange shave ice, covered in mango and guava.

"This is Jay when we all skipped school on his birthday and went kayaking," she says, handing me a picture of the gray T-shirt boy, shirtless and paddling a lime-green kayak. "And Claire on the back of his bike on our way to a Valentine's Day dance our school has every year." She hands me another one, Claire's brown hair and striped dress flowing in the wind, her hands clutching Jay's shoulders, the both of them laughing against a sunset.

Everything she shows me is so fun and exciting. A place I've never been before. A place so different from Huckabee. I'm surprised she hasn't complained more about being stuck here.

I study a picture of her on a surfboard, her smile somehow a little brighter than I've seen it.

"Do you miss it?"

"Yeah," Blake says simply, her eyes dark and serious. "I miss the sand. And the sun. And the water." She lets out a long sigh. A sigh that says the dirty Huckabee public pool definitely does not come close. She shrugs, squinting at the picture of Jay and Claire on the bike. "And my friends and family, most of all. We did everything together. It feels kind of impossible to picture a senior year without them."

I couldn't imagine leaving here before my senior year of school. Leaving Kiera behind. Leaving the familiar hallways of Huckabee High.

Then again, that sounds like it could be a miracle after the past few weeks.

But Blake isn't running from a ruined social life.

"My grandma back there is doing a lot better than Grandma Carter though."

"Is that why you moved? Because of your grandma?"

Blake shifts, leaning her head back against the wall. "Yeah, she hasn't been doing so well since my grandpa died. And my aunt Lisa lives *way* closer than Hawaii, but still a bit too far away to check up on her regularly." I think about seeing her downstairs. The cane. The hollowness of her cheeks. "Plus, I didn't want to feel like I didn't spend enough time with her, you know? Like I did when my grandpa died. I think my dad felt the same."

There's a loud bang from somewhere down the hall, Johnny and my dad up to no good. "That, and I think he wanted to be close to her when I go away to college." She stands with a stretch. We hear another bang followed by some laughter, the two of us smiling at each other. "It'll probably be a good thing for your dad when you head to college too," she says, doubling down on her confidence in me getting out of here. "Not sure about anyone else, though. The two of them together might just bring about Huckabee's demise."

I nod and don't say anything, continuing to look through the pictures. I stop on one of Blake and her friends from back home sitting atop a huge cliff, the jagged edges of the rock illuminated by the sunlight, the distance to the water enough to make me feel dizzy just looking at it.

I spin the picture around to face her. "Did you *jump* off this?"

"Yeah," she says as she stoops down to look at it, her eyes flicking up to meet mine, a mischievous grin on her face. "You ever been cliff jumping before?"

"Have I ever been cliff jumping?" I snort. "Blake, that's like asking if I've ever robbed a bank, or solved pi."

I push down the initial wave of excitement I had upon seeing the photo. I've definitely read articles about cliff-diving accidents. People breaking their necks, or losing their balance and smacking their head on the way down.

I don't need to test my luck falling off anything.

She turns back to me, confused. "I always remembered you as the adventurous type," she says. "Sledding down that huge hill backward, chucking snowballs at those teenage boys who were being jerks, trying to blow up Santa."

"First of all, the last one was all you," I say, raising my eyebrows at her. "And besides, cliff jumping is more than *just* being adventurous. I'm way too afraid of . . ." My voice trails off as I realize what I'm about to say.

"Heights?" Blake finishes, her eyes wide, that mischievous grin reappearing.

"No," I say, shaking my head, even though that's *exactly* what I was going to say.

"Like . . . what's on the list? Like . . . we should *probably* go cliff jumping so you can check it off the list?" she asks.

I start to object, but I can feel the cracks starting to form, the Huckabee Lake trip getting closer and closer with each passing second. It *is* kind of perfect.

"Okay. Fine. It has to be a small one, though. I don't want to break my neck or anything."

"Medium, and you've got a deal," she challenges, holding out her hand.

I stare at it before letting out a long huff of air and shaking on it. "Fine. Medium. ONE jump, and then we're done."

She pauses midshake. "Just one little detail. Are there, like, cliffs around here?"

I laugh and pull my hand away, looking back down at the water in the picture. I know this is an out. I know I can lie and say there aren't.

But I think of the list, and I don't take it.

"There's a bunch of lakes and creeks around here. I'm sure we can find something."

Matt would know. The thought comes to me despite myself. He would be thrilled to hear I was thinking about launching myself off a cliff.

The second-to-last time we broke up, he told me I'd been keeping myself in a little box the past three years.

"Because I won't go backpacking with you this weekend?" I fired back at him.

He ran his fingers through his unkempt hair, frustrated. "It's more than just the backpacking, Emily, and you know it."

I did know it.

Back when we were just friends, we used to go mountain biking in Huckabee State Park, or hiking by the old bridge over Coal Creek. But after Mom was gone, none of it seemed the same to me. Instead of adventures, I'd just see the five most common mountain-bike injuries, or how if we got cut by the bridge metal, a tetanus shot is only 95 percent effective at protection against something like diphtheria.

Why seek out the chance for something to go terribly wrong when life was always threatening to do that without your help?

Eventually, he just stopped asking. I didn't realize he'd felt boxed in with me until that fight. I realized then some part of him was bummed I wasn't as adventurous as I used to be. That he was still hoping to get the daredevil Emily he had a crush on in middle school to reappear.

He was just too nice to outright say it. And I was too cowardly to bring it up again. So maybe if I did this . . . I could get a piece of that back. Maybe that's what's been so off between us.

I slowly put the photos away, watching Blake put together her easel, her dark eyebrows knit together in concentration as she works.

I wonder what someone like Blake is afraid of.

I wonder if she'd think less of me if she knew I was afraid of mostly everything now, the statistics and the unexpected worst-case scenarios.

I wonder if my *mom* would think less of me if she knew I was afraid of mostly everything.

I jump when there's a knock on the door. Johnny's and my dad's heads pop inside, appearing stacked on top of each other.

"Em, we gotta head on down the road," my dad says. "I've got work in the morning."

I tap my phone to see it's already almost ten. Wow, the hours with Blake completely flew by. That's a good feeling in a summer I've pretty much watched the seconds tick away in.

"Thanks for the help," Blake says when they've left the two of us to break down the now empty boxes. "I'm sure it wasn't exactly the most entertaining night."

I shrug as we shuffle off down the hall, each carrying an armful. "Honestly, it was the most enjoyable night I've had in a while."

We drop them off in the living room, all the boxes now reduced to a flattened pile of cardboard.

As we say our goodbyes, my dad jingles his car keys in his pocket, a contented look on his face I haven't seen in years. As we head for the door, Winston's tail droops to half-mast, his brown eyes fixed on me mournfully.

Blake pats him on the head, right between his big, doofy ears. "She's coming back, man. Don't worry."

He wags his tail slightly at her words, comforted by her hand on his head. Something about what she says comforts me, too. The fact that I'll be back here, Blake's friendship not ruined by Matt and the Huckabee Pool.

At least not yet.

"See you," I say, more to Blake than Winston, although he wiggles a bit at my words.

"Medium cliff, Em," she says, rehashing the terms of our cliff-jumping agreement. "Or else it doesn't count. We can't half-ass any of these."

I think of how I felt putting that first check mark down at

Hank's. The rush it gave me. But it also kind of felt like a consolation prize.

I want this one to feel bigger. More earned.

"Might as well find the biggest cliff in Huckabee," I say, and her face lights up mischievously. I'm completely going to regret that, but I can't deny the fact that our small, shared adventure sends a little thrill through my spine, carrying me all the way out to my dad's pickup truck and down the long driveway.

The ride home is dark, the sides of the road illuminated only by lightning bugs, but for once, the shadows beyond the trees feel a little less scary.

11

I usually don't work on Sundays, but when I heard Nina needed apples from Snyder's Orchard for the first batch of apple tarts this season, I jumped at the opportunity to check another item off the list. Especially one that doesn't involve jumping off a cliff.

Although . . . this one isn't exactly going to be easy.

"I never knew why we didn't come apple picking when I was a kid, but I guess now I know," I tell Blake as we each grab an empty brown basket before strolling through the grass to the orchard, the afternoon sun beating down on us. "Take it in, Blake. We're about to get banned."

I still can't wrap my head around the fact that Mom had done this. But it's there on the list. A check mark sitting right next to it.

Was she as nervous as I am right now? I think about the envelope of certificates, the life she had led before her invincible summer.

She *must* have been.

"Banned? Over an *apple*? I mean, there are thousands of them here!"

I can't help but smile as she stops to stare in awe at the rows and rows of apple trees, her brown eyes wide as she takes it all in. Each pair of rows is a different variety, a wooden placard broadcasting the different kinds. She'd never been apple picking before and was beyond excited when I texted her to see if she wanted to tag along.

I feel bad this will be her first—and last—apple-picking experience here at Snyder's Orchard. Going every other weekend in the summers and fall had ruined it a bit for me, but I still remember how fun that first time with Kiera and Paul had been.

"It's not just *any* apple, Blake," I say as I lead her over to the Honeycrisp section. Nina likes to use them for her tarts because they have just the right crunchy texture and sweetness. "It's an apple from the first tree they planted here at Snyder's Orchard. Half the people employed at this place just stand next to it all day, making sure no one picks an apple from it."

"They just *stand there*? Sounds like I picked the wrong summer job," she says, the two of us laughing as we head deep into the orchard, the trees folding in around us, more and more apples clinging to the branches the farther back we get. Families with kids usually peter out by the halfway point.

The closer we get to the tree, the more my heart hammers in my chest.

I try to keep my cool, glancing back to watch Blake as she

carefully inspects each branch, trying to find the perfect apples, the ones with the fewest blemishes, free from worms. I'm way less precious than she's being about the apples that find their way into my basket. They'll all taste the same in the tarts.

We're nearly to the clearing when the sound of laughter filters through the trees from the row next to ours. I peer through the leaves, and my hammering heart stops. Because the first thing I see is Jake's messy blond hair, flying as he dodges out of the way of an ambush of rotten brown apples that Ryan is launching at him.

Seriously? This can't be happening right now.

I duck down, trying to remain out of sight as I creep slowly backward, running smack into . . .

"Matt!" I exclaim, almost dropping the basket I'm holding. I clear my throat and straighten up from my crouch, watching as his face shifts from eyebrows-raised surprise to a pained expression to a look of forced indifference, his jaw locking in the way I knew it would.

I just start talking, the nerves from the upcoming apple theft and now *this* ripping off any barrier I might've attempted to put up.

"Just, uh"—I hold up the basket, giving a weird little shrug—"getting apples for Nina. First batch of apple tarts this season."

"You don't work on Sundays," he says, his voice low, my schedule still memorized.

"Yeah, well, I do today," I say, the words still tumbling out of my mouth. "But not usually! So, you're still good to go to Nina's then, if you want to go but don't, you know, want to see me. I know how much you like her blueberry scones." I peer up at him and see his face soften at that, a look that I've seen after some of our worst fights.

In that look I know there's still a chance. Just like Blake said at bingo.

So why can't I open my mouth? Why does my stomach drop at the thought?

There's a loud crashing sound, and both of us jump as Jake comes tumbling through the trees from the other aisle, all arms and legs. Ryan comes flying around the aisle, rotten apple raised and ready to be launched, Olivia giggling right behind him. Everyone freezes when they see me.

Slowly, Jake stands up, Ryan drops the squishy apple, and Olivia crosses her arms.

All their eyes are on me as they flank either side of Matt defensively, and still I can't form words.

"Hey, guys!" Blake says. I turn my head to the side to see her, basket of shiny, perfect apples tucked under her arm, warm smile plastered on her face.

Her appearance instantly deflates the tension. Everyone relaxes, and Jake slaps on a goofy grin with a pair of borderline-nauseating heart eyes.

I don't think I've ever been more grateful to see someone.

The only one still glowering at me is Olivia, her icy blue eyes narrowed.

Jake saunters over, peering at the basket Blake's holding. "What've you got there? Honeycrisps?" He pokes at them. "I'm more of a Gala fan."

"Yeah, figured I'd pick them instead of wear them." She points to Jake's head, where a blob of brown mush clings to his hair.

"Your loss," he says, reaching up to flick it out. "It's great for your hair. Right, Olivia?"

Olivia is obsessed with hair and skin care. She takes, like, eighteen vitamins a day and is always trying new routines and masks and scrubs she sees on TikTok.

I'm honestly not sure we'd be friends if it weren't for Kiera. They'd become close during home ec class in seventh grade, but we've never exactly been BFFs.

"Yeah, but not if they're rotten," she says, rolling her eyes.

Ryan laughs at that, and Matt cracks a small smile, but then an awkward silence settles back over everyone.

"Well, we better get these back to Nina's," Blake says, nodding to the apples. "I'll see you guys at work tomorrow."

There's a chorus of goodbyes, directed entirely at Blake, before we head in the exact opposite direction of the exit. I glance behind me at Matt as his broad shoulders disappear from view, the look he gave me still fresh in my mind.

"So, clearly," Blake says when we're a safe distance away, "things are not at *all* awkward between the two of you."

Her tone is light and joking, and I breathe an internal sigh of relief. She doesn't know anything new. "Yeah," I say, looking up to see the sunlight filtering in through the trees, my arms getting tired from carrying the basket of apples. "We still haven't spoken since the breakup. Honestly, none of them has spoken to me since the breakup. This one's . . . definitely the worst."

"*This* one?" Blake asks.

"We're a bit like a faulty light switch," I say. "Most times, we're back on before you can tell it flickered. But this time's different."

The other times it had always been small, stupid incidents. Moments I'd ended things because I felt like we weren't clicking in the way I wanted to, the way my mom talked about with my dad. Moments I didn't feel butterflies in my chest. Moments when I felt like he was being too clingy. Or too distant.

That time he said I'd kept myself in a little box the past three years.

I always hoped when we'd get back together that it would bring about a new result. Would make things feel less . . . off.

Would they really this time?

"I mean, it's just my luck we would see them here today." I groan and spin around to face her, turning my back on the tree, on my mom's list. "*Why* did she do this? Why am *I* doing this? What if I trip? Or we get caught? *What will people say?* What—"

"Don't overthink it," Blake says, her voice stopping me from spiraling. "Who cares what other people think? Maybe that's why your mom did it. To get out of her head. To stop obsessing over what other people thought about her. To break the mold she was stuck in."

I think about my mom and her manila envelope of awards. All the years she had spent cementing her golden image in the eyes of Huckabee, this small act of rebellion a sharp turn away from that. A way to break her mold.

A way to break *my* mold. Or at least put a crack in it.

I think about how stuck I feel. Stuck in other people's perceptions of me, in that moment at junior prom, in my mom dying, in my own *friends'* opinions of me, all of it completely weighing me down.

"I'll admit, blowing up Santa may have been my idea," she says, a trace of that mischievous smile lingering on her lips. "But you're the one who *planned* it." She spins me back around to face the clearing. "So, what's the plan this time?"

I look up to see a squishy, worm-ridden apple dangling on a branch in front of me, and like she willed it into existence, an idea pops into my head. I start to unload my good apples into her basket and add the grossest ones I can find into mine, a plan taking shape.

I swear I can hear a choir of angels as the afternoon sun hits the First Tree just right, the red apples practically glittering in the light.

And directly underneath the tree are three guys, hand selected from Huckabee High's football team. Tom Mendoza, Aaron George, and T. J. Widner. They had all just graduated this past June.

If you ask me, bouncers for an apple tree is definitely more than a little overkill. But apparently necessary, all things considered.

Luckily, the warm weather and the weekend has brought a decent crowd of people to the orchard, and my wide-eyed staring at them goes unnoticed. I gulp as T. J. stretches, his biceps rippling impressively.

I peer around the tree to see Blake stationed on the opposite side, hidden just outside the clearing, two baskets of apples in front of her.

One filled with Nina's Honeycrisps.

The other filled with the mushiest apples Snyder's Orchard has to offer.

I reach into my pocket to feel the lucky quarter, my heart dancing in my chest as Blake waits for my nod.

I think about checking my first item off. How great it felt, even though it was so easy. So unearned.

This, though? It's next level. My mom did this. She felt the fear I'm feeling now, and she still stole the damn apple. She pushed past her golden reputation, her stack of awards, her fear of what people would think, and did it anyway.

So, before I can think too much about it, before I can let my nerves get the better of me, I look Blake dead in the eyes and give her the nod.

Then, everything begins to move in slow motion.

Blake begins hurling the mushy apples at the football players, distracting them, while I make a break for the lowest hanging branch. My eyes lock on a perfectly round, perfectly red apple, and I sprint over, apple chunks splattering all around me, people watching on in horror at the scene unfolding.

The moment my fingers wrap around it, the moment I pull it free, I feel a hand wrap around my other arm.

I turn my head to see Aaron George, our eyes locking.

And then a mushy apple pegs him square in the face, his mouth opening in surprise as I wrench my arm free, running in Blake's direction.

"Go, go, go!" I scream.

She throws the remaining rotten apple, grabs the basket of Honeycrisps, and we're running, no, *flying* through the orchard, branches scratching at our arms as we go. We break through the trees into the parking lot, hauling ass up a small grassy hill to where her grandpa's old truck is parked.

I dive into the passenger seat, fighting to close the door as the engine growls awake, and Blake rips out of the spot. She pulls a hard turn, the truck skidding out of the parking lot, kicking up a cloud of dust behind us.

I glance out the window to see Matt, Jake, Olivia, and Ryan standing stock-still in the parking lot by Jake's car, their mouths agape as they watch us speed away.

I lean back in the seat, my chest heaving as I look over at Blake, the two of us bursting out into laughter.

I hold up the perfect apple triumphantly.

"You've gotta try it!" Blake says.

"*Try* it?" I say, raising my eyebrows in surprise.

"Yeah! I mean, what else are you going to do? Let it rot away on a shelf?"

I shrug. That's definitely a fair point. I bring the apple to my lips and take an enormous bite, the chunk falling from my lips as the most bitter, disgusting, rotten taste fills my mouth.

"Oh my God," I say as Blake wheezes with laughter. "Oh my God, that is so bad. Like . . . raw-sewage bad." I grab a Honeycrisp out of the basket, trying to get the taste out of my mouth. "No wonder they don't want anyone picking apples from it."

I hold it out to Blake, and she shakes her head, wiping tears away from the corner of her eyes. "You've got to be kidding me. *This tastes like ass. Here, try it!*"

I roll down the window and chuck the apple out onto the side of the road, watching it disappear in the rearview mirror before I pull the list out of my pocket and press the paper up against the dashboard, grabbing a pen from Blake's center console.

Then I put a small green check next to "10. Steal an apple from the First Tree at Snyder's Orchard," that disgusting apple bringing me one step closer to completing the list, my friends' expressions in the parking lot a moment ago making it more than worth it.

"That reminds me!" Blake says as we pull up at Nina's. "I talked to Jake yesterday at work about cliff jumping, and he said there was a cool spot we could go to at Huckabee State Park. Biggest in the county. You want to go on Wednesday?"

Biggest in the county. My heart jumps at the thought, the bravado I had a moment ago slipping away. Fast.

"I don't know if I'd trust Jake's judgment," I say, hesitating. "I mean, the guy was just covered in rotten apples and happy about it."

She laughs at that, nodding. "I confirmed it with two other people just to be sure."

I think of me practically crouching in a tree to hide from my friends, the softness in Matt's eyes for the tiniest moment when he looked at me, waiting for me to finally say something. I can't keep running away from cliffs. From burly football guys covered in mushy apples.

If Mom got over her fear, if the list made her face what she was most afraid of, maybe it can help me do that too. Maybe this list could be the reset button I've wanted for so long.

The one that would actually make a difference, pushing me to steal sacred apples and tackle giant cliffs and to actually *talk* to unruly-haired ex-boyfriends instead of avoiding them.

"Yeah," I say, smiling at her. "Let's do it."

12

I'M barely through the front door after dropping off the apples at Nina's when my phone buzzes noisily. *Kiera*. For the first time since she left, I totally forgot it was Sunday.

I quickly swipe right to answer, and wow.

"This *quality!*" I say, seeing the freckle over Kiera's left eyebrow, her long, dark eyelashes. This is a first in Misty Oasis call history.

"Todd has a hotspot!" Kiera exclaims, excited. "So we'll never have to worry about a dropped call again."

"What an actual miracle," I say, relieved that things aren't weird after how we left them last week. "How's . . . camp?"

I wiggle my eyebrows to let her know I'm referring to Todd and not an update on that kid who took a poison ivy plant to the eyeball. If she's calling, though, and from his hotspot, it means the news is definitely going to be good.

She glances behind her, checking to make sure the coast is clear.

"It's going *great*. Like, I think we're gonna make this a year-round thing great?"

"Oh my gosh! That's awesome."

This is *huge*. Kiera's never dated anyone before. I feel a small stab in my chest, jealousy that I'm not right by her side at Misty Oasis for it. Her first boyfriend.

"I know! I almost don't want to come back," she says, while I nod, pretending that doesn't cause another small stab, straight through my mental countdown calendar.

"I saw Matt today," I offer as I plop down on my couch, and Kiera leans forward in interest. "We didn't talk for long, but he gave me this . . . this *look*. I don't know. I just felt like it was a sign."

"Was he alone? Or was the group with him?"

I let out a long sigh. "They were with him. Things were super awkward, though. Thank God Blake was there to distract them."

Kiera nods. "Oh, cool. You two been hanging out a lot?"

"Yeah, actually," I say, smiling as I think of our Friday adventure at the bookstore, unpacking at her house afterward, sweat still lining my brow from our getaway this afternoon. "She can speak French! And her house is super cool. Honestly, *she's* really cool. I thought with you away all summer, I'd pretty much just be hiding out in my house, but *I'm not*. I mean, we're going *cliff jumping* this Wednesday. And I didn't read a single statistic about it. And today we even—"

I move to pull the list out of my pocket, to tell her about it.

"Yeah," she says, cutting me off and letting out a short laugh. "Yeah, sure you will."

I wince, her words stinging a little as they silence my excitement from my crazy afternoon at Snyder's Orchard. My excitement about the list I was on the verge of telling her about.

I thought she'd be excited too.

"I just mean from chickening out on our tattoos, to refusing to even *try* a night of camping with me at Huckabee State Park, you're not exactly Miss Adventure anymore. At least not with me."

Wow. I guess Matt isn't the only one missing the old Emily.

"Sorry," she says, her dark brown eyes instantly crinkling with guilt. "That wasn't cool."

"It's okay," I say, shrugging. Then the both of us fall silent.

"How's packing going?" Kiera asks, trying to change the subject.

"Fine," I say. It's almost the truth, though I did have to hide my mom's favorite mug in my dresser this morning before my dad could throw it into a donation box to drop off on his way to work.

He's still on a rampage. It's like he's trying to completely erase her from not only this house but also from wherever we'll end up. Like he doesn't even care that she used that polka-dot mug *every single day*, sipping coffee from it while she leaned against our kitchen counter and checked my homework. I wonder what other pieces of her life are gone that I haven't noticed.

It's a miracle I found the list before he could incinerate it.

I've been avoiding finishing up her closet because I don't want to know what he'll force me to throw out.

Kiera's phone alarm pings loudly through the speaker, her hand reaching quickly up to swipe it away. "Oh, shoot. Ten minutes until my phone goes back in The Locker. I gotta go! I told Paul I'd call him with an update." She gives me a big grin, leaning forward. "Gotta tell him the big news!"

I smile back at her, knowing how big this is for her. "Your first boyfriend, Kiera! This is so exciting."

"I know, I know!" she sings. "Todd. Who'd have thought." She freezes suddenly, her face going from an expression of absolute bliss to deathly serious in a fraction of a second. "I'm sorry, again. About what I said."

I nod, waving my hand like it's nothing. "Yeah, yeah. Don't even worry about it." She doesn't look convinced, so I double down with the most blindingly enormous smile I can muster. "I'll talk to you soon, okay?"

"Okay! Bye, Em!" I barely have time to wave before the call ends, her face disappearing and my phone screen going dark, my reflection staring back at me as I let out a big sigh.

Did Mom and Nina ever fight? Ever struggle to see eye to eye?

I lean back against the couch, my hand sliding into my jeans pocket to pull out the list. I wish I had told her. But her "yeah, sure" keeps ringing in my head.

Carefully, I unfold the list, my finger tracing the small green check next to "10. Steal an apple from the First Tree at Snyder's Orchard."

I'll prove it to her. She's not the only one who's going to come back different.

Two down, ten to go.

In fourteen days they'll all be checked off. And Kiera and Matt will have the old me back.

13

I sit on the steps of my house, shifting my legs back and forth as the warm concrete makes my skin prickle. I know absolutely nothing about cliff jumping, but I would assume today is the perfect day for it, just because today is the perfect day for just about anything. There isn't a single cloud in the sky. The sun is hot, but not unbearable, and the trees rustle gently from a cool, relieving breeze that blows through just as you get a little too warm.

At exactly two o'clock Blake's truck chugs to a stop in front of my house, her tan arm slung casually out of the rolled-down window. I push myself up off the steps, grabbing my backpack, and walk down the path to her truck.

"You ready?" she calls to me as I get closer.

I swallow hard on my nerves.

"Uh, I think so?" I say, wrapping my fingers around the lucky quarter, tucked once more into the pocket of my jean shorts.

"That's the kind of confidence I was going for," she says, laughing as I pull open the door, the hinges squeaking noisily.

I buckle my seat belt as she plugs the state park into her phone's GPS, the automated voice telling her to drive down the street and turn right.

We talk about Huckabee High for the entire drive, and I give her a crash course on the ins and outs of the school. I cover all the different social groups, how the cool people are basically her coworkers at the pool, how our rivals are the Seymour Squids, how only one girl on the school cheerleading squad can do something other than a cartwheel.

"Our football team is trash," I say, serving up some brutal honesty, in case she, like the rest of our town, really cares about stuff like that. "In fact, two of the guys who chased us at Snyder's Orchard were starting varsity last year, if that's any indication. But the stands are still packed every Friday."

"That sounds cool actually," Blake says when I tell her about the actual parade our town threw after we won our first game in five years. "My school was pretty small, so we didn't even have a football team."

"I don't know if that's better or worse than having a crappy one."

Blake laughs, reaching up to push some of her sun-streaked hair behind her ear. "Where do you fit into all of that? What's your deal at Huckabee High?"

I want to ask: Before or *after* junior prom?

But what slips out is more honest than I intend it to be. "Before or after my mom died?"

Blake glances over at me, her fingers opening and closing around the steering wheel. "I guess both," she says, not like I've made her feel uncomfortable or awkward, like she actually *wants* to know.

And I actually *want* to tell her. Someone separate and outside of it all.

"I don't know. I guess . . . My friends and I were always up to something. Always trying to pull off some wild scheme or plotting some fun adventure. I spearheaded the eighth-grade prank of filling the halls with Ping-Pong balls. I set three of Jake's family's chickens loose onto the field during a Huckabee High football game. I helped plan the best eighth-grade formal Huckabee Middle School has *ever* had. If something happened at school, people used to assume I was involved somehow and . . . they were probably right. But now . . . ," I say, turning my head to look out the window at the rolling fields. "It's just different. I don't like the risks anymore, I guess. It stopped feeling . . . worth it."

Blake glances over at me but doesn't say anything, so I shrug. "I try to keep a low profile now. But that's pretty hard to do when everybody knows everybody else, and you go from the girl who was always 'fun' or 'up to something,' the person everyone wanted to be around, to that 'poor girl whose mom died.'"

And, yeah, I mean, it's also pretty hard to do when you kiss someone other than your boyfriend at junior prom.

"What about you?" I ask, reminding myself we still barely

know each other. Why do I keep telling her so many things? "What's your plan for senior year?"

Blake lets out a long huff of air. "I don't know! I'm more of a doer than a planner. Probably just make a few friends. Try to pass my classes. Join the soccer team." The corner of her mouth ticks up as she gives me a teasing look. "Keep a low profile."

I swat at her shoulder. "My friend Olivia plays on the soccer team," I say, before I realize what I'm saying. I think back to her icy glare at Snyder's Orchard. Former friend? "Jake can probably introduce you," I add, quieter now.

"That would be cool."

"Make a right turn into the parking lot in half a mile," the automated GPS voice says. I swallow hard, trying to ignore the destination dot getting closer and closer.

I feel the truck slow as Blake puts her turn signal on and pulls into the parking lot, the sun reflecting off the pool of sparkling water as she parks.

"Are you nervous at all? For school to start?" I ask.

"Why would I be nervous?" she replies. The most Blake answer of them all. Completely free from overthinking.

We both fall silent, peering up at the cliff, sitting atop the lush, green tree line. It is . . . *enormous*. Just looking at it, I can feel my vertigo taking over, Blake's words from a moment ago echoing around my head.

Why would I be nervous?

"All right!" Blake says as she turns the car off, her keys jingling as she pulls them out of the ignition. "That isn't too bad!"

My eyes widen, and I give her a "you have to be kidding me" look. "*That's* not too bad?" I say, aghast.

She ignores this and hops merrily out of the truck, completely barefoot, while I crawl out, wondering what the statistics are on people passing out from fear and falling to their deaths.

I kick my flip-flops off as Blake pulls off her T-shirt to reveal a white-and-orange-and-navy-striped bikini, the colors standing out against her tan skin.

I feel my gaze lingering on the toned lines of her stomach, the curve of her . . .

I swallow hard on *whatever* that was and preoccupy myself with ripping off my own clothes, tossing them onto the passenger seat of her truck. I look down at my black bikini, a stark contrast to Blake's brightly colored one.

Crossing my arms tightly over my stomach, I look up to see she's giving me one of her big, enthusiastic smiles.

"Let's do this?"

"Let's do . . . this," I echo, with markedly less pep.

We start walking through the tree-covered trail that will lead us up to the top of the cliff, the path carefully labeled with light blue arrows etched into small wooden signs. Blake leads the way, her steps smooth and even, despite the small twigs and rocks along the path.

Meanwhile, I'm in my own personal game of hopscotch, the soles of my feet getting stabbed every time I put my foot down.

I watch as the sunlight trickles softly through the branches overhead, casting shadows on Blake's shoulders and legs. We make a sharp turn, then begin the climb to the top. The path suddenly becomes steeper as we near the water, crystal blue eating hungrily away at the shoreline.

"Did you know your mom had a fear of heights?" Blake asks as we walk.

"I actually had no idea," I say between breaths. "I was pretty surprised when I saw it on the list."

We went on a family vacation when I was younger to Puerto Rico, where she did this crazy zip line in Toro Verde. I was too young to go on it, which had really bummed me out at the time. My dad stayed behind with me, the two of us peering up at the tree line, watching in awe as people rocketed past above us. I remember watching her pass by, high above the trees, completely unafraid of the space between her and the ground below.

"That was my mom, though. Never afraid of anything." I think back to months before her diagnosis, when she first started getting bad headaches, writing it off as nothing, even when the pain relievers stopped really working. "Even when she should've been."

I try not to get woozy the farther we go, focusing on the steady rhythm of Blake's feet, falling right, left, right, left, one after the other, slower now as we near the top, the bright blue sky coming into view.

Blake stops short in front of a sign with an arrow pointing directly toward the sky, a shoulder-high ledge separating us from the jumping point.

"Oh, good," I say, pointing at the arrow on the sign. "This is the part where we ascend straight to heaven."

Blake rolls her eyes, but they crinkle with a secret smile. She takes a deep breath and effortlessly pushes herself up onto the cliff ledge like some kind of parkour expert, turning around once she's at the top to offer me a hand. I reach out, our fingers interlacing in the spot where the shadows turn to light, hers soft and cool against my warm skin. She helps pull me up, and suddenly the entire world is far below us.

I instantly feel like I'm going to vomit.

I know, instinctually, that it's beautiful. The blue of the lake, the sun high in the sky, the trees going for miles. Despite all of that, though, I feel *super* dizzy. I'm nowhere near the edge, but I feel like I'm teetering on it. It has to be a good twenty feet to the water below.

"Oh my *God*," I groan, clutching Blake's arm to steady myself, any attempt at remaining cool and collected in front of her suddenly being tossed out the window. "This was a terrible, terrible idea. Like . . . so stupid."

"It'll be fine," she assures me, her voice confident but not dismissive. "What's the worst thing that can happen?"

"Death," I say without even a second thought. "Either from impact, or from some stick down there we can't see stabbing through my chest, or from having a heart attack before I even jump or, or . . . whatever! Blake, my dad only knows how to cook pasta! And eggs! He's done for without me!"

Blake grabs ahold of both my shoulders and leans forward, her face inches from mine. "Emily. You can do this." She looks deep into my eyes, and I've never been this close to her before. Close enough to see the tiny freckle on her chin, the almost golden rays encircling her pupils, the cupid's bow of her top lip. For a moment the fear completely disappears, replaced with a heart-hammering feeling, and I have to look away to escape from it. "You can't obsess over the risks and the what-ifs, or else you won't do *anything*. You'll spend your life five spaces short of a bingo."

I freeze, frowning, my head swinging back around to look at her. "You had me until that last bit. Five spaces short of a bingo? What does that even *mean*?"

"I don't know," Blake says. "I was going for something like 'if you don't even play the game, you can never win.' You know?"

I bite my lip, processing. I *do* know. A bit too well.

She nods toward the edge of the cliff. "Do you want me to go first? Double-check for stray sticks?"

I give her a weak smile, nodding, but then I instantly want to take it back. I don't want to be alone up here. "Well, that would be—"

But without even thinking twice or hearing the rest of my sentence, she lets go of my shoulders, turns, and launches herself off the cliff at a full sprint like an actual maniac.

I take a step back, clinging to the rock behind me as I watch her soar through the air, her arms pulling together in perfect dive form, her body falling for one, two, three—*too many* seconds. Until finally, her whole body disappears into the water.

I watch, holding my breath, waiting for her to reappear, but every second feels like an eternity, my worst fears swimming around my head.

No, no, no.

Did her neck break on impact? Did she crack her skull on something? How many bones did she break?

. . . And then she surfaces, her head finally popping up in between the white foam that formed as she made impact, the both of us taking a deep breath. "No sticks! I didn't even touch the bottom."

"Oh! Great!" I peer down at her, and the world tilts again. The distance seems even more enormous now that she's on the other end of it.

"Come on, Em!" Blake calls up to me, her head bobbing up and down as she treads water. "Don't look! It makes everything worse! Just step back and take a running start."

"I don't think I can!" I call back down to her.

"Don't think! At all!" she calls back. "Remember the apple orchard? Trust me, if you just *go*, everything will be fine. The overthinking is what will hurt you."

"Oh, sure!" I call back to her. *"Everything will be fine,"* I mumble to myself, mimicking her voice as I step back from the ledge, swaying unsteadily as I go.

I take a deep, shaky breath and put my hands on my hips, fixing my eyes on the horizon as I steady myself.

And then I remember why I'm here. Who brought me here.

Mom. But I don't see her as seventeen, not like I thought I would. What comes to me is those last few weeks, holding her hand while she lay down, her eyes closed after hours of testing, doctors poking and prodding at her body.

I thought she had been asleep, but her voice startled me when she began to speak. "I think the regretting is the worst part, Em," she whispered, her weak fingers squeezing mine. "Wishing you could've done more. Wishing you could've done all the things you wanted to do."

I feel tears sting at my eyes, the same way they did that day.

I take a deep breath, the words she said that day settling on my chest.

If I turn back now, I know I'll regret it. If I don't face my fear the same way she did, if I give up on the list, I know I'll regret it.

"On the count of five," I whisper, Mom's lucky number, *our* lucky number.

"One." I fix my eyes on the horizon, locking my jaw. "Two, three, four—"

Before I can even process what I'm doing, I run toward the edge of the cliff, launching myself off as I scream out, "Five!"

The open air makes my stomach lurch, and for a glittering moment, time slows. Or maybe even completely stops existing. I feel completely free. Weightless.

I can feel *her* all around me, hear her laugh, her words and her list pushing me forward.

Then . . . I realize I'm still falling. Still hurtling through the air. *WHAT AM I DOING?!*

I begin to flail my arms wildly, desperate for my feet to meet the water, for the free fall to be over.

I hit the water hard, my legs splayed, my shins and thighs burning from the impact, an instant wedgie shooting so far up my butt, I don't think it will ever come out. And I can't stop to *try* to pull it out, because somehow I'm still going down, my body slicing through the water with twenty feet worth of momentum.

Finally, I come to a stop, completely suspended. I look up to see the sunlight trickling through the water, a sea of bubbles between me and the outside world, a steady stream of them pouring out of my mouth and nose. I paddle my burning legs to the top, and eventually I break through the surface of the water, grateful to be alive and all in one piece. I let out a gasp of air, coughing, the grimy taste of lake water hitting hard in the back of my throat.

"You good?" Blake asks, swimming over to me, her fingers reaching out to lightly touch my side.

"I think I lost a boob on impact," I say, double-checking that my black bathing-suit top is still in place *and* that both my boobs are still there. "Oh, thank God," I add, breathing a sigh of relief. "They made it."

We both burst out laughing, giggling as we swim toward the shore, the water slowly getting shallow enough for us to stand on the slippery, mossy rocks at the bottom. I stumble, and Blake reaches out quickly, grabbing on to my arm to steady me. The two of us tiptoe carefully around the jagged stones and twigs covering the shore and make our way to the trail leading back up to the cliff.

I gaze up in awe, slightly impressed I fell all that way and lived to tell the tale. It was nowhere near as neat as Blake's graceful little dive, but a cliff jump is a cliff jump. I did it.

Blake turns to look at me, her brown eyes glowing almost amber in the sunlight.

"You up for a round two?"

My heart beats loudly in my chest, my shins tingling from the smack of the water, the burn suddenly more intense at the thought of a second jump.

I feel . . . exhilarated, though. Like my body's been asleep and I just woke it the hell up. Like I haven't ever used it properly and it wants me to, long-dormant adrenaline coursing through my veins, making me feel like I can conquer just about anything.

Making me feel the tiniest bit . . . invincible.

My adrenaline rush forces a nod out of me, which provokes a smile so big and genuine out of Blake, I can see every tooth, and the gap between the first two. It's adorable and my heart rate spikes again, because I know that smile's there because of me.

I don't know why that matters so much, but it does.

"You going to do a flip this time?" she asks, clearly joking.

I roll my eyes at her, my legs still stinging. "Blake, I'm honestly just trying not to give myself a permanent wedgie this time. Last jump was a close call."

We make our way back up the trail, faster now, the excitement of the first jump fueling us, even as the dirt clings to our wet feet. Blake pulls me back up onto the uneven rock, and this time I'm able to finally look out at the view.

Really look, now that my vision isn't clouded by as much fear or vertigo.

The lake is glittering, there are trees as far as the eye can see, and . . . Blake's mom was right. From up here, everything does feel small. What happened at Snyder's Orchard with Matt. What happened at junior prom. Even the house that soon won't be mine anymore.

But what she didn't tell me to expect is that by everything else shrinking away, it leaves room for other things to become bigger. Something that sometimes feels so small and far away can suddenly feel closer than it has in years.

Three years, to be exact.

My mom. She taught me to live so fearlessly. And I've spent all this time since her death pushing that away because her words were so completely drowned out by everything that happened to her.

We jump for the rest of the afternoon, each plummet off the cliff less scary than the last. Blake, of course, does a flip or two. I cringe every time she does, holding my breath until her head resurfaces, completely unharmed.

After a while we sit on top of the cliff, our legs dangling over the ledge as the afternoon sun begins to set, sending a shower of deep orange and pink across the sky. I look down at the water underneath us, the surface sparkling in the fading light, and . . .

I'm officially not afraid anymore.

So why the hell am I afraid of the guy I've been dating for *years*? The boy who had always had a crush on me. The boy who my mom always wanted me to give a chance.

I remember the way her face lit up when he came to the hospital to keep me company, sunflowers clutched in his hand as he pulled up a chair next to her. I think, deep down, all my other friends were scared to come. Scared to see someone so young wither away so quickly, a person they knew suddenly skin and bones underneath a blanket, her own cells and body rebelling against her.

But not Matt. He came every weekend.

The second the door closed behind him one Saturday afternoon, she leaned over to say, "You really should give that boy a chance someday, Emily. Sometimes the best romances come from the best friendships." She smiled over at my dad, the two sharing a knowing look. "That boy who has a crush on you could end up being the one you're meant to be with."

I didn't feel . . . that way about him at the time. But I liked hanging out with him. I liked the way he narrated movies, and how he was always there for me, through crazy adventures and pranks and my mom getting sick. So, after everything, I couldn't help but think she must be right.

I tap my heel against the rock underneath me and let out a long sigh.

So *why* is it so hard? What am I so afraid of with him? What's stopping me?

Give him a chance.

I keep thinking I am, but if I'm always halfway out the door, I can't *really* be. And I *know* that if I don't fix things between us, I'll regret it.

If I could jump off a cliff, maybe, just maybe, I can face him. If I dive in completely, without reservations, without overthinking it, maybe it'll be the change we need. The thing that was always missing between us was maybe just me being too scared to actually make the jump.

Maybe we always just felt off because I was never *really* in. Not the way mom wanted me to be.

"Thanks," I say to Blake.

She looks over at me, the sun casting a golden glow on the skin of her face and her body. "For not pushing you off?" she asks, reaching out to grab my arm and fake a push over the edge. I swat her away, laughing, but then her face slowly grows serious.

"Anytime," she says. "I think it's cool that you're doing the list, Emily. Jumping off cliffs, buying books from old guys with impeccable mustaches. That you can still learn new things about your mom. Still make new memories that she's a part of."

I let out a long exhale.

"Sometimes I'm afraid I'll forget things. Like the way she smelled, or the color of her eyes, or the sound of her laugh." I squeeze my eyes shut, trying to picture her face. The outline of her hair. The curve of her eyebrows. The fullness of her lips. It's hard to piece them all together. "Then I have moments like today, you know? Where she feels so close, it's like she's been here all along."

"Well, she has. In a way at least," Blake says with a shrug. "You're a part of her, you know? She can never be forgotten because you exist."

I let out a long whistle. "That was . . . really deep."

Blake nudges me. "I've had a lot of years to think about it." There's a look in her eyes that I recognize. A trace of the sadness that is always there when you lose a loved one. The sadness that changes size and shape, bigger in some moments, smaller in others.

We stand up, stretching, ready to make one last jump down

and head back. We count down from five together, and at the last second, without even thinking about it, I grab Blake's hand, pulling us both toward the cliff's edge as the two of us launch into the air at full speed. Our hands pull apart as we hit the water, but our eyes lock through the sea of tiny bubbles as we swim to the surface.

We paddle to the shore one final time, our legs struggling way more now to fight against the current, until we splash noisily onto the bank, exhaustion setting in. Slowly, we head back to her truck to dry off and begin the drive back to my house.

The sun dips below the horizon as we spend the whole ride home debating which item to go for next.

"Tattoo," Blake says, without even a second thought. "Gotta be tattoo. I mean, how fun would that be?"

"Uh, *no*," I say as I shake my head. Clearly, our idea of fun differed on that particular subject. "Between today and getting chased out of Snyder's Orchard, I need a *break*."

I find a black felt-tip pen in Blake's glove compartment, checking off "2. Get over my fear of heights," as my eyes scan the rest of the list, the next two items jumping out at me.

3. Go on a picnic.
4. Try a new food.

I smile to myself. My mom was a *notoriously* picky eater. This one will be a breeze for me, but I bet this one had been just as hard for her as facing her fear of heights.

"How about we go on a 'try a new food picnic'? Kill two birds with one stone?" I ask as I quickly tally the number of days I have left, Blake slowing to a stop outside my house.

Eleven. Only *eleven*.

"Sounds like a plan to me," Blake says as I scoop up my bag and unclick my seat belt.

"I'll bring the food," she calls out the window as I hop out. "I'll text you this week to make sure it's something you've never had before."

"Deal!" I call after her, waving goodbye. I wait until her truck fades from view before heading inside, my heart feeling full.

Feeling invincible.

I don't know if it is the fact that I've lived through jumping off a cliff with her, or the fact that she seems like she could be friends with just about anyone, but I feel different around Blake. Not only is she practically a ray of actual sunshine, but . . . she doesn't treat me like the girl who lost her mom. The ghost of the girl she used to be.

She's the first person I've felt like I could be completely real with in a long time. Like there's no unspoken expectation, no Kiera and Matt exchanging glances when they think I've looked away. Olivia mouthing "mom" and rolling her eyes to Ryan when I bailed on a weekend trip out of town, worried something would happen to my dad while I was away.

She's the first person I feel like I can talk to about *my mom*, because she understands without being too close. Without there being so much shared grief, like with my dad and Nina, that it's suffocating.

Blake doesn't just want to make me feel better, like my friends do, and she doesn't need me to share her grief. And something about that helps me feel like I'm not so completely frozen.

A couple of weeks ago, when Kiera was leaving for camp and everything was so broken, it felt almost like the last straw. Like I was at the end of my rope.

When I heard Johnny and Blake were moving to Huckabee and we were going to bingo, I never would have guessed this would happen.

But . . . I feel like she's got me back in the game. And for the first time in a long time, I feel ready to play.

14

I wake up the next day still riding the high from cliff jumping and my new, list-inspired goal.

Talk to Matt. I finally feel ready. Like if I stop thinking about it and just *go* for it, the right words will come to me.

The feeling builds and builds through my shift at Nina's, time moving at a glacial pace despite the morning rush and the batch of blueberry scones I spend the afternoon baking.

For once, the familiar rhythm of whisking, and adding ingredients, and shaping doesn't bring me the same kind of comfort, my mind too distracted to fully concentrate on what I'm doing.

"You good?" Nina asks as she peers at my misshapen triangles. "First you get banned from Snyder's, and now you think a triangle looks like a football."

I grin sheepishly. "Sorry, Nina."

I've thought about telling her about the list, but something always stops me. Where my dad can hardly talk about my mom, Nina is . . . almost the polar opposite. The Julie Miller pain is always a sentence away, always just within reach. And it's heavy and awful, the shared grief between the two of us enough to make you feel like you got run over by a train.

So, today, like all the other days, I decide not to say anything.

By the time the clock strikes two, I'm already sprinting out the door. The bells jingle behind me as I grab my bike out of the rack and pedal quickly down the street before I can talk myself out of it.

The pool is less than a mile away, situated just outside the center of Huckabee and down the road from the hospital. I usually make it a point to avoid this route, going through a development and tacking on an extra half a mile, but I don't want to waste another second. I've wasted too many already.

Before I know it, I'm turning into the parking lot and locking up my bike, the too-familiar sound of kids splashing in the water and muffled music pouring out of an ancient boom box filling the air.

Is Blake still working? I know she was here this morning. I don't want her to hear this.

But if I can fix things now, maybe she'll never have to.

I start power walking, skidding to a stop in front of the plastic chair by the front gate, where Jake is sitting, the chair tilted back on two legs, a silver whistle swinging around his finger. His eyes widen when he sees me, and he flails, righting himself before he completely tips over.

"Oh shit," he says, pushing his shaggy blond hair out of his face to give me a once-over. "Look what the cat dragged in."

"Nice to see you, too." I crane my neck, looking past him, my eyes scanning the deck. "Matt here?"

"Uh, yeah."

I go to slide around Jake, but he stops me. "Pool fee?"

I put my hands on my hips, giving him a look. "Jake. You can't be serious."

He doesn't say anything but keeps his hand outstretched. I let out a frustrated sigh and dig into the pocket of my jeans for the tip money I just made, peeling off five ones and handing them to him.

He slips it into a black leather bank bag, nodding toward the rusty vending machines outside the bathrooms. "He's over there."

I follow his nod to see Matt peering through the glass in a pair of red swim trunks, debating between salty and sweet, just like he always does. My heart begins to hammer noisily in my chest.

"By the way," Jake says as he leans back in his chair again, pointing at my left cheek with a smirk. "You've got flour on your face."

"Better than rotten apples," I mutter, rubbing away at the flour as I move past him. I walk right up to Matt without even a second thought, like I'm running straight toward the edge of a cliff.

"Hi," I say, jumping off.

He looks over at me, surprised, a strand of his brown hair falling onto his forehead. "Hi," he says, brushing it away. For a second he smiles, like a reflex, but then he clears his throat, plastering on a serious glower. "What are you doing here?"

My stomach drops, and I feel my breathing hitch. I open my mouth to say something, and wait and wait until I realize . . . this isn't like cliff jumping at all.

I would've hit the water by now, but instead I'm still falling, my arms flailing wildly around, a belly flop damn near inevitable.

"I just wanted to say . . . ," I manage to get out. "I just wanted to say I'm sorry."

His eyebrows fall into full brooding mode. He doesn't say anything. He just crosses his arms and glances to the side at the lifeguard table, where a sea of eyes peer at us intently. Cassie Evans, an upcoming junior who's had a crush on Matt for the past two summers, looks like she's trying to murder me using just the power of her mind.

But that doesn't come close to the look on Matt's face. I've never seen him this upset before.

"Matt," I say, leaning forward. "I want to make this right. Tell me how to make this right."

"I'm honestly surprised you want to, considering you haven't even tried to talk to me in weeks. Never even bothering to give me an explanation." Matt shakes his head in disgust and turns back to the vending machine. I watch as he plugs in a few numbers, opting for salty, and a bag of chips falls to the bottom. He pushes the door in and grabs them, letting out a long exhale before facing me again.

"Matt—" My voice cracks, and I see him pause, see the tiniest hitch in his breathing.

He reaches for my hand, just like he used to. At my locker, or before his football games. But he stops short, and I see his fingers fold into his palm, his hand balling into a fist, his arm recoiling as he turns and walks away.

I don't understand.

I thought the words would just *come*, but they didn't. Still, all I've got is that I want to fix it. Nothing more than that.

But Matt wants to know why it broke. And I still don't have an answer to that.

I watch him go, with his swoopy brown hair and his broad shoulders, tan now from his days spent on a lifeguard stand.

He's beyond cute. Every girl in our grade knows that. He's sweet. He remembers every anniversary and holiday and birthday, big or small. He actually *listens*, and everyone in our friend group, not just me, knows he's the person you go to if you have a problem.

And he gets me, just like I get him. He knows that I like rom-coms more than horror movies, and my favorite triple-layer chocolate cake recipe, and that I get quiet when I'm upset. Just like I know that his favorite director is Wes Anderson, and his favorite Nintendo Switch game is *Fortnite*, and that he *hates* when people are late.

But I still can't stop the feeling that always used to blindside me during our relationship from suddenly swimming back into my bones, settling deep in the marrow.

The feeling that something is . . . *off*, no matter how perfect Matt Henderson is.

Which . . . means that something about *me* needs to change for it all to click. Maybe I've been too busy looking at him, when

I need to look at myself. If what I needed to say didn't just *come* to me, then maybe it's a problem with me.

Is this all because of how much I changed after Mom died? Maybe I still have more lessons to learn from the list before I can figure it out.

Or . . . maybe it's something else entirely?

My eyes travel past Matt to the deep end, where Blake sits, her hair in a messy bun. I'm both relieved and anxious to see her. She pushes her sunglasses up onto the top of her head when she sees I'm looking at her.

"You good?" she mouths, only for me, and the wrongness melts away.

I nod, but I'm really not, and for some reason it feels wrong to lie to her.

I swallow and look quickly away, noticing the lifeguard table is still hard at work, staring at me like I'm auditioning for a Broadway musical. I make a beeline for the exit, eager to get right the hell out of here. I'm definitely not in the mood to stay and give them any more of a performance.

I know now I can't just wait for the right words to come, for the switch to flip. I need to figure out what's wrong and fix it. Only then can I really show Matt how sorry I am. That I can still be the same person he fell in love with.

I just need the list to show me how.

I also don't want to stick around and risk Cassie Evans *actually* figuring out how to kill someone using her glare. If anyone was petty enough to succeed, she'd be the one.

15

I meet up with Blake after work on Friday at the local park for our picnic, eager to be anywhere but home, obsessing over the Matt drama as I sit in my empty living room.

With the uptick in house showings, and our boxes very nearly packed, I would've *thought* we'd be looking at places to move into. But we haven't looked anywhere yet.

When I sent Dad a few listings I'd found online this morning, even one for a nice apartment just above the hardware store in town, he'd just ignored me.

"I've got it handled," he murmured before heading off to work.

Whatever that means.

Blake has gone for the *full* stereotype for our picnic, a checkered blanket unfurled on the big grassy field just up the hill from the playground. I bring some of the apple tarts Nina made with the apples we picked, and Blake brings a square container, her fingers tapping on the edges.

"I called my grandma. The one in Hawaii. She walked me through how to make them," she says as we sit. "And it's her recipe, so I definitely don't think you've had this before."

When she opens it, there's a tiny hiss of steam.

"I think they're best if they're still warm. I pretty much wrapped the nori around them, threw them right in the container, and floored it over here," Blake says while I peer down at the rectangular blocks she's brought for us to eat, rice and a pink hunk of meat wrapped together with a thin piece of seaweed.

"Is that . . . ? Is that Spam?" I ask. I am no stranger to Spam, especially when a twelve-ounce tin is under three dollars at the local grocery store.

But I can't say I've ever had it quite like this.

Blake nods, placing the container down on the blanket in between us. "Spam musubi. You can kinda just . . ." Her voice trails off, and she reaches out, picking one up and taking a big bite out of it.

"My mom would *never* eat something like this. She was such a picky eater," I say as I imitate Blake, reaching out to grab one, the tiny brick warm underneath my fingertips. I bring it cautiously to my mouth, taking a much smaller bite than she just had.

It's a lot of things all at once. Sweet, salty . . . sticky? But it's not bad. I'm surprised to find I actually really like it.

Blake stares at me expectantly, a concerned crease forming between her eyebrows, like she's actually nervous for once.

"It's really good!" I say, and it wipes the crease away as her whole face lights up. "I think my mom would've even liked it, if she could've gotten past the seaweed. It's definitely the best Spam has *ever* tasted."

She laughs at that, and we keep digging in, until the container of Spam musubi is all gone and it's time for the apple tarts, crispy and sweet and delicious.

Afterward, we scour the grass around our picnic blanket while I try to find a four-leaf clover, the countdown clock for list completion now sitting at less than ten days.

My mom had been so lucky, she probably found it in an afternoon.

Meanwhile, I've been staring at the ground everywhere I go for the past two weeks, and still nothing.

"So," Blake asks from behind me. "How was talking to Matt? It, uh, didn't look like it went too well."

"You can say that again," I say, letting out a long sigh. I lean forward, plucking a clover from the grass, dismayed to see it only has three leaves. Just like the last five I've picked.

I try to think of a way to talk to her about all of this, without giving too much away.

"I just want to make things better. Kiera says I'm going to ruin our senior year if I don't, and I know she's right. I'll ruin it for my other friends, too. And . . . I don't know. I really feel like I can now. Like the list is leading me to it. A way to make things *feel* right between us, you know? I just have to keep going."

"Is that why you kissed that other guy?" she asks. "Because

159

things didn't feel right between you and Matt?"

Is that why I—wait. *What?*

I whip around to face her, my heart going into triple time in my chest. "You *know?*"

"Yeah," she says with a shrug. "Since like the first day of work. Cassie Evans told me by lunchtime."

She'd known all along. When we'd gone to the bookstore, and unpacked at her house, and sat atop the cliff at Huckabee State Park. Even now, standing here.

I search her face, but there's no sign of judgment. She doesn't care. She doesn't think of me any differently.

Which is maybe why she's the first person I tell the truth to. "Yeah. It is," I say.

I've always given another excuse for our breakups, cloaked it in clinginess or needing to focus on schoolwork, or Jake's flask. Never the real reason.

I shrug. "But a lot of things haven't felt right the past three years. *I* haven't felt right. Not until the list showed up." I look up at her, smiling. "Not until *you* showed up in Huckabee and made me jump off cliffs and stuff."

She smiles back at me, and I notice she's clutching not one, not two, but *three* four-leaf clovers.

"Blake," I say, pointing down at her hands. "You do know if you pick all of them, there'll be none left for me to find."

"Good point," she says, opening her hands, a small shower of green falling from her palms.

We look around for a few more minutes before I accept defeat.

I lie back on the checkered picnic blanket, pulling the list out of my pocket and unfolding it, using a pink pen I brought from Nina's to check off "3. Go on a picnic" and "4. Try a new food."

No revelations about Mom, or invaluable life lessons here. But at least it was fun.

"So, do you think that's the solution?" Blake asks. "Changing yourself?"

"Well, not exactly *changing* myself," I clarify. "More like *becoming* myself, you know?"

"Just . . . make sure it's for you," Blake says as she plucks a few blades of grass and chucks them into the wind, the both of us watching them float away. "I was in a relationship before and it felt like I changed so much of who I was to fit what I thought she wanted. Like I cared more about what she thought of me than what *I* thought of me."

"She." My skin prickles at the word. *She.* "You're . . ."

Blake whips her head around to look at me. "Yeah, uh . . . gay. I'm gay. Is that . . . ?"

"Cool! Totally cool, of course," I say as I smooth out the blanket underneath us. I had wondered. When Paul had told her he was gay at Nina's, when Jake had flirted with her at Snyder's Orchard. "But you're right. That's not what I want to do."

We sit in silence for a few moments, watching the clouds drift by overhead.

"What are you doing tomorrow night?" Blake asks.

I let out a long sigh, rolling over onto my side to face her. "We've got a few back-to-back showings going on at my house, even though we haven't even *found* our new house yet. So . . . absolutely nothing. Why?"

She gives me a mischievous grin, holding up a red lifeguard lanyard filled with keys. "I'm closing tomorrow."

I look down at the list, my eyes landing on

8. Skinny-dip in Huckabee Pool after hours.

I groan and cover my face with the corner of the checkered blanket. "This list is going to kill me."

16

Front gate in 5.

I peer down at the text from Blake, then look up to watch the last few sets of headlights pull out of the Huckabee Pool parking lot, driving off down the road. When I hear the creak of her truck door and see her climbing back out of the driver's seat, I creep out of the bushes by the bike rack and make a beeline for the front gate.

"You ready?" she asks as she pulls the lanyard keys out of her pocket, using one to reopen the gold lock keeping the gate closed.

"Maybe? I don't know." I groan, resting my forehead against her warm shoulder. "Are you *sure* everyone's gone?"

She pulls the chain out from between the links it's wrapped around. "Positive," she says, using her foot to tap open the gate. It squeaks noisily open to reveal a dark and empty pool deck, not a soul in sight.

We walk inside, stopping at the edge of the water.

I've never seen the pool like this. Completely quiet, the moonlight reflecting off the ripples in the water. If I didn't know just how gross it was during the daylight hours, hair balls rolling around on the bottom, dead bugs floating on the top, I'd actually think it looked kind of beautiful.

"*Why* would she want to skinny-dip in this? I definitely don't understand this one. I bet the water hasn't been cleaned since my mom swam in it," I say, and Blake laughs.

"Not very well, I can tell you that." She shrugs. "Maybe you just have to do it. Maybe there is no why."

I stare at the water for a few more moments, my pulse quickening as I think about what comes next. "Count of three we take off our clothes, okay?"

I look over at Blake, and she nods in agreement. "Deal."

"One."

"Two," she says back.

"Three."

I start to pull off my sundress, stopping suddenly when I see Blake glance over at me. My face burns underneath her gaze, my body suddenly ablaze.

"Blake! I swear to *God*, don't look!" I hit her shoulder and she steps back, clapping her hands over her eyes, the both of us laughing. But something lingers under the surface. This strange new energy between us.

"I won't! Here—" She turns around, pulling one hand away and motioning for me to do the same. "We'll both turn our backs, okay?"

"Okay," I say, following her instructions.

We're both silent for a long moment. I look down to see the skin above my heart dancing, the rhythm uneven.

"Do we have to count down again?" Blake asks, breaking the tension as the both of us burst into giggles.

"Let's just go for it," I say as I rip off my sundress. Two seconds later my rose-colored bra and striped underwear land in a pile on the pool deck too.

"Is it cold?" I ask, cautiously reaching my foot out to dunk a toe into the water. But as I do, out of the corner of my eye, I see her pull her red bikini top off, her back completely bare, the lines of her shoulder blades and dip of her spine a shadow in the darkness.

"It's probably—" She starts to turn around, and I jump as I try to cover my body with my arms *and* snap my gaze away at the same time.

"Blake!" I squeak out, but I'm already losing my balance in surprise and . . .

—*Smack*—

I tumble into the icy water, submerging completely.

"Freezing," she finishes when I come up, coughing, chlorine stinging at my eyes and throat.

I rub my eyes, but a splash next to me soaks me all over again, a wave of water right to the face.

"Really?" I say when Blake surfaces, her hair slicked back. I skim my fingers across the surface to shoot a wave back at her, and the two of us laugh as we push water back and forth at each other, white foam forming at the surface, bubbling.

"All right, all right!" she says when I get her right in the eyeballs, holding up her hands in defeat. "Truce. I call truce!"

I stop splashing, the water quietly hissing as it calms, giving way to absolute silence. My eyes lock with Blake's, and I feel my stomach flutter at the intensity of her gaze, my breath hitching in my chest as she moves just half a step closer.

Unconsciously, my eyes move down to her lips, to the sharp lines of her collarbone.

Something about this moment and the freeness of it, skinny-dipping at the Huckabee Pool, pulling me toward her. To this. To . . .

"Emily?" a voice asks, but I know Blake's lips aren't moving because I'm still looking at them.

I swing my head around wildly to see Matt, his eyes wide with surprise, his phone flashlight smacking me square in the eye.

"Matt! *Don't look!*" I say as Blake and I paddle to the edge, flattening ourselves against it. Matt quickly squeezes his eyes shut.

"I just came back because I forgot my—wait. Are you . . . skinny-dipping?" he asks, incredulous.

I clamor out of the water, Blake following just behind me. I quickly pull on my dress, the water making the fabric suction to my body.

"Maybe?" I squeak back, clutching my bra and underwear to my dread-filled chest.

What will he think of me now? Kissing someone else at prom. Swimming naked in the Huckabee Pool. Oh God, I've just ruined—

And then he starts to laugh.

"That's actually pretty badass," he says, his voice sounding . . . slightly impressed, not pained for once.

"You won't tell anyone?" Blake asks, and I can tell she's nervous, the expression on her face unfamiliar. He pops one of his eyes open, opening the other when he sees we're fully clothed.

"Matt doesn't snitch," I say, and I know this because before he was my boyfriend, Matt was my middle school partner in crime. The one who refused to break under pressure, staying strong even when Kiera tapped out.

"I dare you," Matt had said after lunch in sixth grade, holding up a tiny green garden snake, "to set this loose in math class."

"Deal," I'd said without as much as a second thought.

Half an hour later, Mr. Benson's sixth-grade math class had to be evacuated, each of us getting individually grilled in the hallway while the school janitor, Mr. Wibble, scoured the classroom for the snake.

Matt knew it was me and didn't say anything.

"He won't even rat you out when Mr. Benson threatens detention," I say.

The corner of his mouth ticks up into a smile at my words. "Not even then." His eyes meet mine, and he nods to the main road. "A patrol car drives past in ten minutes to check on the place after a couple of freshmen broke in last month. You may want to get out of here." He holds up a key ring, his eyes flicking to Blake. "I've got a spare. I can lock up."

"Thanks, Matt." I reach out to give his arm a squeeze. He closes off just the tiniest bit, a pained wince, but it's a fraction of what it's been.

Then Blake grabs my hand, and in a blink the two of us run into the night, dripping our way to the exit, happiness filling my chest. The feel of her hand in mine takes me back to that moment in the pool, her eyes locked on mine, her lips . . .

I push it away, giving it a name. A source. *The rush of the list.* That's all it was. I'd gotten swept up in the experience, the exhilaration of skinny-dipping.

I glance back at Matt and he shakes his head, but he's smiling. Our first conversation in more than a month. Well, our first *good* conversation in a month, the list and my mom guiding me in the right direction.

And just like that this night is a step closer to making everything more than right.

Maybe it's a step to making it better.

17

I spend most of the next day hiding in my room while my dad is on the phone with the real estate agent.

There's been an offer on the house.

Definitely a bit of a buzzkill after my whirlwind of a night.

I should be packing the last of my stuff, but instead I'm going through the box of my mom's, laying everything out on the floor around me. I'm still looking for something to help me understand what the list meant to her. I reach out for one of the cassette tapes, even though I have no way to play it, and when I open the plastic box, I see a note taped to the inside in my dad's messy handwriting.

Let me know if you change your mind. I'll be waiting.
Yours, Joe

"Let me know if you change your mind"? What did that mean?

I look toward the door, his muffled voice drifting through from the other side. I wish I could talk to him about it, but I don't even know where to start.

He'd probably have thrown out this entire box if he'd come across it. Just like everything else.

In fact, I've been hiding it underneath my bed, surrounding it with other boxes and blankets, because I'm afraid he'll do just that. He already gets upset with me for "trying to keep too much," for "making excuses" instead of finishing her closet.

I'm pulled away from the note when my phone screen lights up, buzzing noisily on the floor next to me. *Kiera?* That's weird.

It's Sunday, but I wasn't expecting a call from her, since she'll be back from Misty Oasis tomorrow, for our traditional unpack and bake night. I found the perfect carrot cake recipe I *know* she'll love.

I reach out, the green accept button transforming into her face.

"Hey!" I say, pushing aside the old soccer T-shirt and the 2000 yearbook to lean back against the foot of my bed. "Noon? Isn't it a little early for Misty Oasis phone time?"

She nods, holding up a stack of certificates. "End-of-camp awards ceremony is tonight, so I won't be able to call later."

"Ooo, fun." I flash her a big smile. "You're back tomorrow! I can't *wait.*"

She doesn't say anything. She just bites her lip, looking away. "Listen, Em. I, uh . . ." Her voice trails off, and my heart sinks straight to the floor. I knew something was weird about this call.

Had Matt said something to her? "Todd invited me and a couple of the other counselors to his house, and I said yes and—"

"Hey!" I say, trying to keep the smile on my face. "That's super cool, Kiera. I'm really happy for you."

I *am* happy for her. I mean, it's her first boyfriend. Of *course* she wants to spend all the time she can with him.

But I can't deny the fact that it hurts, the fact that she doesn't want to come back to Huckabee. To the carrot cake recipe I scoured the internet for, excited for her return, and our annual tradition.

She's fine and *happier* being away from here. Being away from me and our current mess of a friend group.

She looks up, her eyes round and hopeful. "Really? Listen, I know we have plans and I haven't been there to help with all the Matt stuff, and I'm really sorry about that. But I'll definitely make it up to you."

I wave my hand like it's no big deal. "Don't even worry about it," I say. "In fact, I think things are finally starting to come together with all of that."

Kiera leans forward, looking excited. "Wait, really?"

"Yeah," I say, nodding enthusiastically. I know I'm overselling, but her expression stirs me on. I picture Matt's smile yesterday on the pool deck. "I mean, he actually *talked* to me yesterday."

"He did?" Kiera is practically squealing.

I nod. "He caught me after-hours skinny-dipping yesterday at the pool—"

"Hold up," Kiera says, trying to process what I've just told her. "*You* went skinny-dipping?"

"Yeah, with Blake. Anyway, Matt came back because he forgot something, and—"

"Em," Kiera says, cutting me off. She nods, giving me the same look of admiration that Matt gave me yesterday. A look I haven't seen in three whole years. From any of my friends. "That's pretty badass."

"That's what Matt said!"

Kiera lets out a long, exaggerated breath, filled with relief. "I am so relieved. I'm going to be honest—I was *really* worried."

A wave of guilt washes over me for putting my best friend in the middle of this. But also . . . a wave of frustration that she's more excited about this than about seeing me again.

"I'll be back the day before the Huckabee Lake trip," she says, talking fast, her voice filled with excitement. "I feel like the trip is going to be the *perfect* place to officially get you guys back together."

Not only was it the first time we'd all be back together in one place, but the Huckabee Lake trip definitely had a bit of mythos around it. It was more than a little famous for people coupling up over the course of the weekend.

Including my parents.

"We can fix everything then, and it will all be back to normal by the time senior year starts."

Normal.

That's what I want . . . isn't it?

I think of Matt standing by my locker between classes, and eating breakfast sandwiches in his car on the way to school, and scrolling through the new movies at the historic theater in town on Friday afternoons. But I also think about the countdown clock in my head every time we kiss, and all our little fights, and him talking about *taking things to the next level* when I'm barely comfortable on the level we're on.

My stomach flip-flops though because normal also means more than just us. It means Kiera, and Olivia, and Jake, and Ryan, all of us hanging out in Olivia's enormous basement, and hot chocolate and cookies in the winter at Kiera's house, and going to Hank's for milkshakes when it's someone's birthday.

I miss all of that. I *want* all of that. I don't want it to be ruined.

And, I remind myself, *this time will be better*. This time I'll say yes to weekends away, the small adventures, the pranks. I'll give it a real chance and won't hold back. Like Mom.

I nod, determined, and give Kiera a reassuring smile. "Yeah," I say. "Normal."

We talk about Misty Oasis for the rest of the call. She tells me about how a camper got stuck in a tree, detailing the rescue mission that required Todd, a queen-size mattress, and a climbing rope.

I laugh along and try my best to listen. But deep in my stomach, a tiny whisper of queasiness lingers, familiar and unwelcome. At the thought of Kiera not wanting to come back until I said I could fix things.

When we hang up, I lie down on my floor, watching the sunlight trickle through my bedroom window. I hold up a tiny jar of sand from my mom's box and stretch out my arm, my gaze following the tiny granules running along the side as I flip it upside down, over and over again. The feeling slowly grows with every turn of the jar as I begin to think about Blake, and the list, and the eight days left to complete it.

And a way to figure all of this out so maybe Kiera will actually want to come back.

An idea begins to take shape. With time running out, I was thinking I'd just count the lake trip as my "get out of Huckabee" escape, but . . . maybe now is the perfect time to do it. Maybe I need to get out of Huckabee too.

I roll over and grab my phone, hitting the call button. It rings a few times before she picks up.

"Hey, Em," Blake says, her voice crackling noisily through the microphone. The middle-of-the-woods Huckabee phone service is almost as bad as whatever Misty Oasis is working with. "What's up?"

"Hey," I say, sitting up. "I know I said I was going to pack today, but . . . I changed my mind. You want to get out of here?"

Blake laughs, and I can picture her mischievous grin on the other end of the phone, her fingers reaching up to tuck a strand of her sun-streaked hair behind her ear. "I thought you'd never ask."

An hour later on the dot, Blake's faded blue pickup truck slides to a stop outside my house, two surfboards sticking out of the truck bed, that grin I'd pictured on the phone plastered on her face. She was more than game for a four-hour drive to the beach, just like I was equally game for spending the night when she mentioned her aunt had a beach house nearby so we didn't have to run right back.

If we're getting out of Huckabee, I want to do it right.

I glance behind me to see my dad leaning on the doorframe, his phone still pressed to his ear as the real estate agent drones on. I can't help but hesitate at the top of the porch steps.

What if they convince him to take a bad offer? Where are *we* going to move to? I feel like he's keeping me in the dark with all of this.

He puts his hand over the mouthpiece. "Text me when you get there, okay?"

He was so happy to hear that I had somewhere to go and something to do. His eyes have lit up every time I've asked for his permission these past couple of weeks. Probably because my absence means he can throw out even more stuff.

I watch him give Blake a big wave.

"Will do," I say curtly as I jog down the steps, my feet slowing and then stopping completely as I land on the bottom one.

This is the farthest trip I'll have gone on since my mom died, and I can't help but have all the worst-case scenarios circling around and around in my head.

What if he gets hurt at work, or doesn't put his seat belt on, or forgets to turn off the stove after making dinner?

What if I get back and something terrible has happened?

I spin around to face him, but I fight back the nervousness. Everything I've done so far has turned out fine. I have to trust this will too. "Love you."

His eyes crinkle at the corners. "Love you too," he mouths.

I jog the rest of the way to Blake's truck, yanking open the passenger door to chuck my backpack on the floor, already talking. "Surfboards, Blake? *Two* of them?" I say as I climb inside, moving to buckle my seat belt.

"It'll be fun! Not much harder than riding a bike," she says, which is like someone saying that a middle school play is the same as a Broadway performance.

I feel a surprise wave of excitement at the thought, the effects of jumping off a cliff and skinny-dipping, alongside Blake's calm and assured confidence, muting the risks and the fear, leaving only the thrill of the adventure.

"And to prepare, my grandma made enough breakfast burritos to feed everyone in Huckabee," Blake says as we pull off down the road. She tosses me a foil-wrapped log, hitting me square in the chest. "Never too late for a breakfast burrito."

My stomach growls as I carefully unwrap it, the smell of pico de gallo and cheese radiating off the lumpy tortilla brick.

I take a bite, and *holy shit* is it good. Even after the trek to my house, it's still warm and cheesy and delicious.

"This is incredible," I say, and Blake nods in agreement.

"She makes them almost every morning, and I still haven't gotten sick of them."

I devour it as we drive through the winding Huckabee roads, slowing to pull into an old gas station just before the highway entrance.

"My mom and I used to get scratch-offs here," I say. It startles me how naturally it comes out. That I'm actually *wanting* to talk about her, about moments beyond just the list. I lean out the open car window to toss the crumpled aluminum foil into the trash can while Blake tries to get the ancient pump to accept her credit card.

"I once won *big* on the Bingo Boogie card. I think I was in fifth grade."

"Oh yeah?" Blake asks, distracted as the card is declined yet again. Finally, she gives up and leans back against the truck, frustrated.

I poke her shoulder, nodding toward the store. "You're gonna have to go in and pay. These gas pumps are older than dirt."

"No surprise there," Blake mutters as she heads inside, her flip-flops clacking noisily as she walks.

I watch her go, wondering if this move has been harder for her than she lets on. Gas station pumps that hardly work. Bad phone service practically everywhere. A town so different from where she came from.

It can't be easy.

I pull out my phone while I wait, posting an Instagram story of the surfboards and writing "Blake is trying to kill me" just underneath it. My first of the summer.

I can't help but wonder if Matt will see it. Will he purposefully avoid watching it? I know Olivia will.

I glance up to see Blake pushing through the exit, a white plastic bag around her wrist. She fills up the truck and hops back into the driver's seat.

"What'd you get?" I ask.

She pulls out some Lay's chips, a package of Skittles, sour gummy worms, and a Hershey's chocolate bar. "Aaand," she says, reaching into the back pocket of her jean shorts to whip out two brightly colored scratch-off lottery tickets.

Bingo Boogie. I'd recognize that orange and pink anywhere.

It feels bittersweet to see it after all this time, the hand holding it out to me someone other than my mom.

"Pick one," she says. I reach out, hesitating over the right one before moving slowly over to the left, something about this card calling out to me. "You feeling lucky, Emily Clark?" she asks, stopping me in my tracks.

Lucky. I realize now that's what's drawing me to the card. *It looks lucky.*

I think about the past few weeks. The list. Blake. Matt. All of it.

When I think about it . . . I feel luckier than I have in three years.

I grab the card on the left and pull the quarter with a nick on it out of my pocket.

"Maybe a little."

18

The wind tugs at my hair, whipping wildly around my face as we drive. Blake glances over at me and my Cousin Itt impression, then pulls a hair tie off her wrist and holds it out to me with her free hand. I reach out, noticing just how tan her arm is compared to mine, a thin white line wrapping around her wrist where the hair tie sat. I wonder just how many days she's spent outside in her life, the sun absorbing into her skin, filling her hair with its rays. We don't get that kind of sun in Huckabee.

I smile gratefully before pulling my brown hair into a messy bun, my fingertips struggling to find and tame all the strays.

I look past her at Pennsylvania whizzing by, a sea of trees and farmland, Huckabee getting farther and farther away. It feels . . . good. Better than I could have expected, and with each mile that passes, the weight of the move and the town and everything that happened feels lighter and lighter.

I take a deep breath in, the warm air filling my lungs.

Soon the sun-filled summer will give way to a blistering winter, the trees surrounding us stripped of all their leaves, naked branches sitting against snow-filled skies. I try to picture Blake in the middle of it all, but I can't see it. Her tan shoulders covered up in a forest-green jacket, a knit hat pulled down over her sun-streaked hair. I try changing the jacket color in my mind, exchanging the knit hat for a thick wool scarf, but the image is still hazy.

She seems like she only exists in the summer. Only made to swim in the waters of the ocean, the smell of sunshine and salt clinging to her clothes.

She catches me staring at her, but it doesn't feel awkward. "What?"

I shake my head, turning my attention to the road in front of us. "Nothing." I think asking her what she smells like in winter would definitely cross into awkward territory.

I reach out to turn the music up, St. Vincent pouring out of the speakers. We've been taking turns picking songs, one after the other. I've liked all of Blake's suggestions. "Radio" by Sylvan Esso, "Bury a Friend" by Billie Eilish, "Ribs" by Lorde.

I throw in a couple of tracks by St. Vincent: "Fear the Future" and "Cruel."

"We should go to one of her concerts if she tours nearby," I say, and Blake nods eagerly.

"I hear she's incredible live."

Most of the trip has been like this. So far, aside from the concert, we've made plans to visit Jay and Claire in Kauai over spring break, using Johnny's extra air miles from work, and to *actually* go to Hank's for their meat loaf special, and to make kulolo, a traditional Hawaiian dessert.

It's exciting. Planning for the future. For adventures beyond this list.

"Do you think you'd like going to college in the city?" Blake asks.

I lean back, twisting my ponytail around my finger. "I've only been to New York City once. I went with my mom pretty close to Christmas when I was a kid." I think about the crowds, the energy, the towering buildings, all of it so different from Huckabee.

In a good way.

"But maybe? I think I might?" I shrug. "I haven't been there in years, so I can't really say."

"We should take a trip there sometime! Hang out, see a musical, maybe visit a couple of colleges."

Maybe visit a couple of colleges.

I nod, actually . . . excited by the idea. "We could do like a college road trip, maybe?" The truck engine growls loudly underneath us, struggling to accelerate past fifty-five.

Blake smirks and reaches out to pat the dash. "Totally game. But we *may* have to borrow someone's car for that."

Pennsylvania turns into New Jersey, and the air starts to smell like salt water the closer and closer we get to the beach. The sun slowly nears the horizon as we park, and my swimsuit digs into my skin after the long drive.

I run my fingers along the strap as Blake unhooks the surfboards, handing me the smaller of the two, littered in stickers.

"That one's mine," she says.

"Yeah, Blake. I figured. Something tells me Johnny wouldn't have a sticker that says 'National Parks are for lovers.'"

She laughs and nudges me, the point where her skin meets mine buzzing as we lug the surfboards up to the beach. Everything about her relaxes as the water comes into view. The second we set foot on the sand, it's like a barrier breaks. Her shoulders drop, completely free from tension. I watch her take in a deep breath, her chest rising and falling.

"I missed this," she says.

I study her face, realizing how hard these past few weeks must have been for her. How well she's been hiding how much she's missing home and her friends and her life there.

"You wish you were back there?" I ask, looking out at the dark tan sand, a piece of trash sticking out every thirty feet or so. "I mean, not that Hawaii could ever compare to *this*."

She squints out at the water, slowly letting out a long sigh. "I definitely miss it. I think it was hard to leave the place that had so much of my mom in it, you know? The place my parents fell in love, and the beaches they hung out on, and the place I grew up. Especially when I feel so far away from her already."

I nod. I can *definitely* understand that.

"And, to be honest, I miss my friends. I miss my grandparents. I miss all the familiar places and things and people." She glances over at me for a fraction of a second before looking back at the water, swallowing. "But if I were back there, I wouldn't have become friends with you."

A warm feeling swims into my chest. We're silent for a moment, and I hold up the surfboard.

"You going to teach me what exactly to do with this thing? I mean, if I wanted to drown at the beach, I probably could've found a way to do it without the prop."

"Nope," she says, smirking as we walk down to the surf. "I figured I'd let you wing it."

She shows me how to paddle out, from finding the "sweet spot" on the board to how to work with the wave instead of against it. Luckily, the water is pretty calm at low tide, and I manage to get out to the smoother water on my fourth try without getting absolutely wrecked, the swell of the current not strong enough to pull me completely under.

But I'm not as familiar with the ocean as Blake is, so it's a bit scary feeling the pull of the waves, dipping and fighting the board underneath me. I like the ocean, but I've only been here a handful of times, mostly when I was younger, with my parents, and once with my friends back in eighth grade.

And as I paddle, I realize I . . . don't exactly love being out here, surrounded by *so* much water, my trust dependent solely on a giant kickboard.

But Blake's confidence steadies me, her voice telling me to move with the pull instead of against it, and slowly I'm able to work with the board, with my fear and uncertainty, instead of against it.

I can't help but think of my conversation with Blake at the picnic. About Matt. About me and what *being* me means. Because I see now it isn't just about being daring, and skinny-dipping, and jumping off cliffs.

It's also about being afraid and sad and uncertain, and *all* the parts of myself, even if they're the parts my friends don't want to see. It's about being real and honest, like I am at this exact moment, everything else fading away until there's this moment of calm and clarity, just me, and Blake, and the water around us.

Soon we're sitting on the surfboards just as the sun begins to set on the horizon, my legs dangling over either side as the sky begins to turn orange and purple and deep blue, the water mirroring it, filling itself with the same colors.

I let out a breath I feel like I've been holding for a million years, Huckabee and Matt and the move releasing their grip on me, just for a little while. For the first time in years, so far away from all of it, I feel free. Free of expectations and pressure, fears and worst-case-scenarios, broken friend groups, and senior year, and an entire town that thinks they know exactly who you are.

Free to just be . . . myself. To think about who that actually is.

What was my mom feeling that made her put this on the list?

Did she feel boxed in too? The straight-A student who had bombed the SATs, searching for something more? Something *outside* of Huckabee?

But then . . . I think of my mom as I knew her and how she never really did get out of Huckabee. How she said Huckabee had everything. Was that really true, though? What made her change her mind?

Because, being here, I can't help but think she was wrong. I can't help but wonder what *my* life could be like if I left.

I look up to see seagulls flying overhead, free and happy as they coast through the air.

"Just like your bracelet," I say, and Blake cranes her neck to look up at them, nodding in agreement.

"Here," she says. I look down to see the bracelet in her open palm, seagulls identical to the ones that just flew by stamped carefully onto it.

I reach out and she takes my hand, her fingers carefully moving to wrap the bracelet around my wrist. "Your mom gave it to my dad when they were in high school, and my dad gave it to me when we were moving to Huckabee. He said she got it on a beach trip they went on. I've honestly been trying to find a time to give it to you, and, well . . . this feels pretty perfect," she says, snapping it on. "It's made its way home now."

It's like my question is answered. I look down at the bracelet and realize . . . she did feel like this. She *knew*.

She found that feeling in Huckabee. With Dad and me.

Tears spring into my eyes and I move to wipe them away, but Blake gets there first, her hand finding my cheek, her thumb gently catching them as they fall.

My heart begins to race as I look at her the same way I did last night at the pool, the setting sun painting all her features in a golden light, from her honey-colored eyes to her full lips.

Only this time, I've pulled all my walls down, making room for a realization to swim into my stomach that I've been avoiding since even before my mom got sick.

Blake looks straight at me, her gaze so steady, it nearly pulls the truth right out of me.

19

The summer my mom was diagnosed was the year I did my one-week stint at Misty Oasis.

There was a girl in my bunk. Dominique Flores.

I remember how cool I thought she was. How nice her black hair looked in a ponytail. How my cheeks turned bright red every time she talked to me.

I remember the bus ride home from camp, the tiny pang of something that I now recognize as heartbreak over maybe never seeing her again (or, *definitely* never seeing her again, because I was sure as hell NOT going back to Misty Oasis, no matter how much Kiera begged).

I wanted nothing more than to get off that bus and talk to my mom about it. To tell her while we were unpacking that night, or to sit on the floor of her closet the next morning as she was getting ready, the confusing mess of these unexpected feelings from this past week spilling from my lips.

But the second I saw my mom when I got off the bus, I knew something was wrong. In the car ride home, she didn't talk about the bingo fundraiser happening the next day, and she kept rolling the lucky quarter around and around in her hands.

That's when I noticed it.

The Band-Aid where an IV had been. The dark circles under her eyes. Months of headaches and dizziness and nausea finally investigated . . . and added up to stage IV cancer.

We got so swept up in doctor's appointments, and surgeries, and my mom getting sicker and sicker, withering away before my eyes, that I just ignored it. I pushed it down. Our closet time in the morning turned into her perched on the edge of the bed while I brought her a change of sweatpants or an oversize T-shirt. Our bingo fundraiser Fridays turned into late nights at the hospital, machines beeping noisily all around us while I ran to the vending machine to get her a snack she would be too nauseous to eat. Her brown hair, identical to mine, was cut short and then, in the blink of an eye, gone completely.

Soon the feeling was nothing more than a tiny blip on my radar, something so small and insignificant compared to everything else going on. And then Matt began showing up to keep me company in the hospital, bringing my mom flowers, and holding my hand in waiting rooms, my mom whispering to finally give him a chance. Looking so certain about this one thing. This boy I'd been partners in crime with all through middle school, who had an unyielding crush on me, was there when I'd needed someone more than anything.

So, I finally did.

But the blip never went away. After my mom died, it just became impossible to face.

The sobering thought of Matt and my mom brings me crashing back to reality, to the course set for me all those years ago. Which is probably why I pull away from Blake so hard that the entire surfboard tips and I go splashing into the water.

I get caught in the surf and washing-machine my way to the shore, head over heels, surfboard flying from my grip as my nose fills with enough salt water to make my brain hurt. Just when I think I've regained my footing, another wave takes me out, launching me out of the water like a Fourth of July firework. I lie on the sand, gasping for air while Blake rescues the board, *then* comes over to see how I'm doing.

Nice to know she's got her priorities in check.

"You good?" she asks, trying not to laugh at my dramatically shipwrecked self.

I grimace and sit up, sand plastered to my back, seaweed stuck to the side of my head. "Blake, I swear . . . if you laugh, I will . . ."

My voice trails off as she ducks her head, her shoulders silently shaking with laughter. I peel the seaweed off my face, not in the mood to joke just yet, and grab the surfboard, heading back up the beach to the truck.

"Em! Come on. I'm sorry," she calls, chasing after me.

I don't say anything as we drop off the surfboards and grab our stuff to get changed.

When I'm locked tightly in the bathroom changing stall, I turn around, leaning my head against the back of the door.

Come on, Em.

I'm not going to ruin my night of freedom over a capsized surfboard. And some . . . pretty enormous butterflies.

When I duck outside, Blake is standing there holding two oversize cones of pink cotton candy, the white cone invisible underneath all the poof. She holds one out to me, a sheepish grin on her face.

"Sorry I laughed at you."

I take it, nudging her lightly. "It's okay."

We walk along the worn wood of the boardwalk, dodging in and out of people, the air filled with voices and laughter, the sweet, sugary cotton-candy cloud melting on my tongue. A bell rings noisily next to us, announcing a victory in the water-gun-race game, the reward an oversize bear, roughly the same size as Blake's dog, Winston.

Blake pauses, her eyes following the bear through the crowd. "Do you want to—"

The money is already out of my wallet and in the vendor's hands, her sentence left unfinished. I slide onto one of the open wobbly stools, ready to go.

Blake sits down next to me, two kids and an old man taking up the remaining three spots.

The vendor goes over the rules while I close one of my eyes and line up my water gun.

Shoot water at target. Raise platform with creepy bear on it. Win prize.

Easy.

"Ready to lose, Clark?" Blake whispers as the vendor starts counting down from three.

"You wish." I smack her water gun out of alignment and start firing my own at the sound of the bell, hitting the target instantly, my red bear soaring through the air to narrowly beat the grandpa two seats over.

"Damn," Blake says as the alarm bell rings noisily over our heads. I look over to see her yellow bear hardly moved an inch. "I took my contacts out to go in the ocean and I literally can't see anything. My eyes were too dry to put them back in."

"Excuses, excuses," I say as I'm rewarded with one enormous bear, a bumblebee-yellow bow tied neatly around its neck.

I turn around to see Blake digging around in her backpack. She pulls out a glasses case, grimacing as she flicks it open and puts on a familiar pair of glasses, bigger than the state of Texas and nearly identical to the pair all those years ago.

She. Looks. Adorable.

She groans. "They're awful, aren't they?"

"Definitely not." I shake my head. "They're really cute, actually." I feel my cheeks turn bright red at the words.

But not redder than Blake's.

Her eyebrows rise, incredulous, her eyes slightly magnified by the thick lenses. "Wait. Really?"

"Yeah," I say with a nod. "Very Christmas 2011."

Once her glasses are on, it's game over for me. Literally.

She wins ring toss, balloon darts, *and* Skee-Ball, our hands lightly brushing together as we walk from stand to stand, tiny stuffed animal heads sticking out of Blake's backpack. Every time her fingers graze the back of my hand, it's like a shock of electricity, warm and tingly in a way that's new and unfamiliar.

As we head back to the truck, we stop at a snack stand filled with brightly colored signs shouting, FUNNEL CAKE! BEST ON THE BOARDWALK! and, FRESHLY SQUEEZED LEMONADE! even though I can see the tub of lemonade mix still sitting on the back counter. We get the two-for-five-dollars hot dog special, complete with two plastic cups filled to the brim with not-so-fresh lemonade, and drive the two blocks to her aunt's house, eating the hot dogs along the way.

When we get there, a female Johnny Carter in a white button-down and flip-flops throws open the door to the small white bungalow, directing us to drive around to the backyard. I've only seen her in pictures or heard stories about her from Mrs. Carter. She moved out of Huckabee right after high school and only comes back when she absolutely has to.

"Aunt Lisa!" Blake says, her door screeching open. She hops out to give the woman a hug.

"Nine o'clock," Aunt Lisa says, checking her watch. "You kept me up past my bedtime! You know daybreak is the best time to surf around here."

She smiles at me, one arm still slung over Blake's shoulder. "You must be Emily! God, you look just like your mom."

Should've known it was coming. But it doesn't sting as much as it used to, Blake's words from that day we found the box becoming my reality this summer, keeping her memory alive.

A warm feeling comes with it, radiating across my chest.

I smile politely. "Thanks for letting us stay—"

"In my *backyard*?" She snorts, throwing her hands up.

We're planning on camping out in the back of Blake's pickup truck in an effort to get "6. Sleep under the stars" checked off the list too.

"Oh, come on, Aunt Lisa. You're telling me you didn't do worse when you were our age?" Blake says, the two sharing an identical mischievous look, eyebrows raised, smirks plastered on their faces.

"You got me there, Blake," she says as we head up the back steps and through a screen door to a covered back porch, decorated with blue-and-white-striped outdoor furniture, a white ceiling fan chugging away above us. I pull out my phone and shoot my dad a quick text to let him know we're here.

"So, how's Huckabee treating you?" Aunt Lisa says as we plunk down in the chairs. She swings her feet up to rest on the small wooden coffee table. "I'm honestly surprised you didn't bail to come see me sooner."

"Not too bad. Definitely still getting used to . . ." Her voice trails off as she searches for the right word. "Well, *everything*, I guess."

"Yeah." Aunt Lisa nods. "I don't think I *ever* got used to it. And I was *born* there!"

She asks us about what we've been up to this summer, and while we leave out the list, we fill her in on our cliff-jumping adventure, and skinny-dipping at the Huckabee Pool, and stealing an apple from Snyder's Orchard.

She laughs at the last one. "Oh, you bet your ass I tried that once. Got tackled about halfway through the Gala section. Had a mean black eye for a week."

Soon we all start yawning, and Aunt Lisa takes us inside to get some pillows.

The bungalow is just as cute inside as it is outside. Wooden floors, with white walls and light-colored furniture, high ceilings with exposed beams.

"Bathroom is through there," Aunt Lisa says, leading us down a small hallway. She points to a door. "Spare bedroom is here," she adds, pushing another open with her foot. She starts handing us pillows off the two twin beds just inside. "If it gets too cold out there and you guys weenie out, you're welcome to just pop right in here. I'll leave the back door unlocked."

She throws a buffalo-check blanket onto Blake's pile, completely covering her like a ghost.

"Looks like you're all set," she says, chuckling to herself as we head back down the hallway to the screen door. She holds it open for us as we stumble outside. "Let me know if y'all need anything else. Otherwise, I'll see you for breakfast tomorrow morning."

"Thank you!" we chorus, the screen door closing behind her.

Blake takes the surfboards out of the back and lays the blanket out in the truck bed for us to sit on. Both of us hop up to sit against the cab, the mound of pillows just behind us, what's left of our oversize lemonades clutched in our hands. I can still hear the whisper of the ocean, the tide coming and going.

When Blake's arm brushes up against mine, like it did so many times on the boardwalk, I don't pull away. I don't know if it's purposeful, or purely an accident, but for just a moment, for just tonight, I let myself be right where I am. Right here with her.

It fills my chest up with a feeling that makes the lemonade sweeter, the night alive, the wind tugging at my wet hair as we sit here together, the soft hum of a radio somewhere in the distance.

I look over at Blake as she reaches out to grab a pillow, catching sight of a tattoo just under her black bralette, visible through the hole in her tank top, "I love you" painted neatly across her rib cage.

"I like your tattoo," I say, wondering what it would be like to reach out and touch it. To trace the words. "I didn't know you had one."

Blake glances down at the writing on her side, smiling. "It's my mom's handwriting. She wrote me a letter the day before she went into labor." Her face is thoughtful as she carefully props the pillow up behind her. "It's like she knew, you know? It's like she knew she wouldn't make it."

"Maybe she did. Maybe, on some level, she knew." For the first time in a long time, I think about my mom on the day she died. "The week before my mom died, she was in so much pain." They tried everything. Morphine. Fentanyl patches. None of it worked. "Then, on the last day, she was . . . completely peaceful. There was almost this calm that settled around the room. Like she knew it was coming."

We're both silent for a minute, the only sound the hum of the radio, the crashing of the waves as they roll steadily onto the sand, falling over one another.

"What did it say? Her letter?" I ask.

Blake takes her glasses off and leans her head back. "A lot of stuff. That she loved me. That she wanted me to live a full and happy life. That I was her favorite person in the world and she hadn't even really met me yet." A smile pulls at her lips. "But also stuff that means something new to me *now*, you know? She had a line in there like, 'Take it from me, Blake, even the most unexpected places and people can turn into the greatest adventures.' And then I moved to *Huckabee*, and met you, and it became real in a whole new way. I feel like every time I read it, I get something else out of it."

I can't deny the fact that I literally stop breathing for a second at her words.

"I definitely get that," I say when my air finally returns, and Blake shifts to look at me.

"What's it like?" she asks. "Doing the list?"

"Well, it's kind of like what you said that day at my house. It's made me feel closer to her." I think for a minute, about how much has changed since the day I found the list. How much *I* have changed, the list and my mom guiding me forward in new and unexpected ways. That moment of clarity I had at the beach about getting out of Huckabee. The free fall of the cliff jump. Even this moment now, talking about her. "It's more than that, though. Doing this list has made me feel more like myself again. More like I did before . . ."

My voice trails off and I shrug, shaking my head. "I don't know. It's made me feel like I don't have to worry about losing everything all the time, or getting hurt, or having everything come crumbling down around me. Like I can take a risk and everything won't be the worst-case scenario just because it once was. Like I'm . . . I don't know."

"Lucky?" Blake asks, and the word feels electric.

It's the word my mom would use.

"Yeah," I say, nodding, the word feeling right for the first time in a long time, not a burden or a lie anymore. A feeling I thought had completely run out. A feeling I thought I would never get back. "Lucky."

"That makes it more than a bucket list, then. It's a *lucky* list," Blake says, and I can't help but like the sound of it.

"God, that's so my mom," I say. "She was lucky right up until she got cancer, let me tell you that."

Blake's silent, leaving a space for me to continue or to bail.

For once, I don't bail. I let myself feel everything, let the pain and the hurt come seeping in.

"She was like a walking rabbit's foot, always jumping into things like the odds were already in her favor. Like they *had* to be. I remember going to the Huckabee Fall Festival, and she put *one* raffle ticket in for the grand prize basket. People buy *thousands* of tickets for that, and she won it with one." I shake my head, remembering how outraged Jim Donovan had been. "She was always so sure. Even when she started having these bad headaches and dizzy spells, I think she thought she was fine. I think *I* thought she was fine."

I picture her lying on the couch, a compress pressed to her head while she waited for the pain pill to kick in.

"That summer, I went to Misty Oasis, where my best friend is now. I knew she was finally going to the doctor while I was away, but I just . . . wasn't even worried about it. I didn't think anything of it."

Tears spring into my eyes, but I fight to keep going, words I've kept hidden inside tumbling out. "I *should* have been. Stage four. Glioblastoma. I should have pushed her to go to the doctor sooner. I should have stayed by her side every minute. Even after her diagnosis, I thought she would beat the odds, because she always had. I thought she would beat the odds because *she* thought she would. Up until the last week."

I take a deep breath, picturing my mom, her body frail, her face sunken in, the way her hand felt in mine on that last day. Bony and weak and fragile. The unfamiliar look on her face, *knowing* what was coming. Saying it was fine when it *wasn't*. We could've at least had a fighting chance if she had been more careful. If she had gone to the doctors sooner. "It was like all the bad luck she never had hit at once. It wasn't one of those small miracles where they say you have weeks to live and you get months, or a year, or a decade. They gave her six months, and she didn't make it two." I look over at Blake. "Her luck ran out, Blake. *My* luck ran out."

"Hey," she says, reaching out, her hand finding my forearm. "Emily, you can't think like that." She scoots closer, our legs touching. "You can't measure a person's life like that." I look up to see her face is serious. "I mean, if that were the case, then I would have to live my life thinking I was the reason my mom died, you know? That I was the worst and most unlucky thing to ever happen to my parents."

I think about Johnny and the way he looks at Blake like she's every good thing in the world balled into one. Which she really might be.

"Even though our moms lived such short lives, think about how much *good* they had in them. The people they meant something to. The lives they touched. The adventures they had. The lists they finished. They were lucky, Em. We're *all* lucky, not because everything works out, but because we get to wake up in the morning and take chances and make mistakes and keep trying not to."

I keep quiet, letting her words ring through me. I want to believe them so badly.

Every moment of this summer so far runs through my mind. From frantically searching for answers on a page, to jumping off a cliff, to skinny-dipping in the Huckabee Pool, to right now—not running away from what might happen but running toward something, some new vision of who I could be. The person that I've been too scared to imagine without her here.

But *I'm* still here—I still have time to try.

I want to.

I take a deep, grateful breath, for the glittering stars above us, for my mom and the lucky list, bringing me here. But also for Blake Carter, the girl who suggested I do the list in the first place. The girl who has been by my side every step of the way, speaking French, and encouraging me to try new things, and assuring me *everything will be fine* with that mischievous grin of hers. The girl whose hand is only a finger length away from mine, resting on the red and black blanket she laid out on the bottom of her truck bed.

Just the idea of reaching out and touching it feels like an entire firework display is going off inside me.

And I wouldn't be holding it as she helps me climb to the top of a cliff, or grabbing it to run off the pool deck before a patrol car can catch us.

I'd be holding it because I . . .

I stop breathing as I reach for her, Blake inhaling sharply as our hands finally find each other's in the dark, our fingers touching ever so gently, my hand dancing around hers to slide slowly into her palm. Neither of us is looking at the other, but I can feel the electricity in the air, my head swimming in a way I have never felt before as her thumb traces circles on the back of my hand.

This time the only counting I'm doing is how many seconds I can make this moment last.

20

The first thing I feel when I wake up is Blake's hand still in mine.

Then, opening my eyes, I see her face, inches from mine, eyes still closed. She looks completely peaceful, so beautiful and serene in the morning light, a strand of her sun-streaked hair tangled in her dark eyelashes.

I reach out with my free hand, wanting to brush it away, but there's a loud bang as the screen door flies open. My fingertips recoil quickly into my palm, as Aunt Lisa's voice calls out to us.

"Breakfast is in five, ladies! Get it while it's hot!"

Blake's eyes slowly open, meeting mine. I hold her gaze for a long moment, then finally look away when my cheeks begin to burn. I don't want her to think I'm creepily watching her sleep.

I pull my fingers out of her grip and sit up, sliding carefully to the edge of the truck bed, my eyes searching the light blue horizon, the magic from last night still lingering in the air, but fainter now in the light of day.

She groans, following just behind me. "Listen, I'm not saying that wasn't fun," she says as she slides past me, hopping down onto the grass, rubbing at her left shoulder. "But sleeping in the back of a truck was not one of our best ideas."

I laugh and jump down after her, my back letting out a sympathy twang of pain. The hard metal of the truck bed was pretty unforgiving. We collect the pillows and the blankets, shuffling toward the screen door.

"Admit it," Blake says over the top of her armful of pillows. "How many times did you think about bailing to sleep inside?"

I snort and hold the door open for her. "Only seven times. Maybe eight. You?"

I don't add that I don't know if it was because of the hard truck bed, or the fact that it was hard to get any sleep at all with her so close to me.

"Not even once," she says, stopping me in my tracks. I don't want to think her words mean more than they do, but I still feel a tiny swell of hope in the pit of my stomach.

I mask it by narrowing my eyes suspiciously at her as we drop the pillows off in the spare room. "Bullshit," I say, and she breaks.

"Practically every hour on the hour," she admits as she slides past me into the hallway, close enough to send goose bumps up and down the length of my arm.

"We must be getting close," I say to Blake as the smell of manure comes wafting into the truck. As if on cue, the both of us start frantically rolling up our windows to block out the scent.

She nods, glancing at the GPS on her phone. "Under half an hour."

I press my forehead against the glass and watch the familiar farmlands roll by, my long sigh condensing on the glass of the window.

I almost understand how Kiera must be feeling. I mean, after yesterday, I don't exactly want to go back to Huckabee either.

It was hard to leave Aunt Lisa's this morning, the beach and the sun and the possibilities. My return to Huckabee feels like crash-landing into reality in a lot of ways, but even still, the closer and closer we get, I feel . . . hopeful.

I tuck my leg underneath me as I scroll through my pictures from our trip. I keep scrolling back, through the photos I've taken this summer, through every item I've ticked off the list, through junior and sophomore year, farther and farther and farther until I find myself face-to-face again with Mom and her tattoo.

In the midst of winter, I found there was, within me, an invincible summer.

The words that I couldn't make sense of then suddenly mean something to me now, the same way they had meant something to her. After everything that had happened, I was so . . . stuck. So deep in winter, it didn't seem like I'd find a way out. All I saw was the ways I could break.

But when I'm riding around with Blake, or sitting in the bed of her pickup truck, or tackling a new adventure, I feel it. I feel invincible.

Like she did.

That summer, and raising me, and even on that very last day, her hand in mine, the room filled with absolute calm. The cancer couldn't even touch her anymore.

And it's that invincible feeling that nudges me to flip from my mom's tattoo to the Sycamore Street Tattoos Instagram account. Immediately, I see a cartoon pair of tighty-whities, complete with arms and a face, holding up a sign reading: NATIONAL UNDERWEAR DAY TATTOO SPECIAL!

I mean, *who* would get a tattoo for National Underwear Day? Except, well . . .

"Blake," I say, not wanting this adventure to end just yet. "Let's do this." I hold up my phone, and she glances quickly at it.

"National Underwear Day? What even is that?"

"What, you've never celebrated?"

"Has *anyone*?"

I glance down at my phone, the tiny cartoon underwear eyes in the Sycamore Street picture staring back at me. "The tattoo parlor in town always has these discount specials around random national holidays." I double-tap the photo, giving it a like. "You can get a tattoo for, like, fifty bucks. They've got a huge clearance binder and everything."

"Wait. A *clearance* binder? A clearance binder of tattoos?" Blake asks. "That's . . ."

"That's Huckabee," I say with a laugh.

"Valid point." She nods, pausing to scan the farmlands all around us. "What are you going to get?"

"I have a good idea," I say, reaching out to plug Sycamore Street Tattoos into the GPS.

The inside of the tattoo parlor is surprisingly dark, considering the detail I imagine is required for tattooing.

The walls are lined with brightly colored designs, framed in an attempt at preservation, but the corners are still yellowing with age. Black fold-out chairs sit underneath them, the seats off-kilter. It's a Russian roulette game to pick the one that won't collapse underneath you.

I peer past the big counter to the room behind it, where, in front of a faded red curtain, a huge guy with a big gray beard and a red bandanna is in the middle of tattooing an intricate heart on the wrist of Katie Moore, the older sister of a girl in my grade.

You would never think that the best offensive lineman Huckabee High had ever seen could tattoo something so delicate, but Big Eddie is a real artist. And also a total softie. I think he maybe cried the hardest at my mom's funeral, and they'd only been in homeroom together at school.

"Hey, Big Eddie!" I call out to him.

He glances up, beaming when he sees it's me, his eyes practically disappearing behind his round cheeks. "Emily! You here for the special?"

I nod, patting the enormous binder sitting on the front counter, pages of designs overflowing out of it. Blake leans over my shoulder, her face lighting up when she sees the faded black Sharpie on the cover: CLEARINSE BINDER.

"Let's hope he tattoos better than he spells," she whispers to me.

I elbow her in the side, and she elbows me right back, a big grin appearing on her face.

"You're not gonna chicken out this time, are ya?" Big Eddie asks, the tattoo gun buzzing again as he leans back over the girl's wrist.

I grimace, cringing. I look over to see Blake open her mouth to tease me. "Say a word and I will never talk to you again."

"That'll be pretty tough considering I'm your ride home," she says, leaning casually against the counter.

I give her a look before turning my attention back to Eddie. "Can I maybe get something *not* in the clearance binder?"

"No can do, Em," he says, his eyes focused on the tattoo he's doing. "You know the rules of the special."

My heart sinks, but I refuse to turn back now. Yeah, this is an invincible summer. But it's *mine*.

Maybe my tattoo doesn't have to be the same as Mom's.

Maybe this should be for me.

Determined, I lean over the pages of the binder. A purple butterfly, a devil smoking a cigarette, a cup of coffee with a halo, a disheveled-looking goat. I have no idea how these were all squeezed together on the same sheet of paper, but all the pages are like that.

No theme. Just tiny, random drawings spread out on a blanket of white.

Blake points at a piece of pizza wearing sunglasses, amused. "Where would you even put a tattoo like that?"

"Oh, that's a definite butt tattoo," I say.

"Well, pizza does go straight to your ass."

We keep looking, the binder slowly passing the halfway point. I feel a small pit of dread deep in my stomach, as I begin to worry that I won't find anything. Nothing that really *means* something.

I put my hand into my pocket, fingers wrapping instinctively around the quarter.

Two more pages go by. Then another three.

Nothing.

I turn the page once more, and suddenly there it is, calling out to me. A small sunflower, the deep yellow the same warm color as the sunflowers in my mom's garden. The same ones my dad lays on my mom's grave every year.

It's like a *sign* from her. Something real and significant in this massive binder of comical images. Lucky.

I push away from the heavy binder, nodding determinedly, the dread releasing its grip on me.

"You picked one?" Blake asks, her eyes scanning the page eagerly.

"Yeah, it's—"

She grabs my arm, stopping me. "Shh! I want to guess."

She narrows her eyes but doesn't pull her hand away, looking between me and the images, her dark eyebrows furrowing as she makes her way down the page.

Finally, she taps the sunflower, peering up at me eagerly. "Sunflowers! Like your mom's garden." I nod, a warm feeling filling my chest at her validation.

"I mean, it was a tough call between that and the dancing donut. . . ."

"Fair," she says, sliding out of the way as Big Eddie lumbers over with the freshly tattooed girl.

"What'll it be?" he asks as he reaches under the counter to grab a clipboard.

I point to the sunflower and he nods, giving Blake a quick look before grabbing some paperwork and sliding it into the metal clasp of the clipboard.

"You getting one?" he asks.

Blake shakes her head. "Not today! May come back for the slice of pizza in the sunglasses, though."

Big Eddie holds out the clipboard to me and lets out a low chuckle. "You'd be surprised the number of people that get that one." His eyes shift over to meet mine. "Where you getting yours at, Em?"

I tap the bare skin of my forearm, trying to imagine that space no longer smooth and blank. I wonder if it felt weird to her too, if she chose that spot because she'd always see it and be reminded.

He nods to the black fold-out chairs. "Look over all these documents and give them a signature. I'll get everything ready."

I manage to pick the structurally safe fold-out chair, but Blake, on the other hand, has the plastic seat buckle almost completely out from under her. She perches unsteadily on the edge of the chair, her eyes wide as she waits for a total collapse.

Her expression cracks me up so much that it takes everything in me to turn my attention back to the clipboard in front of me.

I scan it while Big Eddie rings up Katie, then preps everything for my tattoo. Most of it is pretty self-explanatory, talking about infection and how Big Eddie always sanitizes everything and uses clean needles and all that.

Even though I can literally *see* him doing it now, a month ago I would have been running for the door after Googling tattoo-related infections, the worst-case scenarios guiding my decision.

Like this past February when I came with Kiera.

There's no denying the fact that the thoughts still come this time. But, when they do, I think about just how great this tattoo will be. How another list item will be checked off. How my mom must have felt in this exact moment.

The weight of these thoughts far outweighs the worst-case-scenario ones, pushing me forward as I sign on the dotted line, my fear no longer debilitating.

Big Eddie heads back up to take the clipboard, motioning to the faux-leather tattoo chair sitting empty in the middle of the room.

I walk over and slide into it, my legs squeaking noisily against the leather as I perch on the edge. Big Eddie has me put my arm up on the armrest, cleaning it with rubbing alcohol. I'm surprised when he pulls out a razor to shave down the faint brown hair on my right arm, the skin underneath prickling. He puts down a stencil of the sunflower, transferring it onto my arm with water, his thick fingers working carefully as he slowly pulls the paper away.

And suddenly there it is. My soon-to-be tattoo. I exhale slowly, taking it in.

"Look all right?" he asks. "There's a mirror over there if you want to double-check."

I push myself up and walk over to the mirror attached to the back of a worn closet door, turning my arm right and left in the reflection. The flower stands out against my pale skin. A lot. My eyes find Blake's in the reflection, and I hesitate, but she nods with absolute certainty, her arms crossed.

"It's the perfect thing to get. Your mom would love it."

I swallow hard on the tears that begin to bubble up at her words and head back to the tattoo chair, putting my arm back up on the armrest.

Big Eddie gets all the ink ready while Blake wheels a stool over, sitting down across from him, and suddenly he's asking me, "You ready?"

And that's when my eyes find the glimmering silver needle.

"Uh," I manage to get out. Big Eddie stops in his tracks and gives me a once-over.

Am I ready to do this? I think of all the other items on the list. How I don't regret doing a single one.

Everything my mom had on it has led me to feeling closer to not only her . . .

But also to the person I actually want to be. And this is a reminder of that.

Blake scoots the stool closer and holds out her hand to me. The same hand I held last night, underneath a blanket of stars. "You can squeeze it when it hurts, okay?" she says. "It'll be over in no time."

I pry my fingers off the armrest, placing my sweaty palm in

her very dry and very soft hand, her fingers folding safely over mine, the feeling familiar and dizzying and distracting.

"All good?" Big Eddie asks again, the tattoo gun buzzing.

This time I nod.

He presses down, and the pressure goes from nagging to unpleasant to painful. I grimace, squeezing Blake's hand tighter as the pain swells from an uncomfortable prickle to blindingly overpowering.

Even when my grip tightens hard enough for her fingers to lose color, or the bones to pop straight out, Blake never pulls her hand away. She sticks by me, just like she has this entire summer.

I squeeze my eyes shut and count to five, over and over again in my head, until the buzzing stops, giving way to absolute silence.

I pop one eye open and then the other, peering down to see the result.

It looks different from the one drawn on the page of that thick binder, something about the colors and the shape transforming underneath these dim tattoo parlor lights.

The sunflower on my arm looks *alive*. Like it was plucked straight from my mom's garden. The petals are an identical, glowing yellow, the stem a soft green.

"Good?" Big Eddie asks hesitantly.

I nod, trying again not to cry. "It looks *just* like the flowers from my mom's garden. Thank you."

It's a part of her. A part of me. A part of *us* that can never be taken away. No matter where I go, I'll always have this.

He puts a clear wrap over it, taping it carefully down as he goes over basic care instructions. For once in my life, I hardly listen, my eyes fixed on the sunflower and the bright red skin around it. My vision blurs as I think about my mom's forearm, her tattoo in the same spot as mine, another shared experience we've now had.

I didn't think we'd have any more of those, and now I have so many of them.

I finally relax and let go of Blake's hand as we walk to the front, my palm tingling without the constant pressure of hers against it. She flexes her fingers, grinning at me.

"They all still work! I'm shocked," she teases.

I smile at her as I pay Big Eddie. A warm, happy feeling begins to build, swelling like a balloon until it takes up my entire chest.

Soon I am pushing through the front door, the bells looped around the handle ringing noisily behind me.

"I fucking did it! I got a tattoo!" I scream to the empty street, adrenaline coursing through my veins.

Blake gives me a big smile, watching with an amused expression as I dance around.

Before I can process what I'm doing, I throw my arms around her, my skin buzzing as her hands wrap around my waist and my chin rests on her shoulder.

I pull away before she can feel how fast my heart is beating.

21

When we pull up to my house, I'm surprised to see that my dad is home, his truck sitting in the driveway.

"That's weird," I mutter as I slide into a zip-up hoodie from my backpack.

It's a Monday afternoon. He should be at work. He's *always* at work.

I feel my stomach flip-flop with nerves, the worst-case scenarios inevitably swimming into my head. I hope everything is okay.

"Thanks, Blake," I call as I throw open my door, scooping up my enormous teddy bear. I pause to meet her warm brown eyes, my stomach flip-flopping for a different reason. I glance toward the house and let out a long sigh. "I kind of . . . don't want to go."

She flashes me a smile that lights up her whole face, the gap in her teeth showing. "You could hop back in and I'll head right back to

Sycamore Street Tattoos. Turn that sunflower into a whole sleeve."

I laugh, the two of us falling silent as we look at each other, the same energy from last night filling the air.

"See you at the lake trip?" she asks.

I nod. "Wouldn't miss it."

I close the door and wave before jogging quickly up the driveway and the porch steps to throw open the front door.

"Dad?" I call as I kick my sand-laden flip-flops off and cross the threshold. "You here? Is everything all right?"

"Em!" He pops his head out of the kitchen, like he's been waiting for me to get back. I study his face, relieved to see he's fine. Everything is fine. "Drop your stuff! I've got a surprise for you."

I drop my backpack by the stairs like he said, placing the bear on top of it, but narrow my eyes at him, suspicious. "A surprise?" I ask, watching as he grabs his car keys off the entryway table. He opts for his nonwork boots instead of his work boots, the only difference being distinctly less mud, yet *another* weird sign. "You have off today?"

"Took the afternoon off," he says, spinning the key ring around on his finger, like this is totally normal. He's still in his white Smith & Tyler T-shirt, a smattering of dirt on his chest, but an enormous smile is plastered on his face. He tilts his head eagerly as he pushes open the screen door. "Come on. I've got something to show you."

I frown and spin around to jog after him, jamming my feet back into my flip-flops as I go. All I want is a shower and a *real* nap, not in a truck bed, but I haven't seen him with this much pep in his step in about a hundred years.

"Where are we going?" I ask as I slide into his truck, buckling my seat belt while he zips out onto the road, the truck engine revving.

"You'll see!" he says, turning the radio up, Billy Joel crooning at us while we drive past the McMansions and the gas station and the highway entrance, straight into south Huckabee. I peer out at the sea of identical town houses, doors barely hanging on their hinges, torn screens in the windows.

I'm surprised when my dad flicks on his turn signal, pulling into a parking lot and driving past a row of yellow and blue town houses to park right in front of a row of white ones, wilting flowers and bushes lining the paths to each door.

He flashes me a big smile and swings open the truck door. "Ready to see our new place?"

"Wait," I say, my insides turning to ice as I fumble for the handle, hopping out and following him toward a small house on the very end. "Our *what*?"

"Our new place!" he repeats, nodding toward the handwritten SOLD sign staked straight into the dying flower bed. "We move in two weeks."

Sold. Not pending. Not for sale. *Sold.*

I feel the ground shift underneath me.

Stunned, I follow him inside. I try to register everything, but it's like I'm underwater, a wave pulling me down and holding me there. Faded white carpet. The worn linoleum of the breakfast bar in the kitchen. A sliding door in the living room that falls off the track when he opens it.

I clutch the banister as he takes me up the narrow steps, trying to fight my way to the surface.

My room is to the left now instead of the right. The handle gold instead of silver. I walk across the hardwood and push through the door to see the walls are a bubblegum pink, the tiny space closing in around me as I gravitate to the window.

The view is . . . the parking lot: rows of cars and the communal Dumpsters in the corner, currently overflowing with trash.

Not a sunflower in sight besides the one on my arm.

My fingers find the windowsill, grabbing on to it as I hear the sound of my dad's boots on the floor, walking toward me.

"We can paint this, of course," he says. "White. Or beige. Or yellow, even. Whatever you want."

I squeeze my eyes shut, trying to keep my shit together.

I think about this entire summer, boxes and boxes of my mom's stuff thrown in his truck to donate, and now *this*. I thought we'd look at places together. The places I sent him. Places we decide on together. Places other than the town houses my mom's family had been offshored to when their farm had been bought out from under them.

I thought he'd at least *talk* to me. I thought even when the offer came in that we'd have *more time*. It's like he's hit the fast-forward button on everything.

"It'll be good, Em! You've got a bigger closet now, and you'll be closer to school. It's a new start," he says, his hand landing on my shoulder.

A new start.

I push it away, whirling around to face him. "Are you *kidding* me? Please tell me you're joking." My voice cracks unexpectedly on the last syllable.

His eyes widen and he takes a step back, stunned. "I don't—"

"I mean, I know we don't ever talk about *anything*, but you didn't think to talk to me about this? About *any* of this? What good is a bigger closet when all we've been doing this summer is getting rid of *everything*! All her stuff! Like she doesn't mean anything anymore!" I say, my hands balling into fists.

"I thought you were . . . fine with all of this. You've been so happy this summer, I just thought—"

"Yeah! And you want to know why? Because of the list. *Her* list. The list you would barely talk to me about," I shout. "I'm not fine with *any* of this, Dad. I don't *want* a fresh start. I don't want to move into a place so completely different from what she would have wanted."

He softens, his eyes filling with so much disappointment, it makes me feel awful about being mad. Awful about ripping his enthusiasm to shreds. Awful about feeling like this is such a total and complete betrayal.

But it is.

"Em . . . ," he starts to say, but I shake my head, cutting him off.

"Forget it, Dad. Let's just . . . let's just go," I say, pushing past him and walking down the narrow steps, across the faded white carpet, past the SOLD sign.

We don't speak the entire ride home, or for the rest of the day. My words opened a box that we usually keep tightly closed.

As I'm drifting off to sleep that night, I hear his footsteps coming down the hallway, the door to my room creaking open.

"I love you, Em," he whispers into the dark.

I want to say it back, but if I talk, I don't know what else will come out. How could he be so *fine* with any of this? Fine with just packing everything up and moving on and forgetting her. Fine with moving into a place she hated.

I know the bills. The debt. I know it's the only choice we have, but why is he so happy about it?

I squeeze my eyes shut as the tears begin to fall, my fingers finding the leather bracelet around my wrist, sitting just below the tattoo I was so excited about only a few hours ago.

She felt so close then. But now? Now I cry myself to sleep in the house that is no longer my home.

22

Kiera's home.

I fly across town, putting the past two days with my dad behind me with every stroke of my pedal, the thought of seeing my best friend after what has felt like an eternity able to push everything else away. Even some of the frustration and anger I felt when I found out she wasn't coming back until the day before the lake trip ebbs.

For the first time in a while I just . . . need to talk to someone who understands. Who knows my mom. Who knows what those town houses mean. Who has experienced these past three years.

I swerve into the center of Huckabee, past Hank's, past the library and Nina's, to where the historic houses sit, red brick and white siding, tiny plaques nailed beside each door declaring they are old enough to have had George Washington breathe on them.

I see her from down the block, sitting on the front steps, her hair pulled back, an oversize heather-gray Misty Oasis T-shirt on.

"Kiera!" I scream as she jumps up, waving frantically.

I skid to a stop in the driveway, hopping off the bike as she launches herself at me, scrapes on both her knees, chipped red nail polish despite all the bottles I sent her. "Oh my gosh, dude! I missed you!"

"I missed *you*!" I say as we giggle our way inside. Nina peeks out of the kitchen, used to me stealing Kiera away as soon as she gets back, a small smile on her face.

"What've you two got planned to bake this year?" she asks.

"Carrot cake!" I call back as we kick off our shoes and start up the creaky wooden steps to Kiera's bedroom.

We push open the door, dodging around the huge, dented suitcase sitting on the patterned carpet, and launch ourselves onto her bed.

"Welcome back to the twenty-first century," I say with a laugh.

Kiera giggles, nodding. "I missed cell phones. And warm showers. And *Netflix*."

"So, how was camp? How was Todd's house?"

Kiera rolls over on her side, grinning at me. "Camp was . . . probably the best year yet? None of the campers was seriously injured, which was a bit of a miracle. Not a single squirrel incident." She smirks, the both of us remembering a pack of squirrels that had completely trashed a bunk two summers ago. The story had gone viral after a local news company tweeted a picture of one squirrel stuck in a pair of polka-dot underwear. "My entire group got along.

We went on, like, a million cool hikes, which you know is my favorite part. *And*, hanging out at Todd's house was so amazing, Em. *He's* amazing."

I roll over to see a dreamy look plastered on her face.

"It was just like camp, but with Wi-Fi, and pizza, and a roof that doesn't leak. Good people, fun times, no drama, you know?"

No drama. I feel a small jab at that.

"Plus, he only lives forty-five minutes away, so it shouldn't be too hard to see each other this year. I think the group will really like him. *And*, we both want to go to Colorado State next year, so it'll definitely be easier then."

Wait, what?

"*Colorado State?*" I ask, surprised, reaching up to push my hair behind my ear. "I didn't know you wanted to go there."

Since *when*? It's so far away, it makes my chest hurt already.

"Yeah, there's a ton of hiking around there, and—" She freezes, her eyes locked on my arm. "Holy shit. Is that a tattoo?"

"Yeah, I . . . got it a few days ago. With Blake," I say as she sits bolt upright, reaching out to grab my arm.

"You got a tattoo with Blake?"

"Well, not *with* Blake. I mean, she was there, but she didn't . . ." I can see the glint of jealousy in her eyes, so I continue quickly.

"Anyway, I did it because of this." I pull my arm out of her grasp, reaching into my pocket to pull out the folded list. I hand it to her and she carefully unfolds it, her eyes widening when she sees what it is. "I found it in a box of my mom's high school stuff. I've been trying to get it done before the end of the Huckabee Lake trip."

I reach out, pointing at all the different colored check marks, the new red ones from my trip to the beach, and sleeping under the stars, and getting a tattoo.

"This is so cool," she whispers, her eyes getting a little teary, and I know she gets it. "You've been doing them? Just like she did?"

"Yeah," I say, nodding. "And it's so crazy, Kiera. I feel like I'm *myself* again, you know? I feel like she's been guiding me this whole summer, back to who I was. Who I should be."

"What do you have left to do?" she asks, her thumb moving down the page.

"Just two more and then I'm done," I say, watching as she stops at "7. Go on the Huckabee Lake trip" and "11. Find a four-leaf clover," and . . .

She completely unfolds the paper, revealing the hidden number twelve. "Kiss J. C.," the one I've been intentionally ignoring all summer.

I don't know what to think about this one now.

I can't help but have Blake's face pop into my head.

"No way," she says, turning it around to face me.

I know in a nanosecond Matt's popped into hers.

"Oh, well, the initials don't even match his. . . ."

"This is *scarily* perfect, dude," Kiera says, cutting me off, her voice going up half an octave with excitement. "The Huckabee Lake trip. A *kiss*? It's like your mom knew. Like she knew you'd need to make things right with Matt. That the trip tomorrow would be the *perfect* way to do that."

I freeze, my eyes flicking between my best friend and my

mom's handwriting, the promise of everything going back to normal. Everything being okay, our friends' angry faces and Matt's silence gone, a drama-free senior year actually possible. It is what I want. Isn't it?

I think about what just happened with my dad two days ago. What's been happening this entire summer. The town houses. Packing. My life being uprooted from underneath me. How I want nothing more than uncomplicated *normalcy* after all of this.

"I mean, your *parents* got together during the Huckabee Lake trip, didn't they? Talk about a sign."

A sign. It does feel like that, doesn't it?

I roll onto my back to look at the glow-in-the-dark stars we put on her ceiling when we were in elementary school. I think of the stars that night at the beach with Blake, that invincible feeling that something more could be possible. But all of it seems so distant now, my real life, my life in Huckabee and all the expectations closing in around me. The house still slipping away.

If I don't listen to her now, about this, about Matt, I'm no better than my dad, throwing her stuff into boxes, forgetting her, ignoring her. The list has led me in the right direction this entire summer. Why would it not now?

23

The second Nina pulls into the parking lot at Huckabee High the next day and I see the navy-blue and silver charter bus, my heart starts hammering in my chest. It's about to be filled with classmates I haven't seen since June. Classmates who know what went down at junior prom, Matt somewhere in the hustle and bustle, and, on top of it all, Blake just . . . *being Blake.*

This is like eighteen cliff jumps and six tattoos rolled into one.

I pull my mom's black cardigan closer to my body as Kiera and I hop out of the car, duffel bags slung over our shoulders. The last person to wear it was my mom, and I can already feel the worn wool giving me strength.

Or maybe I'm just *hoping* it will.

"Have fun, ladies!" Nina calls, holding two bags of chocolate chip cookies out the driver's-side window for us.

I grimace at the word "fun" but manage to plaster a smile on my face before she can see.

"Molasses?" I ask as I peer into the bag at the cookies.

Nina shakes her head, yet another rejected secret-ingredient guess. "Nice try!"

I tuck my arm into Kiera's as we head toward the bus, half hiding behind her as we wade through the line and check in with Mr. Sanders, what feels like a million eyes following my every move as I bend down to slide my bag into the under-bus compartment. It's better now than it was at the end of school, their gazes less scalding, but it still makes my skin crawl.

Just wait, I tell myself. In a few hours I'm going to put this right. And no one will care anymore.

I take a deep breath and square my shoulders as I straighten up, the list making me stronger. Making me ready for any judgment that comes my way, ready for all the whispers, ready for—

I spin around and run smack into Blake.

She reaches out to stop me from toppling over, all honey-brown eyes, and messy sun-streaked hair, and full lips. . . .

"Blake!" I say, the feelings from the night in the truck bed slowly starting to swim back into my stomach. I quickly push them away, turning my head to scan the crowd for Matt. "Hey. Hi."

She pulls her hand away from my shoulder, glancing to the side at Kiera, a warm smile unfolding onto her face. "You must be Kiera," she says, charming and friendly and nice like there wasn't a distinct shift in the quantity and tone of our texts since I went over to Kiera's yesterday. "It's nice to finally meet you."

"Yeah! Hey. Nice to meet you," Kiera says, giving her a once-over. "Blake, right? Our parents went to high school together."

"Seems like that's the case for just about everyone around here," Blake says, and Kiera laughs, nodding in agreement.

"Tell me about it."

Mr. Sanders pokes my shoulder with the pen he's using to sign students in with. "Clark. Biset. On the bus if I've already checked you off."

Kiera rolls her eyes at me when he looks away, shooting him an if-looks-could-kill glare. Mr. Sanders is her sworn enemy. He gave her a B– on an essay last year, and she still isn't over it.

"See you on there," Kiera says, grabbing my arm and tugging me toward the bus. I hesitate for a fraction of a second, opening my mouth to say something.

Does she want to sit with us? Will she come sit with us?

"See you," Blake says, her eyes moving from Kiera's to mine before she looks away. I stumble after Kiera into the small line.

"Oh my *God*, Em. You didn't say she looked like *that*," Kiera hisses at me while we squeeze inside.

I glance behind me to see Blake stooping to stuff her bag into the under-bus compartment. "Blake? I mean, I guess. . . ."

We slide into two seats halfway down the bus, Kiera beating me out for the window despite an elbow I throw to try to squeeze past her. "You *guess*," Kiera says after she plops down, eyeing the front of the bus as Blake steps on, trailed by Jake. I watch as Blake laughs at something Jake says, but I'm distracted when a head appears behind them. . . . *Matt*. "You better hope Matt isn't as googly-eyed as Jake. I mean, Jesus, Jake. Get a grip."

And of course the second I start thinking about Blake again, Matt looks up, his eyes meeting mine and widening in surprise. The last place I would've been at the end of school last year was on a bus about to go on the Huckabee Lake trip.

But I'm different now. I need to show him I'm different now, so *we* can be different this time.

In my peripherals, I see Blake glance back to see what I'm looking at, and her smile fades ever so slightly.

"Emily?" Jake's voice rings out, perfectly encapsulating Matt's incredulousness. I see his head pop past Blake, then Olivia's and Ryan's faces appear just behind him. "Didn't think I'd see *you* on the lake trip."

I'm about to say something when Kiera jumps in, coming to my rescue as always. "Honestly surprised you see anyone, Jake, with your head so far up Blake's ass."

Jake snorts, but his cheeks redden slightly as he moves past us toward the back of the bus. Bantering with Jake is one of Kiera's favorite pastimes.

Blake slides into the seat across the aisle from me while I reach out to lightly grab Matt's arm. He turns back to look at me, his dark eyebrows rising.

"Can we talk later?" I ask, keeping my voice low.

"Uh," he says, hesitating. I hold my breath, but I can tell from his face that something is different. "Yeah." He nods. "Okay."

Relief floods through me, and I let go of his arm. He gives me a small smile before heading to the back of the bus, Jake following just behind him. Olivia, though, turns to shoot me a narrow-eyed glare around Ryan as she passes by.

"He's definitely not over you," Kiera whispers. I turn back to face her, and she gives me a little shake of her head. "You'll be back together by the end of this trip, for *sure.*"

I nod, wrapping my cardigan tightly around me as Mr. Sanders hops on to make general announcements about not being giant assholes for the duration of the ride. The entire bus of students collectively zones out.

I don't look over, but I can *feel* Blake next to me, like she was that night in the truck. Just the thought of her sitting across the aisle makes my face hot. I stare at the weirdly carpeted back of the seat in front of me, trying to ignore the pounding in my chest as the bus chugs to life and we pull out of the parking lot.

I don't even know how I can pretend to be just her friend, but I need to.

I need to pull myself away.

When we hit the highway, she leans across the aisle. "You find a four-leaf clover yet?" she asks.

I shake my head, still staring straight ahead. "No, but I need to by the end of this weekend. Right, Kiera . . . ?"

My voice trails off as I look over to see she's already fast asleep, her face smooshed up against the glass of the window, her mouth agape. Mr. Sanders's words were apparently stronger than any sleeping pill known to man.

I snap a quick picture, and Blake smirks as I post it to my Instagram story. Kiera will roast me over it later, but it's worth it.

I glance past her out the window, watching as the trees fly by, my hazy reflection staring back at me. I can see the outline of Blake's arms and legs, and her hand reaching out to lightly touch me on the arm.

I turn my head, and she holds an earbud out to me, giving me a small smile that makes me melt just the tiniest bit. I take it, slipping it into my ear, and she scrolls to the top of a Spotify playlist, turning it to face me.

Beach ride.

It's a whole playlist of songs, pulled from our trip to the beach.

Oh, Blake.

I tap on the first song, and it begins to play "Coffee" by Sylvan Esso.

I try to focus on Matt in the back of the bus, on figuring out what I'm going to say to him, on showing him how much I've changed, the promise of everything being normal and easy and right, but Blake holds my gaze, and the song sings, "Do you love me?" and I . . .

I don't know what to feel.

All I can do is shove whatever *this* is deep down and pull my eyes away.

24

Henry Huckabee Lodge looks like it was made out of Lincoln Logs.

Everything is made out of wood. From the steps to the walls to the ceilings, this place is the definition of a fire hazard.

Because we were late additions to the trip, Blake and I are sharing a room, while Kiera is bunking with Olivia, which . . . should be interesting.

With the current rift in our friend group, and their opposing sides, I would *hate* to be a fly on the wall in that room.

I glance down the hall while Blake is opening our door to see Kiera looking back at me, the look on her face saying, *Fix this. Now.*

"That's not creepy at all," Blake mutters as the door swings wide, both of us stopping short as we come face-to-face with an enormous deer head nailed to the wall.

"Can't wait to try to sleep tonight," I say as I slide past her, avoiding any and all contact as I claim the twin bed by the window, the fake glass eyeballs following me across the room. I narrow my eyes, staring back at it.

We both unpack, and when Blake ducks into the bathroom, I get changed into my suit super quick. The optional afternoon kayak trip is just around the corner, and Matt will definitely be there. I've barely had time to pull a shirt on when the door opens and Blake emerges in a white tank top and shorts, a yellow dish-washing glove in her hand.

I straighten up, raising my eyebrows at her. "What the hell is that for?"

She nods at the tattoo on my forearm, shrugging as she holds up a roll of waterproof tape. "Gotta put this on it to keep it safe." There's an amused twinkle in her eyes, that mischievous grin of hers pulling at the corners of her mouth. "You know how much bacteria is in a lake?"

I shove her shoulder, rolling my eyes. How dare she quote *me* back to me.

I take the glove from her and slide it on, struggling to get the tape around it.

"You need help with that?" she asks, stepping closer. Reflexively, I take a step back.

"No. Thanks. I, uh . . ." I head for the door, trying to put as much space between us as possible, racking my brain for an excuse. A believable lie. "I got it. I think I'm going to go meet . . . Kiera . . . before kayaking, so she can . . ."

My voice trails off and I hold up the glove, the entire thing flopping limply to the side as I slide out of our room like the most awkward person ever, the door clicking shut behind me.

I groan, rubbing my face. I've got to find Matt. And fast.

I head down the stairs and outside, past Aimee and Ashley Campbell. The pair intentionally turn their backs to me and make a huge show of whispering back and forth, in a pointed display that could only be about one thing and one thing only.

Sighing, I step out into the afternoon sun, its rays bright and warm as it shines on the winding path down to the lake, wooden signs leading the way through the trees.

I pass a few classmates as I walk, all of them giving me pointed looks while I try to focus on the sunlight filtering through the tree branches, the path just in front of me, *Matt in a gray T-shirt and turquoise-blue swim shorts.*

"Matt!" I call out, and he turns around to face me, Jake next to him. "Can you talk?"

He nods and smiles faintly at me, but there's a small barrier still between us. A barrier I need to find a way to get over.

"I'll just . . . go. . . ." Jake's voice trails off, and he points behind him with his thumb, disappearing down the path and out of sight.

I take a deep breath, knowing I need to be honest with him. About what happened at junior prom. About this summer. About the list, preparing me for this moment. I can't just skate past it and ignore. "Listen, I am *so* sorry. What I did was . . . really terrible."

He swallows, his thick eyebrows furrowing, his eyes guarded.

"I think I just felt like things . . . didn't feel right between us. And I think that was all on me. *I* didn't feel right, and I did something really, really stupid." I want to be on the same page. So for the first time in our entire relationship, I lay it all out on the table. "But this summer I found my mom's bucket list from the summer before her senior year of high school, and it *changed* things."

I see his face soften at the mention of my mom, and it keeps me talking.

"I've changed. *Really* changed, Matt. I spent the summer checking off all the items, and . . . I'm out of that little box I've been keeping myself in," I say, repeating his words from that one fight we had. The thing at the core of all our problems. "And I know you haven't seen me much, but I know you've noticed. I know you know I'm more like . . . well, like how I *used* to be. I'm *on* this lake trip. And, I mean, you caught me *skinny-dipping* at the Huckabee Pool. I think we both know that Emily from two months ago would have *never* done that."

"Yeah, that was surprising, to say the least," he admits, and I know I'm getting somewhere.

I take a step closer, looking up at him. "I know we've broken up before. I know you've given me a lot of chances in the past. But this time is different. *I'm* different."

He takes a deep breath, looking away from me. "I don't know, Em . . . I just . . ."

"Let me prove it to you," I say quickly. "This weekend. Let's just, I don't know, *hang out*. Let me show you I've changed."

He's silent for a long moment, and I hold my breath, counting the seconds. Finally, I see him frown, and my insides turn to ice. "What's with the dishwasher glove?"

Relief floods through me. I sheepishly hold up the glove in

question. "I got a tattoo a few days ago, and I need to keep it covered for kayaking." I hold out the tape to him, hope pushing me forward. "You want to help me with it?"

He nods, reaching out to take it from me. "What'd you get?"

I hold out my arm and he takes it, his fingers lightly holding my wrist.

"A sunflower," he says. The corners of his mouth tick up into a smile as he gently pulls the glove over the tattoo and tapes it down. "Just like your mom's garden."

"Just like it," I say, holding his gaze for a long moment.

He exhales and lets go of my arm, spinning the roll of waterproof tape around on his finger as he looks away. "I just . . . I don't know. It was more than just that. I always felt like you were pulling yourself away from me. From us. Always finding problems and making excuses, always pushing me away when I wanted to get closer."

"I definitely was," I say. His eyebrows arch up in surprise at my admission. "And I'm sorry. I think it was really hard for me to be open and real with *anyone* the past three years. You, Kiera, my dad. *Myself*, even."

He stops spinning the tape, his face thoughtful as he looks at me. Finally, he holds it out to me. "You'll prove it to me? This weekend?"

I reach out and take it from the open palm of the boy I'm meant to be with. "Absolutely."

Kayaking is a complete mess in the best possible way.

Sending twenty kids out, half of whom have never kayaked

before, for two hours of barely chaperoned fun is bound to be.

Jake tries to kill everyone the whole time, ramming into people's kayaks at full speed, until Blake manages to knock the paddle out of his hand, stealing it and leaving him stranded in the middle of the lake.

I want to cheer, but since I'm trying to put some distance between us, that would probably not be the best idea.

Kiera coasts to a stop next to me, grinning as she watches him try to hand paddle his way back to shore. "All right, I'll admit it," she says, glancing over at me. "My summer FOMO aside, Blake is . . . pretty great."

I nod, my gaze meeting Blake's just past Kiera's head, the smile on her face making my skin burn more than the afternoon sun.

I'm afraid to put into words exactly what I think of Blake, but I know "pretty great" isn't enough.

I swallow and look away, at Matt paddling in circles around Jake, and set off after him to help, knowing that it'll have to be.

25

The next forty-eight hours pass in an absolute blur.

From kayaking, to unsuccessfully scavenging for a four-leaf clover, to flinging myself off a rope swing into the water, I barely stop moving. And Matt is alongside me the whole weekend, Kiera pushing us closer and closer together every time we move even a foot apart.

It's slowly starting to feel like how things used to be.

"Do a flip!" I call to him as he soars on the rope swing.

"Race you to the dining hall?" he asks, pushing me into the water before we go laughing up the path back to Huckabee Lodge.

And slowly but surely, the rest of the group begins to find a new rhythm, even with Olivia and half the students glaring at me during mealtimes and activities and in the taxidermy-filled Henry Huckabee Lodge hallway.

I try to keep a distance from Blake and our shared room, but she always finds her way into whatever we're doing, even though she's already made friends with just about everyone else in our grade too.

It's a welcome relief when I find myself peacefully floating atop a donut-shaped pool float on Huckabee Lake, my legs still sore from a hike Kiera led us on before lunch.

I raise my head, flipping my sunglasses up and squinting against the bright afternoon sun at the glittering water, the circle of trees around the perimeter, and Henry Huckabee Lodge peeking through the branches. I scan the throngs of students, taking a quick inventory. Kiera is a few feet away from me in an oversize inner tube, Blake is lounging on the dock with a sketchbook, and Matt, Jake, and Ryan have convinced half the boys on the trip to launch themselves off said dock in a *very* intense belly-flop competition. I can see their fire-engine-red arms and legs from here.

I grimace, watching as Jake slaps the water flat as a pancake, my skin burning as the boys cheer like he just scored a game-winning touchdown.

I slide my sunglasses back on and go to shift farther up in my donut float, but the plastic screeches noisily and as it wobbles past vertical, it tips sharply.

"Shit!" I squeak out as I flip backward off it into the lake, my mouth and nose filling with bacteria-ridden water as I claw my way back to the surface, pushing through the murkiness.

Coughing, I'm about to chalk this up to a bit of bad luck when I feel something lightly tap my shoulder.

Looking over, I see a red lifeguard float sitting atop the water, Matt at the other end of it, a playful grin I haven't seen since before junior prom plastered on his face.

"Looked like you needed rescuing," he says.

I push my hair out of my face, glaring as I toss the float back at him. "Rescue yourself, Matt!"

He laughs, and I splash him square in the face, but his hands reach out to grab mine, stopping me from splashing again as he takes a step closer to me. His normally unkempt hair is slicked back with lake water, his shoulders and chest red from belly flopping.

Despite myself, I think of Blake in Huckabee Pool, my breath hitching as she took that step closer to me. How different that moment felt compared to this one. How much . . . more.

Almost instinctively, I pull my hands out of Matt's, but I know even before I see his face fall that it's the wrong move.

Stay on course, Emily.

I look back up at him, giving me a small smile as I hold up my freshly tattooed arm, the dishwashing glove lost somewhere in my tumble. "I need to go disinfect this," I say, offering an explanation as I grab my donut float and turn back toward the dock. "And *you* need to go lose your belly-flop competition."

He grabs my arm, stopping me. "You going to the bonfire tonight?" he asks.

The Midnight Bonfire. It's a Huckabee Lake trip tradition. One that's gone on since the very first trip a bajillion years ago. The teachers turn a blind eye for the night, and all the students sneak out, heading to the lake for a bonfire and some after-hours fun.

I nod and he smiles, letting go of my arm. "Good," he says, pushing off onto his back. "I'll see you tonight."

I look just past him to Kiera in her inner tube. She shoots me two thumbs-up, a huge grin plastered on her face. "See you tonight," I echo.

I head back to the dock, chucking the donut onto the worn wood, purposefully avoiding Blake's gaze. I go to push myself up, stopping short when her hand reaches out to help me.

My fingers slide into her palm, and she pulls me up until her face is inches from mine. My gaze moves from her honey-brown eyes to her lips, then back again.

The same moment with Matt a moment ago.

Only this time, my heart can't keep time in my chest.

I pull my hand away, quickly stepping back.

"You heading back up?" she asks.

"Uh, yeah," I say, pushing my hair behind my ear.

"I want to grab some water from the dining hall," she says as she grabs her sketchbook off the dock.

We head up the forest path to the lodge, the trees wrapping around us as we walk, her hand bumping lightly against mine. I cross my arms to stop it from happening.

The path narrows so she steps ahead of me, and I watch as she tucks the pencil she was using behind her ear, calling back to me, "Can I ask you something?"

"Yeah," I say, unsure of what she's going to say.

"Are you avoiding me?"

"What? No!"

She turns around to look at me, her eyes searching my face for a long moment. Finally, she nods, clearly not buying it. "All right. Sure."

We keep walking, but I can tell she's upset. I reach for her arm as we step out of the woods, the lodge coming into view. "Blake, I—"

"Why Matt?" she asks, cutting me off as she whips around to face me. "You told me that it didn't feel right that day we had the picnic. If it didn't work out the first time . . . if it didn't *feel* right the second time or the third time or the fourth time . . . why do you still want to be with him?"

"I . . ." I hesitate, opening my mouth to reply, my mind scrambling for an answer. "Because he's a great guy, Blake. He's nice and sweet and reliable and my mom *always* wanted me to be with him, especially after she got sick. And now, after doing the list, I feel like *this* is what she would want me to do. I feel like all of it has led me to this moment, where it's actually going to work."

Blake nods, holding my gaze as she processes what I'm saying. "So, you think that by doing the list and by becoming more like the person you were, things are just going to suddenly work out between the two of you?"

"Yeah," I say, rising to the challenge. "I do."

"Doesn't that completely erase what you've been through, though? Who you've become because of what happened? Who you are *now?*"

I don't have an answer for that.

I cross my arms and look away, at the path leading back to the lake.

"Let me just ask you. Is this what *you* want, Emily?" she says.

She's asking more than just that. I can see it in her eyes and in the way she says it.

"Yeah," I say, drawing a line in the sand. "It is."

"Okay," she says, nodding. "Got it." She turns on her heel and heads quickly up the steps of Huckabee Lodge, leaving me standing there, watching her go.

26

"Tonight's the night, Em," Kiera says as she leans back, appraising her makeup-application skills. I turn right and left, checking myself in the bathroom mirror. Kiera cuts me off though as she leans forward, sweeping on another layer of mascara for good measure.

I'm wearing an off-white floral-print dress that I am not a huge fan of, but Matt said he liked it this past spring on a date, so it feels a bit like a good-luck charm. My long brown hair is half up, and gently wavy thanks to Kiera's skills with a curling iron.

With a satisfied nod, she turns to meet my eyes, pointing the mascara tube at me. "This list is getting done tonight at the bonfire. The grand finale. You're officially getting *your* J. C. back."

Done. I can hardly believe it. I look at the paper, unfolded on the bathroom counter, the multicolor check marks next to almost every number.

"And, I mean, we can find a four-leaf clover before we board the bus tomorrow," she says with a wave of her hand. "It can't be that hard."

I'm going to have to get up pretty damn early. I've *literally* looked the entire month of July. This thing is about as elusive as you can get.

Unless you're Blake, I think, remembering her stack on our picnic.

I lean against the counter as she zips up her makeup bag, biting my lip warily. Is it okay that I still haven't found it? Am I ready for this next step with Matt, the "grand finale" as she called it, even though I haven't?

I look at myself in the mirror one more time, letting out a long exhale before following Kiera out of the bathroom. Blake's sitting on the edge of her bed, and my jaw nearly drops when I see her.

I've seen her a million times this summer, but not like *this*.

The thin line of eyeliner and the gloss on her lips and the coating of mascara emphasize her features and sweep them into a level of beautiful that is both hard to look at and impossible to look away from.

Kiera lets out a wolf whistle, nodding, and I remind myself my admiration is totally normal. Blake is objectively hot. It doesn't have to mean anything. "Looking good, Blake!" she says, before rubbing her hands together in excitement. "All right, team! Game plan for item number twelve. Sealing the deal with Matt."

She grabs my hand, plunking me down on the bed next to Blake. My cheeks instantly turn red as Blake's shoulder brushes against mine. I shoot a sideways glance at her, and she gives me a small, thin-lipped smile.

Kiera puts her hands on her hips and starts to pace around the room, her feet padding along the green carpet. "Three words." She spins around, her hair swaying behind her. "Truth or dare."

"Truth or dare?" Blake asks, raising her eyebrows.

"Yes," Kiera says, nodding eagerly. "*Truth or dare.* I start a game around the bonfire. No one is going to pick Emily right now since she's the school pariah." She stops pacing and shoots me a sympathetic look. "No offense."

I roll my eyes. "None taken."

"So," Kiera continues, zeroing in on Blake. "Whoever gets picked first between the two of us dares *Emily* to kiss someone—"

"Uh," I say, cutting her off with a raise of my hand. "Quick little thing. Given the fact that I . . . kissed . . . another guy publicly, is this really the best . . . ?"

Kiera waves her hand, brushing my words away. "That's kind of *why* this'll work, you know? It's a good way to make amends. Right the wrong, by kissing the *right* person this time."

I frown, processing. Does that make sense? It probably would in a movie, but this is real life.

"*Okay*," she continues, zeroing in on Blake again. "So, we dare her to kiss someone, she kisses Matt, there are fireworks in the sky, bing bang boom, mission accomplished."

Mission accomplished. Just like that, everything will click back into place.

For a long moment Blake doesn't say anything. She's quiet,

and the two of them are pretty much left just staring at each other.

I watch as Kiera blinks, waiting for Blake to match her enthusiasm. "So, are you in?"

Blake runs her fingers through her hair, hesitating, her expression unreadable. I get distracted by the faint highlighter on her cheekbones as I try to decipher it. "Yeah. I mean . . . I know how much the list means to Emily, so . . . of course I'm in."

"Sweeeet!" Kiera claps, satisfied, throwing herself onto my bed and checking her phone.

"We've got half an hour until midnight," she says, rolling over onto her back. "This is the first time in my life I'm actually early for something."

"If you want to kill some time, I found something cool this afternoon," Blake says as she turns to look at me. "I think you'll probably want to see it."

With nothing else to do, we creep quietly out of our room and tiptoe down the long hallway after her, phone flashlight guiding the way as we loop through the lodge. Around one corner, we come face-to-face with a ginormous stuffed bear, its pointy teeth illuminated in the light.

I let out an unintentional squeak, and Kiera claps her hand over my mouth, shushing me.

"Emily Clark," she hisses. *"Shut up."*

Stifling our laughs, we head around another corner and up two flights of steps before squeezing through a tiny, dusty door to the attic.

Blake feels her way to the corner and flicks a light switch. A tiny light bulb pops on, and the sloped, cobweb-covered walls are brought to life in the soft light. They're filled with *writing*, words and pictures carved into the ancient wooden rafters.

"Oh my gosh," I say as I take a step closer, finding a heart, and HUCKABEE LAKE TRIP 1966, and HEATHER AND TIM 4EVER. "This is *so* cool."

"It gets cooler," Blake says, walking over to the corner and tapping a section of the wall. Kiera and I shuffle over, squinting to read in the dim light.

No. It can't be.

I gasp, reaching out to touch the initials in front of me. J. M. + J. C. '99. My parents. They were up here all those years ago, on the weekend they officially got together.

It's the final sign. That this plan, that Matt, that *all* of it is the right thing to do. Four-leaf clover or not. That *this* is my way to my own version of what they had.

We're all silent for a long moment, Kiera slinging her arms around me and Blake as we stare at the wall, taking it all in.

"We should carve our names up here!" Kiera says, whipping a pocketknife out of her pocket like this is an episode of *Naked and Afraid*.

"Whoa, there, buddy," I say, holding up my hands.

She grins sheepishly. "My bad. Still in Misty Oasis mode."

We find a free spot by my mom and dad's initials, going one at a time, our own small part in this massive tapestry spanning generations and generations. Kiera giggles excitedly, peeking out the tiny attic window as Blake finishes her *C*.

"I see people heading out. It's time!" She turns and grabs me firmly by the shoulders. "You ready, Em?"

I look at my parents' initials on the wall and all of ours below it, nodding. "Let's do this."

27

This is exhilarating.

My adrenaline is pumping as all of us pour out of the building, tiptoeing our way through the halls and through the forest as we find our way down to the lake. We're near the back of the pack, Kiera leading, Blake just behind me, the night alive around us with whispers and laughs and the sound of twigs snapping underneath our feet.

Ahead of me, I see the light of the bonfire start flickering through the trees, and finally a whoop echoes through the air. We made it.

I'm surprised when Blake's hand grabs on to mine, stopping me. The feeling of her fingers lacing through my own is familiar enough to recognize.

I look back at her in the soft glow of the moonlight as people slide around us.

There's an uneasiness in her gaze I've never seen before. Something is unsettling her.

"Can I talk to you?" she whispers, an unfamiliar twinge of urgency in her words.

I hesitate as a wave of nervousness blindsides me, my excitement swallowed whole. I look between her and the light of the bonfire, debating.

Finally, I nod, calling out to Kiera to let her know we'll be there in a second. Kiera yells something back to us over her shoulder, but her words blend together with the noise of the bonfire as her flip-flops fade into the distance.

Blake pulls me off the path, through the trees, a safe distance away from everyone.

And then . . . it's just the two of us, the air around us prickling as Blake looks at me.

"Emily . . . ," she starts, her voice trailing off as she swallows. "I don't know. I just, uh . . ." She looks down at her feet, shifting uneasily like she's working up to something. I've never seen Blake scared of anything, and something about that terrifies me. "I know there's this whole plan tonight, but if I've learned anything this summer from your mom's list, it's how important it is to put yourself out there and take chances. And . . . this right here is literally the last chance I have to tell you how I really feel."

I freeze as the air gets punched right out of my lungs. I want to pull my hand from hers and clasp it over her mouth before she can say it. Before she can say exactly what I want to hear and exactly what I don't.

She looks at me with those warm brown eyes that find their way into every single one of my thoughts. "I like you, Emily. I *really* like you. To be honest with you, I was pretty scared to move to Huckabee. But then I sat down next to you at that bingo fundraiser, and you smiled at me, and I knew almost instantly everything was going to be okay." The corner of her mouth ticks up into a smile as she talks. "I've loved every minute of this summer with you. I've loved planning with you, and listening to you talk about your mom, and how brave you've been when you have to jump off a cliff and you really don't want to. I love how you tell jokes when you get nervous, and the way you smile when you talk about baking, and how it feels when you look at me. And I love all the things about you that you're scared to show people. Your sadness, and your pain, and your fear, because without it, you wouldn't be you."

All at once I'm hit with two overwhelming emotions.

The first dances around my chest in a way I have never experienced with anyone, the stars above us shining brighter than ever. It feels *real*, and overwhelming, and so dizzying, my entire world shifts.

The other is an overpowering dread that sits heavy in my stomach, the feeling the same as when I stepped off the Misty Oasis bus that summer and saw that something was wrong with my mom.

I never got to tell her what I felt, and who I felt it for. Never got to know what she would have said. What she would have wanted for me.

So I shoved it down so deep, I could pretend it never happened. If I was with Matt, though, I could know. I could know she would've been happy.

And I could pretend I was fine with her never knowing, because maybe there was nothing to know in the first place.

But there was.

There is.

I stare at Blake, words escaping me. Both sides fighting within me.

"I know," she says, when it's clear I can't form a sentence. "I *know* you think your mom wanted you to be with Matt. I know you think that finishing the list and being with him is how you can keep her with you and live your life the way she wanted you to live it. I can understand that. But—" Her grip tightens on my hand and she takes a step closer. "But, Emily . . . from everything you and my dad have told me about her, from everything this list has taught me about her, what she would have wanted, more than *any* fairy tale, is for you to be *happy*. For real. She would have wanted you to try your luck on something real."

I pull my hand from hers, taking a step back.

It's not that simple, Blake, I want to shout. But . . . she can't possibly understand. She didn't grow up in Huckabee, where *this* is still pretty far from the norm. More important, though, she didn't have her dying mom tell her how right things could be if she gave this one specific boy a chance, like she'd given my dad a chance all those years ago. A boy that was pretty close to perfect, bringing flowers to the hospital and being there for me during the hardest moment of my life.

But not perfect for you.

The thought comes to me like a traitor, from the part of me

that wants nothing more than to kiss her right now. The part of me my mom never knew. Can never know.

The part that for all those reasons . . . I can never be.

"Blake, I . . . I can *try my luck* a hundred times, but I can never bring her back. I'll never know what she really wants. Except for this."

It takes everything in me to break this pull between us, but finally I turn, pushing through the trees, everything hazy as I fight my way along the path to the bonfire. I break into the clearing, the light and the sound overwhelming me, colors and shapes all morphing together. I take a deep breath, trying to steady myself.

"Em," I hear Kiera say, feel her pressing a beer bottle into my hand. "You're just in time to play truth or dare!" She leans in as she pulls me over to the group, whispering now. "It's showtime."

I sit down on a giant log, joining the circle formed around the bonfire. Looking up, I see Matt sitting across the way, his lips pulling up into a knowing smile as Kiera ushers more people over. She's always able to get things going, and tonight is no exception.

"I like your dress," he mouths, motioning to his torso and then to me.

I smile back at him, but it feels so forced and wrong, just like this white floral dress he likes so much.

I try to match everyone's enthusiasm, but I feel . . . completely thrown off-balance, the ground unsteady underneath me.

But, with or without me, the game still begins, the plan set into motion.

It's a blur of dares lobbed back and forth across the circle, truths spilling out of people's mouths. Leah Thompson confesses to cheating on her bio final, and Brad Hammond eats a worm, and Jake strips down to his underwear and jumps *through* the bonfire like an actual lunatic.

I watch as he grabs a beer from someone, chugging the rest of it before spinning around and pointing the empty bottle at . . .

Blake. I hadn't even noticed her come join us, my mind still spinning from her words a moment ago.

"Blake Carter," he drawls, a shit-eating grin on his face. "Truth or dare?"

She crosses her arms, raising her eyebrows at him. "You know I'm always game for a dare, Jake."

Jake laughs, an evil glint in his eye. Everyone goes quiet with a palpable excitement, watching the exchange, eager to see what the new girl will do. He points to the rusty lifeguard stand at the end of the dock.

"I dare you to jump off that. Into the water."

Blake doesn't even bat an eye. And she definitely doesn't look at me.

Everyone cranes their necks to watch as she walks down the dock, some even stand up to get a better view. I watch her climb the rickety ladder up to the top, silently praying that she doesn't follow through with her part in the plan.

Blake steadies herself, the stand creaking underneath her, and Jake starts a chant.

"Bla-ake! Bla-ake! Bla-ake!"

There's a collective intake of air as she soars off the top, doubling down on the dare by flipping *backward* into the water, everyone clapping and cheering as she surfaces. As fearless as she'd been when we went cliff jumping.

So totally unlike how she'd been just a few moments ago in the woods. Her confession was scarier to her than this . . . but she did it anyway.

Kiera's fingers dig into my arm, and I swing my head to look over at her. She gives me a big, excited smile, knowing what's coming.

My chest feels tight as I watch Blake swim back to the dock, the mischievous smile I expect to see missing from her face, her words ringing in my ears as she pushes herself out of the water.

Try your luck on something real.

She pulls her wet hair into a bun as everyone crowds around her in excitement, her social status at Huckabee High cemented after one dare.

Don't ask me. Don't ask me.

I silently will her to pick one of them. To pick Matt, or Olivia, or *anyone* other than me.

She doesn't, though. She pulls her hands away from her hair and looks directly at me, through the crowd of people, her wet shirt clinging to her upper arms and her stomach.

"Emily," she says, my skin prickling when she says my name, so different from back in the woods. Everyone falls silent, turning to look at me. "Truth or dare?"

And just like that, it's not a game anymore. How I answer this is a choice.

I look down at the grass surrounding the log I'm sitting on, wishing it would swallow me up. Wishing for a way out and . . .

There. In the grass.

A four-leaf clover.

I reach out, plucking it, and just like that the choice is made for me. I say the word I know will change absolutely everything.

"Dare."

I look up and I know, because I know *Blake*, that she's going to do it. I know she follows through, whether it's backflipping off a rusty lifeguard stand or enduring a night of sleep in the back of a pickup truck.

"I dare you to kiss someone," she says.

There's a chorus of "ooo"s and someone shouting, "Don't see any underclassmen here!" but it's all background noise as I hold Blake's gaze, her eyes darker than I've *ever* seen them, not giving anything away.

I stand up, my hand clenching around the four-leaf clover like it's my lucky quarter, my connection to Mom, what she must have felt here on this spot so many years ago. My grip tightens until I feel a wave of every single emotion from this past summer.

But they aren't about her at all.

The free fall of the cliff jump. The feeling of Blake's hand in mine in the back of her grandpa's truck. The achingly beautiful ceiling of stars above us. Her face when I walked away from her.

I want to throw this stupid clover away and choose her, and that terrifies me. I want to close that space and kiss *her*.

But that's not why I'm here. Not why I started this list in the first place. I can feel the weight of everyone's eyes on me. The weight of their expectations.

The weight of my mom's expectations, the person I trust more than I trust myself.

So I need to trust her now, just like I have all summer long.

My feet find their way without any instruction, two steps, five steps, my movements feeling almost robotic.

Soon I'm on the other side of the blazing fire, my heart pounding loudly as I take a deep breath and look down at Matt. For a moment I watch the firelight dance across his face, his eyes nervous and hopeful now that I'm an arm's length away from him. He stands slowly, taking a small step closer to me.

And then, before I can think about it anymore, I lean forward and kiss him.

He smells like his favorite cologne, the one he only wears on dates, and on Valentine's Day, and when he's got something planned. His mouth tastes like whatever beer Jake sneaked onto the bus in a duffel bag. His hand feels soft but firm as he finds the small of my back. It's familiar. The same person I've kissed the same way since freshman year.

But just like every single kiss since freshman year, there are no fireworks. No rush of dizzying love. No puzzle piece clicking perfectly into place.

My mind starts the countdown it always has.

But for the first time, I finally realize what I hope it's counting down to.

I realize deep down, I'm waiting for it to *fix* me. Like I thought the list fixed me. To make everything right. To make this part of me, the part that my mom never knew, right.

But it doesn't.

When I pull away, my eyes search for Blake just over Matt's shoulder. She's looking away, out at the dark lake, her jaw set, hurt painted onto every feature on her face.

Automatically, I take a step back, and Matt's hand falls from my waist, his thick eyebrows jutting up in surprise at my reaction. Everyone around us is cheering their approval, but I think he can tell something is wrong. I think we both can.

Blake turns and pushes past our classmates, walking out of the clearing and into the woods, disappearing into the darkness of the tree line.

I watch her leave, my unlucky heart ripping like a sheet of paper, a list being torn apart.

28

I sit silently through the rest of the bonfire, Matt next to me, Kiera shooting me questioning looks from across the circle.

"Is something wrong?" Matt whispers in my ear. "Was it what Kevin said about the underclassmen?"

I shake my head. "I think I'm just tired."

I look around me, and everything . . . should be fine. I mean, everything is fixed. My reputation. My friend group. The glares and the snide remarks completely silenced.

I mean, Jake is acting like nothing happened. Ryan and Olivia are even perfectly fine with hanging out with us.

But nothing *feels* fine. Not to me.

I slip away early, making up an excuse about going to the bathroom, but by the time I get back to our room, Blake is already asleep.

I want to wake her up. To say something. But I made a choice tonight that I can't undo. Everything is ruined.

I don't have a list to make this right.

My phone lights up with texts from Matt and Kiera, but I crawl into bed, squeezing my eyes shut. The look on her face as she walked away circles around inside my head, replaying over and over again beneath my eyelids, until inevitable stomach-aching sobs force their way out. I bury my face deep in my pillow in an attempt to muffle the noise.

Slowly, slowly, the sobs give way to sleep.

When I wake up the next morning to my alarm going off, Blake is already gone. Her bed empty, her things packed, the only sign she was ever here at all is the mess of white sheets, a lingering outline in the mattress.

It takes more effort than I could possibly imagine to get ready and packed, the bus rumbling noisily outside, waiting for all of us to board.

When Mr. Sanders's voice rings through the halls, letting us know we have five minutes to get on, I take a deep breath, trying to keep it together. I check my phone and see all the unread messages, and it only pushes me closer to the brink, the air hiccuping as it passes through my lips.

I need to go home. I just need to go *home*.

The thought pushes me out of the room and down the stairs, the bus doors hissing open to let me on. The first person I see when I step inside is Kiera. Her eyes widen in alarm, knowing in an instant something isn't right. I look away, searching the bus for . . .

Blake.

She's sitting two seats up from Kiera, the hood of her sweatshirt pulled up over a baseball hat, a pair of earbuds in her ears.

I pause as I pass her, but she turns away to look out the window, ignoring me.

I stand there in the middle of the aisle, completely immobilized, until I feel Kiera's hand wrapping around my wrist, pulling me into the seat next to her.

"Emily. What's wrong? What happened?" she whispers, her voice concerned. Her gaze flicks between me and Blake, trying to make sense of what's going on.

Home. Just make it home.

I shake my head, squeezing my eyes shut, forcing the tears down. "Nothing," I say, but my voice betrays me, breaking on the last syllable.

"You wanna sit with me?" a voice asks, and I open my eyes to see Matt right in front of me, Jake peering around him to wiggle his eyebrows up and down.

There's a long, awkward pause as I stare up at him.

"Nope, sorry, Matt!" Kiera jumps in, saving me, finding words when I can't find any. "Playing the best-friend card here. I haven't seen her all summer." She waves him along, and I barely have time to register the confusion on his face, my head spinning.

"Em. What the hell is going on? Why are you being like this when we just fixed everything? I mean, why are you trying to wreck everything again when you *want* to be with Matt?" Kiera whispers once he's out of view, but I shake my head.

"Do I?" I whisper back, angry. "Or do *you* want me to, just so you can have a perfect senior year? Bet it's a real shame you can't just spend the whole year at Misty Oasis, with Todd and all your drama-free friends."

We stare at each other for a long moment, both of us stunned. Finally, she grabs her backpack, nodding. "Yeah. It's a real shame. At least I know they'd actually talk to me instead of just shutting me out."

My eyes fill with tears as she slides past me, moving to a free spot three spaces up.

I put my earbuds in as we pull out of the parking lot, alternating between staring out the window, trying not to cry, and glancing in the driver's rearview mirror at Blake.

I need to talk to her.

The rest of the ride I try to come up with something to say, but just like last night, none of it feels like it's enough. None of it feels like it can fix this.

I know, though, that I need to at least try. After all this, I can't lose her from my life entirely.

When we arrive, she's the first one off the bus. I grab my backpack and fly up the aisle, following just behind her, a few people sliding out of their seats in between us. She notices me when I step off and makes a sharp turn in the opposite direction, grabbing her duffel quickly from the underneath compartment and beelining for her truck.

"Blake," I say, pushing through the throngs of students as I run across the parking lot after her.

She doesn't stop when I call her name. She just keeps her head down, ignoring the sound of my voice.

"Blake!" I call again, reaching out, my fingertips barely meeting the skin of her arm before she pulls it away.

"Leave me alone, Emily," she says, without even slowing down, her voice low.

"Blake, please. I just want to talk about—" I reach out, grabbing for her hand again, but her fingers slip through my grip.

"I don't want to talk about it!" she says, whirling around to face me, her brown eyes angry as she rips out one of her earbuds in frustration. "Okay? I don't want to talk about the list, or about Matt, or about the kiss. I don't want to talk about how you were my friend all summer long because your friends ditched you, and then you dropped me and ignored me when it was no longer convenient for you. I get it, okay? You got what you wanted."

"Blake, I'm sorry, I—"

"*I don't want to talk to you at all, Emily,*" she says, finally making it abundantly clear. "I don't want to talk to you," she repeats, softer this time, her voice crackling slightly on the "you," her words making me feel sick to my stomach.

We stare at each other for a long moment before she turns on her heel and walks away from me, throwing her bag into the back of her truck and slamming the car door loudly behind her.

I feel like my legs might give out from under me.

I watch her drive away, her truck fading into the distance. My head swims as I turn around, willing myself to walk back over to the bus, one foot in front of the other. Right, left. Right, left.

I fight through the sea of arms and legs for my bag, breaking out into the open air, my eyes landing on my dad's truck in the parking lot.

I hear Matt saying my name, but I keep moving, keep walking.

Dad waves enthusiastically out the window at me, calling out to me as I get closer, still trying his best to patch things up after our fight.

"Well, how was it?" he asks as I close the truck door behind me, a huge smile on his face.

"Fine," I say. I put my seat belt on, pulling my legs up and wrapping my arms around them as we drive away, hoping I can literally hold myself together until we get there. Until we get home.

"You okay, Em? Midnight bonfire got you a bit tired?" he asks, shooting me a concerned look. "Did something happen? Are you still upset about the house, or—"

"I don't want to talk about it," I say, trying to keep my voice steady.

I wait for him to ask another question, to say *something*, but like always, he doesn't push.

For once, though, some part of me wishes he would.

But I shove that aside, focusing on the only certainty I have. The only thing that can get me through this drive, and through *all* of this, is my mom's closet. Being completely surrounded by the one place I can feel her. The only safe place I still have in the entire world.

If I can make it to the closet one last time, I'll be fine. I'll be able to make sense of everything if I can just get there.

My dad pulls onto our street and into the driveway, and the second we're parked, I unfurl and head inside.

I drop my bag in the entryway, my vision blurring as I run up the stairs and down the hall. My hands reach out for the handle to my parents' bedroom, and pushing inside, I stumble to the closet, yanking the door open with a desperation that fills every single fiber of my body. I step through the doorframe and turn on the light to see . . .

Nothing.

The shelves are completely cleared. The wire hangers are empty, pushed into the far corner.

"Oh my God," I say as I rip open the drawers, jerking them all the way out of the dresser as I try to find something. Anything. They clatter to the ground as I spin around and around, searching. *"Oh my God.* No, no, no."

There's nothing left.

This can't be happening. This can't be happening.

My dad appears in the doorway, a concerned look on his face. "Emily?"

"Where are her clothes?" I shout at him, frantic. I stoop down and pull out the last dresser drawer, the last *empty* dresser drawer, his voice stopping me dead in my tracks.

"I donated them. About two or three weeks ago . . . I guess you haven't been in here for a bit, but I noticed there was still some stuff left after you were in here with Blake, and you kept pushing it off, so I thought I'd make it easier on you by—"

I whirl around to face him, my ears ringing. "You *what?*"

"I donated them," he repeats.

"Everything?" I whisper.

"Yes, but, Emily, I—"

"No," I say, shaking my head as the room begins to tip, my insides concaving. He reaches out, his hand gently wrapping around my arm. "Get off me!" I yell, pushing past him and out into the hallway.

I have to get them back. I have to get the clothes back.

I grab my bike from up against the porch, my dad calling out my name behind me, but I ignore him. Houses and cars whizz by, my tears blending everything together as I go.

They can't be gone.

They can't be gone.

I pedal as fast as I can, past cornfields and housing developments, my lungs heaving, my breathing forcing its way out in gasped sobs. I fly down Pearl Street, turning right onto Main, my eyes searching the horizon for the blue and white sign.

The Goodwill.

Skidding into the parking lot, I throw my bike down and run up the concrete steps. The automatic doors don't open fast enough, so I force my way in through the gap, desperate to get inside.

The store blurs around me. Colors jump out at me underneath the fluorescent lights.

I push through the shirts, stripes and polka dots and solid colors, trying to find a part of her in the middle of it all. The old jeans she would always wear to do housework in and prune her garden. The maroon dress she wore one Christmas, with the tie around the middle.

Wait. Had it been green? Suddenly, I can't even picture it.

I frantically attack another rack, the hangers clattering noisily against one another as I move down the row, pausing on a button-down, a floral maxi, a wool cardigan, none of them feeling right.

Was this hers? Did she wear this?

I can't even tell. *I can't even remember.* And just like that, my worst fears have come true. List or no list, I feel her slip away from me.

I squeeze my eyes shut, my chest heaving as a hopeless feeling settles into my bones, aching and staggering and disorienting.

Weakly, I stumble out the front door, a sob escaping my lips as I clutch at the metal railing, making my way down the stairs. Looking up, my eyes find my dad's. He's standing in the parking lot, confusion painted across his face.

The second I see him, the wave of anger resurfaces, the pressure of it making my head pound.

"Emily," he says, stepping toward me.

"How could you?" I shout at him, pushing at his arms as they try to hold me, thrashing out of his grip. "How could you do that? Why are you so obsessed with some fresh start? How could you be fine with throwing out your old life and just *forgetting* her?"

"Em, they're just *things*. I'm not—"

"They're not just things!" I shout. I cough as I gasp for breath, tears streaming down my face. "They're parts of her!"

He grabs ahold of me, and this time I collapse into his arms, my body giving way. He holds me tight as I cry, my tears staining his shirt, my stomach aching as I bawl.

"*You're* a part of her, Emily. *I'm* a part of her. Not any of that stuff," he whispers. "I could never forget her. Ever. I'm close to her every minute I'm with you. And I want a new start because I know your mom wanted that for you. For both of us."

I think about the past three years and how frozen I've been. Never taking chances. Never trying my luck. Always afraid of the worst-case scenarios. Almost like I could have stopped it from happening, like I could have stopped her from getting sick, if I had just stayed home.

The list started that way too. I thought I knew where it was leading me, back to the person I was before it all. Back to her.

But then . . . I think of Blake holding out the yearbook to me, the list falling from it. Her smile in the kitchen when she suggested I actually *do* it. How she was with me every step of the way, her face stitched into every memory, the list pressing play on my life, which has been paused for so long.

And then it hits me.

The list wasn't leading me to Mom. It wasn't leading me to Matt.

It was leading me forward. It was leading me to *her*.

I can't keep Mom here with clothes and secrets and things I never got to say. If she's really with me, like I felt all summer long, then I have to trust that she knows. That she can hear my feelings now. That she'd understand even if she can't tell me.

The sky darkens around us as my tears finally dry out. My chest is hiccuping as it slowly stops. I sniff and my dad tightens his grip on me, holding me close, not running away to work or hiding behind pancakes, a barrier between us broken.

"I've got you, Em," he says. "I've always got you."

29

The second I walk into Nina's the next day, Kiera storms off to the back room, leaving me standing in the doorway watching her go. I catch Nina peering at us from the kitchen, her brow furrowed in concern. Paul is just behind the counter, his pen frozen midair.

"Kiera!" I call, following after her. I reach out and stop the door from slamming in my face, slipping inside and closing it behind me.

She crosses her arms and turns around to look at me. "What?"

We both stare at each other for a long moment, the cracks in our friendship that we've ignored for so long suddenly a cavern between us.

"I'm sorry," I say, trying to cross the divide. "I'm sorry about what I said."

"Honestly, it was a bit of a welcome relief. You're always shutting me out and refusing to open up," she says, glowering across the room at me. "It was nice to actually hear what you thought for once."

I nod, thinking about that little box that I kept myself in. How it impacted everything in my life. My relationship with Matt. My friendship with Kiera.

"I think I just felt like you were so obsessed with fixing everything so we could have this shiny, wonderful senior year, that you just . . . stopped seeing me completely."

"Well, you wouldn't let me *see* you, Em," she says, understandably frustrated. "I mean, *what is going on?* I thought this is what you wanted! I mean, our plan *worked*, didn't it?"

"It worked," I say as I take a deep breath. "But I . . . I don't think it was the right plan."

Kiera is silent, leaving me a space to continue. To tell her the thing I kept from her that would have made a world of difference.

I feel my heart hammering in my chest, the truth I've never told anyone before on the tip of my tongue. The part of me I never got to share with my mom.

"I don't *like* Matt, Kiera," I say, and her mouth falls open in surprise. "Not like that. No matter how *hard* I tried to. No matter how hard I tried to not be like *this*, it's no use."

"'Like this'?" she echoes.

I take a deep breath, the truth coming out in a whisper. "I like Blake."

I wait for the storm. For the world to come crashing in around me.

But it doesn't.

Kiera crosses the divide and pulls me in, her arms tightening around me as tears unexpectedly begin to stream down my face, completely soaking her Nina's T-shirt. "Oh, Em. I'm . . . I'm sorry I was so wrapped up in senior year, and making everything right, and all the shit with our friend group that it felt like you couldn't tell me. Or that I wouldn't care unless you were with Matt," she says as she rests her chin against my head. "You know I've always got your back."

"I know you do," I say, giving her a tight squeeze. "I'm sorry, too. For shutting you out. For not being honest."

We stand there in silence for a few minutes, feeling closer than we have in a while.

Soon there's a light knock on the door. When we pull apart and open it, Paul and Nina are standing there, the open sign turned to closed, Paul holding up a bag of bittersweet chocolate chips.

"I think maybe we should just make some chocolate chip cookies today," Nina says, wrapping us all up in a hug. "How does that sound?"

"Will you tell me the secret ingredient?" I ask, my voice muffled against the fabric of her shirt.

"Yep," Nina says.

I whip my head off her shoulder, my eyes wide. "Wait. Really?"

She nods, all of us laughing. "Really."

We get all the ingredients together while I tell them everything.

About this summer and the list and Blake. Reliving the night at the beach, and what she said to me before the bonfire. How I swooned when I first saw her at bingo, without even really knowing I had.

"I realized how much I like her," I say, taking a deep breath. "I realized that I . . . that I like girls."

My eyes flick over to meet Paul's, and he gives me an understanding smile. "It may be a little tough in a small town like this one," he says, knowing from experience. "But I wouldn't want to pass on the post of resident gay of Huckabee to anyone else."

I laugh and shake my head at him. "Thanks, Paul."

"How long have you known?" Kiera asks as she measures out the brown sugar. Not in an accusing way. Not in a *doubtful* way. She just . . . wants to know.

I feel a smile creeping onto my lips. "You remember Dominique? From Misty Oasis?" I ask her.

She drops the measuring cup she's holding. "Dom Flores? You had the hots for *Dom Flores?*"

"I did *not* have the hots for Dom Flores," I say, chucking a chocolate chip in her direction. "Maybe a tiny, *tiny* crush, I don't know."

We all laugh, and I shake my head. "I think . . . I think I suspected something, but when we got back from camp . . ."

Nina nods, catching on. "Your mom was sick."

"Yeah," I say, thinking of how I was swept up in doctor's appointments, and surgeries, and my mom getting sicker and sicker, withering away before my eyes. "I just ignored it. I pushed it down. Until, well . . . until I couldn't."

I meet Kiera's gaze over the mixing bowls. "Kiera, I couldn't be honest with you because I couldn't be honest with myself. And I couldn't be honest with myself because I couldn't tell the truth to the one person I wanted to tell more than anyone."

She reaches out and takes my hand, giving it a sympathetic squeeze.

I let out a long sigh. "I think I just thought that being with Matt was what my mom would have wanted," I say. "All the years she had nudged me in his direction when she suspected he was crushing on me. And then telling me right at the end that I should give him a chance. But it's always felt wrong. It's always felt off." I pull the list out of my pocket, unfolding it and giving it a long look before laying it on the counter. "Doing the list changed me *so* much, I just thought that, well . . . that things would finally fall into place the way they did for her that summer. With Matt. With all of it."

Nina smiles and picks up the list. "Em, I *still* tell your mom stuff," she says as her eyes scan the paper. "When I'm walking around the grocery store, or baking a cake, or brushing my teeth. Even though she's not here, she's still *here.*" She points to her heart, the place where my mom will always have a space. "Your mom was my best friend, and I know for a fact she'd only want you to be *happy*. Whether that's with Matt, or whether that's with Blake," she says, folding the list down to look at me. "Besides, you've still got some summer left."

A small smile creeps onto her lips. "Who said your mom got it right the first time?"

"What does *that* mean?" I ask.

All she does is shake her head, reaching into her apron to reveal a tiny jar of maple syrup.

"That's not my story to tell. You've gotta ask your dad," she says as she pours some into the mixing bowl.

"Maple syrup?" I ask, my eyes wide, my lifelong quest to find the Secret Ingredient finally coming to a close. *Really?*

"Your mom spilled some in a batch we made when we were kids," she says as she screws the lid back on, holding the jar up to the light. "Haven't changed the recipe since then."

30

The next afternoon I bike to Matt's house, wanting to put things right. For real this time.

I coast along the familiar back roads, this trip so different from the hundreds before it.

Different from the hundreds that will hopefully come after it.

If he doesn't hate me.

As I turn into his development, I see him sitting on the front porch, in the same spot where we used to sit and wait for my dad to come pick me up. He's on his phone, still wearing his white life-guard tank top from the pool.

I slow to a stop, hopping off and kicking the kickstand into place. He looks up, surprised to see me.

"Hey," I say as I sit down next to him on the top step.

"Hey," he says, resting his arms on his legs and interlacing his fingers, just like he always does when something is serious. Like he can tell what's coming.

We're both silent for a second, like we're afraid to poke a sleeping bear. I look over at him, squinting into the afternoon sun.

"I'm sorry," I say, meaning it more than those words can convey. "I am *so* sorry, Matt. For the kiss at the lake and ignoring you the past few days instead of giving you an explanation. Instead of just being honest with you, like I said I would be."

He nods, his brow furrowing slightly. "Can you be?" he asks finally, looking down at his hands. "For real this time?"

I let out a long exhale.

"I was scared," I say, telling him the truth. "All along, I've been scared to admit the fact that something was missing on my end, so I just came up with these stupid excuses to break us up instead of being real with you. Like the night of junior prom. I was scared to tell you I didn't *want* to take things to the next level. So I did something stupid to push you away instead of just talking to you. And then I thought the list would help me find the missing piece but . . . it didn't. At least not the way I expected."

Matt looks over at me, his jaw locking in a way that's so familiar to me. "You could've," he says. "You could've just talked to me, Em. We used to talk about everything. If I'm honest . . . I think that's been missing for me, too. I think I thought if we took it to the next level, it might click back into place."

I think about all the years we've known each other. Our adventures in middle school. Our group of friends, all piled together at a lunch table.

"I know," I say. "And I should have. I should have then, and before that, and long before now."

"So this is it? For real this time."

"Yeah," I say, nodding. "Breaking up, getting back together, trying to make it work. It's not working."

He lets out a long exhale, pushing his unruly hair out of his eyes. "Did I do something wrong? Like . . . this weekend? Or during our relationship? Or—"

"No! No," I say, shaking my head. "Not at all. It's not you at all. You're the best guy in this whole damn town. It's . . . well. It's me. I just . . . I don't *like* guys, Matt. And I didn't know how to admit that . . . until now."

He stares at me for a long moment while I hold my breath. I watch the gears turning, see him putting two and two together in real time.

"Oh," he says, his eyes lighting up with understanding. *"Oh."*

"You don't hate me, right?" I blurt out, worried that even our friendship will be ruined because I couldn't be honest. "I would get it if you did. I am *so* sorry, Matt. I mean, I should have—"

He shakes his head, but I can tell he's in shock. "Of course I don't hate you. I just . . . this is a lot."

We're both silent for a long moment, watching as a car passes. "Is it cool if I maybe just have some space?" he asks, and I nod, standing up, my stomach falling through the floor as I walk down the steps.

"Matt, I . . ." I spin around, but my words trail off into silence. There's nothing left to say. "I'll see you around."

I grab my bike and pedal away, biting the inside of my cheek to stop myself from crying. But even as my heart breaks a little further, I can't help but feel like I finally did it.

Even though we aren't together, I finally made it right.

31

The day of the move is here before I know it, a week of packing gone in the blink of an eye. I keep wanting to talk to my dad, to ask him about what Nina said, to tell him, but I can never find the right time.

I wanted to do it in our old house, since it feels sacred in a way, but . . . I'm scared, especially after what happened with Matt. Out of everyone, I really don't know what my dad's reaction will be.

Johnny comes over to help us the day of the move, and I spy Winston's furry head sticking out the passenger-side window, but Blake is nowhere to be found. When Johnny opens the car door, Winston comes running over to where I'm sitting on the porch, tail wagging.

At least someone is happy to see me.

I scratch behind his floppy ears, giving him a sad smile. "She hates me, huh, bud?" I whisper.

He whines and rests his chin on my knee, his big brown eyes

drooping even more than they usually do as he looks at me.

We spend most of the day lugging furniture out to the moving truck my dad rented, a few of his coworkers at Smith & Tyler helping us out too. Gradually, right before my eyes, the house becomes empty and echo-y. Even though, maybe, in a lot of ways, it's been empty since she left us. Tears fill my eyes as I think of how she used to fill this space, with her voice, and her laughter, and her warmth.

But as I go through each room, I still find things. The marks on the carpet where something used to be, tiny holes in the wall where pictures were hung, the lines on the doorframe where we'd measure my height every year.

The small scorch mark revealed from lifting up the carpet in the living room, a reminder of the Christmas a decade ago with Blake.

All signs we were here. All of us.

Soon my dad and I are standing in the entryway, our only claim to this house the memories we made in it.

He puts his arm around my shoulder, letting out a long exhale. "I'm gonna miss this place," he says.

I nod, taking in the steps and the living room and the worn wood floors for the last time. Taking in Mom's house for the last time, before, together, we close and lock the door.

My fingers drag along the flowers of the garden as we make our way down the walk. I stop to carefully uproot a sunflower to replant, although with my tattoo, I'll always have a part of her garden with me, no matter where I may go. I smile as the tattoo peeks out from underneath my mom's black cardigan, pulling the sleeve down as my dad appears over my shoulder with a mug from his truck for me to put the flower in.

My mom's polka-dot mug. Not gone forever, but here.

We pull out of the driveway for the last time, the house fading from view as we drive off down the street, the mug clutched in my hands, everything I need from the house right here with me. All the important stuff.

Every step I take is a step toward a new, uncertain chapter in my life, something about a fresh start feeling good. Inviting. A new beginning waiting just around the corner.

After we unload the moving truck at our new house, I climb the steps to my room, surprised when I step inside and see that the bubblegum-pink walls are gone, replaced with the same eggshell white as my old room, a blank slate for me to fill with posters and pictures of cake designs and handwritten recipes.

Dad.

There's a light knock on the door, and I look over to see Johnny peeking inside. He gives me a small smile, the wrinkles around his eyes crinkling.

"I'm gonna head out, but"—he holds up a wrapped, rectangular object, about the size of a textbook—"she wanted me to give this to you."

My heart jumps at the thought of Blake. I reach out and take it, my fingers wrapping around the solid edges.

Clearing his throat, he runs his fingers through his hair in a way that is painfully familiar. "I know something happened between the two of you. I don't exactly know the specifics, Clark, but I sure hope you two find a way through it." He smiles at me before patting my shoulder and leaving.

Slowly, I sit down on my bare mattress and carefully slide my fingers through the tape on the gift. The wrapping paper falls away to reveal . . .

A painting. Of my old house. The white exterior and the sash windows and the front porch with a swing, and . . . colorful sunflowers growing in the garden just underneath it, and . . .

My *mom* on the front lawn, gardening.

The most important part of the home, the exact memory I want to remember it by brought to life by Blake.

Of course she knew.

My thumb traces her name scrawled onto the right corner, tears stinging my eyes. I sniff, wiping them away.

It's perfect.

That night I carefully hang Blake's painting on my eggshell-white wall. It feels *impossible* for everything to ever be like it was between us. But this feels like a start.

"That's an awful nice painting," a voice says from behind me. I turn around to see my dad leaning in the doorway, a big wooden box tucked under his arm.

"It sure is," I say, plunking down on my bed and wrapping my mom's cardigan around myself.

He slides down next to me, putting the box in between us. I nod to it, raising my eyebrows. "What's that?"

He motions for me to open it, and I crack the lid to see a pile of odds and ends. Sort of like a junk drawer.

But when I look closer, I realize what it all means. A baseball he caught for my mom at a Phillies game, the necklace he bought for their first anniversary, an ultrasound of me as an amorphous blob.

And for the first time in three years, he *talks* about her, telling me stories as he tours me around the box, the both of us smiling and laughing, tears stinging at our eyes.

Things I don't even know about, like a receipt from the French restaurant all the way in the city where my dad proposed to her and a piece of notebook paper with a ton of tick marks that they'd used to count the weeks she was pregnant.

It's such a random and wonderful assortment of stuff. Stuff that holds so many memories of her that I didn't have before, just like the list did. Memories of my mom and pieces of her that *aren't* gone, even beyond the list. That I still have yet to find.

And he kept them.

"It's nice to talk about her," I say quietly as I look down at the baseball.

"I'm sorry," my dad says, rubbing the back of his neck. "I'm sorry for how much I've failed you these past few years. Not talking about her. Keeping all this in a box. I mean, we've never been . . . great . . . at the whole talking thing. That was always you and your mom's thing. It was hard for me, but . . . it still wasn't right."

"From now on, we'll do a better job of that," I say, smiling up at him.

He pulls out an envelope from the box, and I watch as he wipes at his eyes with the back of his hand, smiling as he takes a piece of paper from inside. "Your mom knew I was going to be in over my head," he says, chuckling as he unfolds it. "So she made this little cheat sheet for me."

He holds it out to me, and I see it's covered in my mom's hand-writing, his very own list, filled with advice and reminders. All of them about me.

> *What to do if she gets sick: Get the chicken noodle soup from Hank's, black tea (tbsp of honey, 2 sugars), ask Nina for her biscuit recipe. You can figure it out.

> *What to do if she gets her heart broken: Ice cream, Joe. Ice cream is always the answer.

And at the very bottom, a little note.

> *What to do if she comes to you with something I didn't mention: Tell her you love her. No matter what. And that I love her too. Always.

My tears begin to fall on the paper, fat and heavy, my dad reaching out to grab it before wrapping his arm around me. "Hey! I still need that." He laughs, pulling me close as I dissolve into a blubbering mess as I think about stepping off the Misty Oasis bus and seeing her there, swallowing the words I never got to say to her.

I think about the clothes and all the donated items, things I thought were pieces of her. Things I thought were what made Julie Miller, Julie Miller.

But it's *us*. Me. My dad. Nina. The people who would always tell me stories about her. The things she did and the places she went and the lives she touched. It's *talking* about her instead of hiding in a literal closet, shutting out the world. It's learning new things about her and finding ways to honor her without living exactly the life she wanted me to live three whole years ago.

If I can learn new things about her after she's gone, maybe she wouldn't be disappointed there were things she never knew about her daughter.

Which is why I pull away, knowing it's time to tell Dad.

I reach into my pocket and pull out the list that I've taken with me everywhere for the past month and a half. I don't need a pile of clothes, or a closet, or a whole house to feel close to her, when I can have moments like *this*.

Moments like I had all summer.

Carefully, I unfold it and hold it out to my dad.

"I spent the summer doing the list I showed you," I say.

"'Julie Miller's Senior Year Summer,'" he reads, a smirk appearing on his face. "That explains the sunflower tattoo."

The *what*? How—

My mouth drops open. "You knew about that?"

"Em, you're terrible at hiding things," he says with a laugh. "That, and you have a habit of rolling up your sleeves."

I look down to see my forearm skin on full display, the cardigan sleeves pushed up to my elbows. I laugh, sniffing as I wipe my tears away with the back of my hand. "No more, though," he says, in full Dad mode, a stern look plastered on his face. "You get another one, and we're gonna have problems."

I think of that glittering silver needle and swear my life on it.

"You going to tell me about it?" he asks as he hands the list back to me.

I let out a long sigh, everything blurring together in my head, a montage of feelings and emotions, of Blake's eyes and sparkling water and the summer sun.

He opened up to me tonight, so . . . I open up to him. I tell him about the book, and cliff jumping, and the beach, all the times I felt my mom right there beside me, guiding my footsteps. How much this list has changed me. How much it has made me the person I was too afraid to be again.

He listens. Really *listens*. Smiling and laughing and nodding as I recount my whirlwind summer to him, everything leading up to item number twelve.

"So, I kissed him. And . . ."

I look at the list in my hand, the lucky list that was my mom's.

But now I need to make it *mine*.

Because there's something I have to do if I'm going to really be the person that this list helped me to see I am. I have to tell him the truth about Matt and Blake and . . . me.

My heart skips into double time. Maybe even triple time.

"And it was all wrong. Just like it's always been," I admit. "It's . . . not like what you and Mom had. It just isn't, even though I know she wanted that for me."

"But with Blake . . . ," I start to say, stopping to collect myself. "But with Blake, things have always felt right."

I look down at the leather bracelet on my wrist, those seagulls flying free.

"I thought that I could change who I was. That I could *fix* what was wrong with me and Matt, and that things could finally fit into place like they did for you and Mom. But I couldn't do it. I can't change who I am, Dad. I can't change the fact that I . . ." I take a long, deep breath, all the air disappearing from the room. "That I'm gay."

Holy shit. I—I said it. Even though I told Kiera and Nina and Matt, this is the first time I let myself say the word. My ears start to ring as I wait for him to say something. Anything. I can't even *look* at him.

Am I going to throw up?

Am I going to—

I hear him rifling around in the box, worried he's just going to pack it up and leave. Glancing over, I see him pull out a Polaroid picture. He holds it out to me, and there, in all their faded glory, are my mom, Johnny Carter, and my dad, arms slung over one another's shoulders, goofy grins on all their faces.

I read the handwritten caption, in my mom's neat cursive: *Julie, J. C., and Joe.*

Wait a second—I grab the photo from him, looking between it and the list, my mind exploding.

J. C.

Johnny Carter? Not Joe Clark?

I think of the cassette tape from the box, the note on it: "Let me know if you change your mind."

Nina's words a week ago: "Who said your mom got it right the first time?"

I look up to meet his gaze, understanding. Twenty years ago that kiss had meant exactly the same thing to my mom as it meant to me.

It wasn't about kissing the person who we were supposed to be with. It was realizing who we *wanted* to be with.

My dad reaches out, his rough hand cupping my cheek. "I love you, Em," he says, his brown eyes getting a little teary, and making *my* brown eyes a little teary. "No matter what, okay?"

I nod, the tears spilling out of my eyes and down my cheeks as he pulls me into a hug. "And I'm not just saying that because your mom's little instruction list told me to," he says, the both of us laughing. "I would have said it anyway."

I stare at the painting on the wall, just over his shoulder, thinking of how happy I'd been this summer. How, even after getting my luck back, I'd still been too afraid to take a chance on Blake. All because I was scared.

I was scared because . . . to be with Blake meant that there couldn't be any more hiding.

But I don't want to be scared anymore. I'm *not* scared anymore. I don't want to change who I am.

I need to be willing to play the game. I need to be willing to put myself out there, and be vulnerable, and take chances, even though I might lose.

And if my mom taught me anything this summer, it's that maybe, just maybe, that's exactly what I need to do to fix this.

And I know just who to call.

32

"You ready?" Kiera asks when I slide into the car.

"As ready as I'll ever be," I say, clicking into my seat belt. "Did Olivia give her mom the bask—"

"Yes," Kiera says.

"And does she have th—"

"Em," she says, reaching out to grab my arm. "Olivia gave her mom the basket and the numbers. Jake is making sure Blake will be there. And . . . Matt got us the seat in the back corner in case things go south and we gotta get the hell out of there."

I look up in surprise.

Matt.

She smiles at me. "Like he'd miss out on a good scheme."

I feel tears sting at my eyes, one thing a little less broken.

I try to fight the queasiness in my stomach the whole ride to the elementary school for the "Back-2-School Bingo Fundraiser," the feeling so strong that not even Kiera playing some Billie Eilish can completely quash it.

Three years ago this was the absolute worst day of my entire life. August 20. The day my mom died.

And now, just maybe, with the help of my friends, with the help of my mom and her list, this anniversary doesn't have to be all bad memories.

The parking lot is already packed by the time we get there, and Kiera circles a few times to find a spot while I peer at everyone walking inside, searching for Blake's face.

After we park, we join the throngs of people heading into the cafetorium, all the regulars already there.

Tyler Poland with his collection of lucky rocks, Jim Donovan ready to fight to the death, Principal Nelson perched at the main table selling cards.

I crane my neck, trying to get a better look at the people coming inside, my eyes jumping from person to person, but she's nowhere to be found. I catch sight of Olivia's mom, Donna Taylor, and she gives me a curt nod, the basket cradled tightly in her arms.

When we get to the front of the line, Principal Nelson hands me my mom's card with a smile, and I pause, reaching out to pick up another card, number twelve. For the list. "I'll take this one too," I say.

A new chance, just like the one I hope I have tonight.

We buy a few more cards for the table before heading toward the back corner, the seats already filled with my friends, Matt, and

Olivia, and Ryan, and . . . *Blake*. She's sitting down next to Jake, her sun-streaked hair pulled back into a bun, just like it was that day in the kitchen, a charcoal, vintage band T-shirt hanging loosely on her torso.

My heart starts pounding in my ears, louder than all the voices in the room.

"Come on," Kiera whispers. She grabs my hand, pulling me forward.

"Hey!" Matt says when we get there. "Look who's here!"

Blake glances up in surprise, a slight furrow forming in her brow when she sees me. I forget how to breathe, her brown eyes knocking every single thought from my head.

She looks between me and Matt, then quickly away, shooting Jake a look that screams, *"Really?"*

"We've got the cards," Kiera says, nudging me into action. She hands out her half while I hand out mine, keeping card number twelve for myself, and holding that fruit-punch-stained card number 505 out to Blake.

She reaches out to take it, mumbling a thank-you.

We sit as the microphone crackles to life, Donna Taylor's voice announcing the start of the night.

The ball cage begins to rattle, and I look behind me to meet Donna's gaze as she plucks one of the yellow balls out. She takes a deep breath before calling into the microphone.

"*I*-twenty-three!"

It takes everything in me to not look at Blake as the familiar numbers begin to pile up, her hand reaching out to take red chips from the center of the table. I look down at Kiera's leg, bouncing nervously up and down next to me, Olivia staring up at her mom, her eyes wide as she waits for the next number.

Ryan is too distracted to even pay attention to his own card, but that's nothing new.

Soon there's only one left. One more number to be called.

I reach into my pocket, my fingers wrapping around the lucky quarter, my eyes flicking up to see Matt swallow nervously as Donna calls out, "*B-nine!*"

And without skipping a beat, Blake calls out, "Bingo!"

I stop breathing as she reads her card off, all of us watching as she heads up to the front of the room to claim her basket. I watch as she walks down the row, stopping short in front of the basket I spent hours putting together.

Two Bingo Boogie cards. Lay's chips, a package of Skittles, sour gummy worms, and a Hershey's chocolate bar, the snacks she bought at the gas station on the way to our beach trip. A dishwashing glove. Her lifeguard sweatshirt, perfectly folded at the bottom. A tin of Spam. And, in the exact center, a list that reads:

EMILY CLARK'S SENIOR YEAR BUCKET LIST
1. Tell Blake how I feel.
2. Go to a St. Vincent concert.
3. Take a trip to NYC.
4. Go on a college road trip.
5. Make kulolo.
6. Go to prom.

7.   Make a plan for life after high school.
8.   Eat meat loaf at Hank's.
9.   Go to all of Blake's soccer games.
10. Spend a week at Aunt Lisa's beach house.
11. Plan a Senior Skip Day adventure.
12. Kiss B. C.

Things we talked about doing on the way to the beach. That we talked about all summer. That I want to do with her, and no one else, by my side.

And then, right there, in front of all of Huckabee, I get up from the table and walk right up to her. I reach out and grab her hand, and she turns around to face me, the entire room disappearing around us. Her eyes are wide, her mouth falling slightly open.

"I'm sorry, Blake," I say softly. Then, like I'm launching myself off the biggest cliff in the entire world, I tell her what I've wanted to say since that night at the beach. Since she told me how she felt the night of the bonfire. "For not being brave enough to admit that I like you."

She swallows, giving me a look that sends butterflies scattering across my chest, everything about her, and this, and *us*, feeling right. The list leading me to this moment.

To her.

"Blake. I *really* like you," I say. "I like you a lot. I like your eyes, and how you smell like a day at the beach, and how you make me feel like I can do just about anything. I like that you paint these *insane* pictures, and that you make the world seem so much bigger than here, than *Huckabee*. I like that you give me butterflies, butter-flies that I never even knew were possible, just by looking at me the way you are *right now*. The way you have this entire summer. You make me want to go on a million adventures, like . . . like . . ." I lean past her to pull the piece of paper out of the basket. "Like all of *these* things. And so many more, Blake. That I *want* to do. With *you*."

She looks down at the list, and then back up at me, and then . . . she smiles. That smile that knocked me off my feet at the very first bingo night. That smile that is in every one of my memories from this summer.

She takes a step forward, her hand reaching out to touch my waist, sending a shock of electricity through my whole body.

"Can I ki—"

The words aren't even out of her mouth before I pull her closer. And . . . it's everything I never knew a kiss could be. Her lips are soft and warm and absolute magic, all the voices and the other people fading away, like there's nothing else in this world but us. And I don't count down to anything at all.

We pull apart and I hear a "Whoop!" from across the room, both of us turning to see Kiera at the back table, grinning like it's Christmas morning, Jake letting out a wolf whistle, Olivia and Ryan clapping just behind them. I meet Matt's gaze and he gives me a smile and a small nod, the best ex-boyfriend a girl could ask for.

Then Jim Donovan's voice rings out from just behind us on the stage. He must've crept onto it while everyone else was distracted. I brace myself for the worst.

"They rigged the game!" he screams into the microphone,

picking up a tiny piece of paper with the numbers I'd told Olivia to give to her mom. He waves it madly around in the air, all hell breaking loose in the cafetorium.

Tyler Poland launches his lucky rocks at us as Jim catapults himself off the stage in our direction.

I grab Blake's hand, our fingers lacing together. "Run!"

We bolt for the back doors, Matt holding them open for us, all of us laughing as we fly through the parking lot, running in between the parked cars, the wind tugging at our hair as our shoes slap against the pavement.

Blake looks back at me with that mischievous smile that completely upended my world for the better. She looks ahead and so do I, as she pulls me forward along with her, everything clicking perfectly into place in exactly the way that my mom always talked about. A way that makes me feel . . .

Well.

Lucky.

Acknowledgments

My solo debut! I have a mountain of thanks to give to all of the people who helped this book land in your hands today.

First, I am eternally grateful to my amazing editor, Alexa Pastor, who is undoubtedly the absolute best there is. This book was crafted, start to finish, during a GLOBAL PANDEMIC, and it would definitely still be an amorphous blob stuck in draft #1 if it weren't for Alexa. That can probably be said for all my books, past and future.

Thank you to Justin Chanda, Julia McCarthy, Kristie Choi, and the rest of the team at Simon & Schuster. It is a true gift to know that my books are in such great hands.

To my incredible agent, Emily van Beek, at Folio Literary, for supporting me and my writing. I have so much gratitude for you, and I am beyond excited for the many books and years to come.

Huge thanks to Lianna, Ed, Judy, Mike, Luke, Aimee, Kyle, Alyssa, and Siobhan (matchmaker and ordained minister extraordinaire!) for friendship, and family, and unfailing support, all of which were needed in large supply this past year.

To my mom, who read to me every single night growing up, and planted the seeds that would turn into both a passion and a career. I love you.

And, as always, to Alyson Derrick, my wife, who is somehow even more swoony than Blake Carter, and makes me feel like the luckiest girl in the world every single day.

Stella and Will are in love, but there's just one minor complication – they can't get within five feet of each other without risking their lives . . .

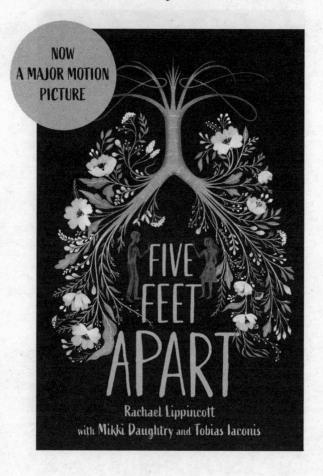

NOW A MAJOR MOTION PICTURE

FIVE FEET APART

Rachael Lippincott

with Mikki Daughtry and Tobias Iaconis